FEDERIGO, or,

THE POWER OF LOVE

By Howard Nemerov

THE IMAGE AND THE LAW (poetry)
THE MELODRAMATISTS
GUIDE TO THE RUINS (poetry)
FEDERIGO, OR, THE POWER OF LOVE

FEDERIGO, or, THE POWER OF LOVE

by Howard Nemerov

For speculation turns not to itself
Till it hath travell'd and is mirror'd there
Where it may see itself. This is not strange at all.
— SHAKESPEARE

An Atlantic Monthly Press Book

Little, Brown and Company · Boston · Toronto

ATLANTIC–LITTLE, BROWN BOOKS
ARE PUBLISHED BY
LITTLE, BROWN AND COMPANY
IN ASSOCIATION WITH
THE ATLANTIC MONTHLY PRESS

*Published simultaneously in Canada
by Little, Brown & Company (Canada) Limited*

PRINTED IN THE UNITED STATES OF AMERICA

for my Mother and Father

BOOK ONE

As silent as a mirror is believed
Realities plunge in silence by . . .
— HART CRANE

Chapter I

YOUNG MEN in our country are brought up to believe that they have a destiny, a guiding idea shaped like a star; most of them pass their lives in unawareness that this destiny is gradually becoming the sum of everything that has happened to them, and need not have been represented by a star in the first place, being perhaps more like the false beacon set up by smugglers to direct a vessel toward a convenient disaster. Disaster, *dés,* from, *astre,* a star.

Of those who become aware, most do nothing; they thankfully accept a life which offers the safety of indistinction, and have a grateful but erroneous impression that they might have been summoned to the impossible and were not. A few others of this class, however, take upon themselves the obligation of ruin. It is not a matter of responding to the summons of destiny, though, for the obligation of ruin is like any other human destiny in that it has first to be invented.

Julian Ghent was thirty-six years old, no longer such a young man, before he had more than an obscure and distorted awareness of these simple things. It came to him in a bad moment of revelation while he was standing alone in the midst of a cocktail party. He looked down into his martini, saw the pearl onion at the bottom of the glass, and said aloud in a voice of naïve amazement: "I am exactly like all these others, if you come right down to it."

One of these others, a small round old gentleman, happened

3

to be passing. "Has it just struck you?" he inquired. "Die early and avoid the rush." He winked rapidly twice in a row, and before Julian could say anything squirmed away between the nearly touching behinds of two tall ladies, one of whom was Julian's wife Sylvia.

On another such occasion, turning away for a moment from the person with whom he was speaking, he saw down a long, gloomy corridor off the room a woman bending to a mirror flanked by two electric candles which gave a reddish, dull illumination. The woman was perhaps applying lipstick, or searching through a handbag on the table before her, and all he could see was her back. This image, so religiously staged in the frame of the hall, so quiet and remote from the noisy room in which he stood, was like a door opened upon some secret world, like a strange reproach. It captivated Julian's mind, and in an instant he imagined himself in love with this woman, having a hidden understanding with her, an apartment perhaps near Gramercy Park, a separate life in which love alone would form the reason of existence. In the moment of his fancy he had already reached the point at which this relation too must begin to cool, when the woman turned away from the mirror and advanced up the corridor into the room; even before her face entered the light he recognized his wife. This little incident, which he could not altogether forget, began to seem the epitome of his mode of existence at this time, and the place from which might begin either self-examination or the examination of others.

He took to watching his own face earnestly in the mirror while he shaved, and in consequence cut himself badly a number of times. So long as he regarded this face of his as no more than an irregularly contoured knob which periodically presented itself for shaving he had run into no such trouble, but the moment he began *watching* the face it seemed to become another being, whose hostile glance was making his hand nervous. "You are your own worst enemy," he said to it across the impenetrable glass. But beyond this remote index of an attitude — that the sight of his own face wrought him to accidental violence — or that the sight of him worked on this face in the same way — the face told him nothing much. Perhaps he had carried it about in too many sorts of weather, adjusted its expression to meet too many people, for it ever to tell him anything again, a face which would never again be caught, as people used horribly to say, with its bare face hanging out.

"And it is with this that for over thirty years I have deceived the world."

He considered this assertion, and its object, in communion over the bathroom sink one morning. The face which returned his stare was shaven down one side and lathered down the other, like a drawing by Picasso, or like the wartime poster showing one half a cheery English gent in tweeds and one half a German officer with a sinister fraction of mouth. Julian had been for some reason mightily taken with that poster (which advertised by this means the need for security), and dated from his first view of it the habit — compulsion, he would have agreed, not seriously, to calling it — of shaving in exact halves, from which he never departed. Another thing he always remembered while shaving was something which had been told him by a friend, say rather a good acquaintance, named Marius Rathlin, a person of psychoanalytic or otherwise devious predilection of thought, that "the lather is the white beard which we put on in symbolic expiation of the black beard which under its cover we furtively remove — we take the curse off the shaving away our manhood." Marius had probably been making an elaborate joke — it was hard to tell about Marius's jokes, and shaving was surely not so

5

complicated as all that — but Julian had been unable to rid himself of that statement, which ritually traversed his mind at the midpoint of the morning shave.

The face did not, to an objective view, look able to deceive a world; but that would be, of course, the prime requisite in any face able to deceive a world — just as your true Machiavel begins his career by writing a tract against Machiavelli. Not that Julian's face proclaimed innocence so very extravagantly, but a keen observer might think to detect there a certain want, not of experience, perhaps, but of penetrative experience. A good face, still quite young, with a strong, broad brow (not high) balanced by a strong but not outrageously strong chin. A nose slightly hooked, large, yet of relatively delicate structure, somewhat a beak but not a prow. His eyes were set quite deep, adding shadow to their own darkness; people had estimated them variously (in Julian's presence) as *honest* and as *intense*. He had dark brown hair, which since the war he had got in the habit of having crew-cut, following in this the fashion which made advertising men and interior decorators resemble nice eagles and lost athletes. His mouth was evenly shaped and moderately though not ascetically thin of lip; he had, however, bad teeth which had given him — as they would continue to do — a good deal of trouble not to mention expense, and his by now unconscious wish to conceal this fact made his smile a trifle more grim and sardonic than it generally intended to be. This was the face with which, as he had just observed, he had deceived the world for more than thirty years; whether the round number was merely a convenience or referred to some five or six years during which he had not, or felt that he had not, deceived the world, would be hard to say.

The question now came up as to what he had deceived the world into doing, or not doing. No answer immediately returned from the mirrored face, both halves of which regarded him with an inscrutable cold honesty that committed neither of them to anything.

In one way, Julian acknowledged, the mere being alive was answer enough — alive and of a fortunate fate so far. A dangerous acknowledgment, as many tragic examples tend to show; call no man happy till he dies. But Julian was unprovided by religion with any apotropaic gesture such as crossing oneself or spitting back over the left shoulder or walking widdershins three times around the house; and as a private citizen he had surely no more private place for such a thought than his own bathroom, the inner and anonymous temple, no doubt, of many a modern home, with its altar and its holy ikon (reflecting the deity in the devout) and its facilities for purgation, baptism, regeneration. What he meant, anyhow, or in earnest, incredulous humility thought that he meant, was that he had not been born, in this century, a German or Polish Jew, a Negro in Florida, a faithful Nazi, or any of a number of things which if one at all believed in fate, and he vaguely did, might just as easily have been his fate. He had not even been killed in the war, and that could quite well have happened on a few occasions he knew about, by a difference of a few centimeters, and probably on a number of occasions he knew nothing about.

Moreover, he made his way in the world. That, perhaps, was the answer; that the outward Julian, the one to be observed (by others) as in a mirror, was getting on quite comfortably, making a go of what commonly represented itself as life, lived well, appeared successful, was married to a handsome and charming woman, had a number of good friends; while the other Julian, who did the observing, who looked out of the deep eyes but could never, by any arrangement of mirrors, look into them, did not quite believe in the truth, the solidity, the reality (if that word must enter the discussion) of what was going on. This Julian, the one under the lather, so to say (for so he said, as he had resumed his shaving), the German officer behind the bluff and tweedy gent, felt, had always felt without ever having been able to make out a good reason for it, like a spy, a secret agent. If people knew, they would destroy him, and it was this alone, doubtless, which gave success in the world a slight but dangerous charm, allowing to a dull respectability something of energy and *élan*. Did others, he wondered, feel this in themselves, the secret subversion mining away at everything they stood for? He supposed they must, and at the same time could not see how they could. "I alone, I am the man" (and the arms outstretched waiting for someone to bring the cross).

The razor nicked him bitterly at the Adam's apple, and he watched in the surprise of slight shock the blood begin to spread in the white lather. It was a quite extreme cut, to judge by the rapid flow of blood; Julian bemusedly wondered just where one drew the line between "I cut myself shaving" and lonely farcical death in the bathroom. Nevertheless he continued shaving, and when he had finished entered the shower.

If the bathroom could be compared to a place of worship (undenominational), probably the shower was its confessional. For Julian at any rate it briefly became every morning the warm, liquid medium in which thought was born again out of the night, and the personality assembled once more by means of the missing fragments which somehow the shower returned to him, often enough as occasions of contrition and remorse. If he had been drunk the previous night it would be in the shower that suddenly and without consciously willing it he recalled as by revelation what he had said, what he had done; often, too, dreams of the night before were held in abeyance until with the rushing water they came flooding back,

8

bearing on wave after wave their odd assortments of junk and people he had not seen for years, and dead people. Julian did not "know too much" (as people say nowadays when they mean they know nothing at all) about psychoanalysis, but because Sylvia his wife was under a species of such treatment, at some expense to himself, he maintained even to himself a kind of faith in it as "letting all these things come to the surface" or "not keeping things all locked up in there." Besides, the images from his dreams were frequently attractive or amusing; and as neither friend nor analyst nor even the remarks of his wife had convinced him he was responsible for his dreams along with everything else in the world, these images may have been the only pure pleasure in his life. So he stood in the shower and let them run as they would, with a charming inconsequence.

Julian put his fingers to his throat, which hurt. It was impossible to see, with water flying everywhere, if the bleeding had stopped. Doubtless it had not, for in entering the shower he was behaving exactly, though on what he hoped was a smaller scale, as suicides did who slashed their wrists and held them in warm water.

"Creature of habit," he said to himself. "You might be bleeding to death." But he thought that was probably not the fact.

But did the world know it was being deceived? Did it care? *Mundus vult decipi,* a view formerly held in much esteem among learned and superior people, who had very likely, however, not meant it exactly as Julian did. And did, or would (if it knew) the world wish to be deceived by Julian Ghent, of all people? It seemed doubtful. More likely, they — not a lapse in grammar but meaning of course the bureaucracy and cartel of everyone, anyone and no one, who are (is?) all-powerful in this world, its trinity in fact — most likely that

They were watching, had always been watching, just as They (or He, or It) had always been said to watch the fall of every sparrow, the progress of Julian Ghent through time, space, kindergarten to college, the war, the marriage, work and pleasure; watching his growing fondness for scotch instead of bourbon, his aversion from pipes and increasing affection for an after-dinner cigar; watching his dreams, his varying preferences in movies, women, games and subjects of conversation; watching his wishes to be someone else, to begin a new life far away under another name, to be unfaithful to his wife with this one that one and the other one; watching his vanity and remorse, his only slightly expanded waistline and few gray hairs, his admiration for the harpsichord, discomfort among small children and most secret feeling that he ought to have been a monk or priest.

They, then, watched all these things — and the Lord alone knew what, if anything, They said. But it seemed to Julian certain, just now, that what he regarded as his good fortune, what socially speaking he could regard in no other way (though he might wonder what, exactly, he was going to do with it), consisted not in Their approbation but at the very most in Their noncommittal silence. Quite possibly They were giving him enough rope, with which he would one day, in the most natural way in the world, hang himself. Or, as he had once heard it said, "The future is in the lap of the gods, and they are standing up to see what is going to happen."

Under the hot shower Julian tried to produce the image of his liberty. He found himself unable to achieve any satisfactory representation of his robbing a bank, smoking opium habitually (though he might try it once) or even arguing with a policeman. Nor could he convincingly sign on as a deckhand for a long voyage (or any voyage). A vision of his losing everything he owned at cards produced a better result; he could

10

see quite clearly the gray dawn outside the window, but the faces around the table remained vague. Now he had an affair with Alma Alter, the wife — though nearly divorced at this time — of his best friend Hugo (she had recently, it seemed, had a nervous breakdown; which might mean, for all Julian knew, that she had gone insane), and all at once the two of them were found dead in a hotel room as the result of a suicide pact. Even this had a reality of only a rather remote sort; mostly Julian imagined Hugo and Sylvia talking the matter over in quiet, earnest tones, so quiet in fact that he could hear nothing they said. He would have liked a greater display of feeling after his death by his own hand, but could not bring them to it. So much for doing as one pleased.

He turned the shower abruptly off, for to have finished with cold water would have seemed sacrilegious — that absurd dancing about — and at the same time too transparently moral for what was after all, as the world goes, his rigorously moral nature. The bathroom was hot and steamy, the mirror clouded over so that he could no longer see himself in it. No religion, probably, could have done more for a man, but Julian must needs wipe at least one spot clear, in which he perceived that the wound at his throat continued to bleed, not so much as at first but quite steadily. In spite of remedies — the styptic pencil hurt a good deal and did not quite stop the flow, the wound must have been deeper than that; and the patch of toilet paper he applied curiosity forced him to remove too soon — a little blood fell on the collar of his clean white shirt, which he therefore changed. Then, when he had dressed and readied himself for the world, pulling his black knit tie to a mean, hard knot like a midget fist at his throat, he joined his wife in the dining room for coffee.

JULIAN HIMSELF seldom had more than toast and coffee for breakfast, and he experienced this morning the usual slight twinge of indignation on seeing that his wife had already finished a plate of what seemed to have been fried eggs; moreover, in the corner next the kitchen door the two dogs were noisily eating large portions of horse meat, the mere idea of which nearly turned his stomach.

These two dogs, handsome afghan hounds of a *café au lait* color, had been given to Julian and Sylvia for a wedding present by Hugo Alter; there had always seemed something ironical in the gift, but as Hugo was not an ironical sort of person Julian concluded that these hounds merely typified his wealthy friend's propensity for doing people favors which were not only imposing but also something of an imposition. Neither Julian nor Sylvia had ever cared much for dogs, but in the first enthusiasm over these two, whom they had incautiously named Troilus and Cressida, they seemed to have made a commitment which they could not go back on even after, as a matter of domestic policy, Troilus and Cressida had been properly gelded and spayed. So the dogs remained, an emblem of something in their master and mistress which was at once aristocratic and faintly ridiculous, to eat quantities of horse meat, to be taken for walks twice daily, to spend the nights locked in the hall bathroom with the light on (they whimpered in the dark) and to form a subject of reproach among acquaintances who said, "It is wrong to keep such large dogs in an apartment in the city." Julian thought it probably was wrong, yet the elegance of these animals satisfied his pride enough so that he submitted to the inconvenience of their keep as to a just penance; while Sylvia, since she had undertaken

12

psychoanalysis, believed that they were a "surrogate" for having children.

Julian kissed his wife, who smiled a bit absently and reminded him that Hugo's party would be that same evening; then he sat down and conspicuously straightened the newspaper which she had slightly disarranged. The stream of communication between them, even at its best not a torrent, dried up at breakfast to the thinnest trickle of news items and the arrangement of schedules and occasional ill-humored remarks. They did not quarrel, being reasonable people, but there would be usually, in the morning, an air of ill-temper and sullen constraint somewhere in the space between them. At the same time, life had to go on, which it did by means of observations like these following.

"You've cut yourself shaving again."

"Yes. I was thinking about something else."

"Shall I get some Mercurochrome?"

"No, I don't think so, thanks."

Sylvia, who would have felt better for being allowed to put Mercurochrome, or even iodine, in her husband's wound, poured him his coffee. As she leaned over him to do so, she kissed him very lightly on the forehead and he looked up at her with an ambiguous grimace rapidly turning into a small smile.

"Do you have a headache?" she asked, as she sat down.

"No, I don't, thank you," he replied (it was his habit to add "thank you" at this time of morning to any phrase of hers which had a rising inflection). "I just haven't quite woke up." He spread the newspaper out over his toast and coffee, and scanned in a cursory way, as if making sure of the world's continued existence, its columns of orderly violence: the ships gone down, the gangsters shot to death, the young men who jumped from high buildings.

13

"I wish you would not do that," Sylvia said. "Rest the newspaper on the toast, I mean. It gets in the butter."

"There is nothing of any use on the last page," Julian answered, but nevertheless folded the paper to one side.

"You don't feel very well, do you, poor thing?" she continued. "I thought you were drinking a great deal, even for you."

"You believe I drink too much?" Julian inquired, in a tone that was meant to be quietly dangerous but in fact sounded merely petulant. Still, Sylvia withdrew before even this approach to a direct challenge.

"It's entirely your business," she said. "I'm sorry you don't feel better."

"I feel perfectly all right, I guess," he said, torn between resentment and the wish to be pitied. The newspaper, which he continued to scan, served to generalize his thoughts just now, so that he was wondering in how many apartments through the city this same scene, or one recognizably like it, was being enacted. Is this the only way in which it is possible for human beings to live? he asked himself silently, and rattled the newspaper in slight, involuntary emphasis, whereat the dogs turned to look at him as though about to ask intelligent questions, then went back to their horse meat.

"The mail should be in by now," Sylvia offered. "I'll go down and get it."

Julian was just about to say that he did not wish his wife to walk through the front hall of the building in her bathrobe or housecoat or whatever, but he recollected just in time that a most important letter would almost certainly arrive in this mail. So he said nothing, and in this way was enabled to enjoy the mail and his resentment both at the same time.

As it was the first of May, there appeared a large stack of bills, and these he leafed through quickly without opening

14

any of them, only permitting himself an ironical smile as he passed the one from his wife's psychiatrist, Dr. Mirabeau. When he came to the letter he had expected, he opened it decisively, after having noted with approval the cheap quality of the envelope — "such as might have been procured from any one of a hundred stores" — and the indistinctive typing of the name and address. Inside, on paper of the same sort as the envelope, was a message composed of letters snipped from magazines and pasted together. Julian read:

> SIR —
> A word to the wise. Your wife, sir, is too much alone. And not always alone.
> Your friend,
> FEDERICO

The calm with which Julian received this sinister communication was owing entirely to his having composed it himself, in his office, the afternoon before, and posted it on his way home. The full range of his intentions in doing so was obscure even to himself, and in fact the entire idea, which yesterday had aroused him to enthusiastic assent, this morning appeared very dubious, the product of a mind not at all points touching reality.

Briefly said, what he wanted to do was to give the nature of things, with which he was extremely bored, a slight push. The plan, of which his imagination had not at all taken in the cruelty, was to allow his wife to see this letter as if by accident, the effect being the same as if he should have said to her, as he could not have done nor would in any case have dared to do, "You see, if in future I should be unfaithful to you, there is an excellent reason for it — turnabout is fair play," or at least, "You can see that I was honestly misled by this

15

dreadful letter" or "those dreadful letters" (for there were to be more).

Julian's problem, as he himself suspected, was that morally speaking he was a coward. It is the essence of cowardice not simply to be afraid, but to shilly-shally and willy-nilly, not to be wholehearted in either desires or aversions; cowardice, which thus relates to irony, urbanity, sophistication and a whole host of civil virtues, is in love with the might-have-been, the between-state, the long, long chance of having everything both ways, or twenty ways at once. We might go on: cowardice is reasonable, and temporizes; cowardice is long-suffering; cowardice is perhaps everything the apostle claimed for charity, except charitable.

To a more courageous man, several courses of action would have been open. He might simply have gone ahead with an infidelity, trusting to discretion, luck and the outlay of considerable sums of money that his wife would never get to know, or would not get to know for a long time. He might have announced to his wife that he no longer loved her and would not any longer live with her (he might have finished by saying dramatically but not altogether wildly that marriage under these circumstances was a sin) and they would have arranged for a divorce or a separation according to her response — a certain quantity of stark emotion, of ugliness, would have to be faced up to. Or he might simply have said to himself: Very well, this is what marriage is, love is replaced after a number of years by boredom. We have made our bed, let us continue to lie in it, like the rest of the world — which we did not make. And he would take up tennis or golf instead, or do chess problems in the evening.

There is one more solution, which is found, probably, by very few: to discover again in one's wife that essential strangeness which was the beginning of love, and which is never lost but only gets forgotten, not replaced but overlaid by a number of dangerously familiar details. But, for this, courage, though still necessary, is probably not sufficient by itself; a certain ingeniousness, perhaps a certain perversity, would also be required.

Julian, regrettably, did not possess the requisite clarity of soul for any of these actions, some of which, while quite possibly vicious in the eyes of the public morality, are nevertheless erotically, or *charitably*, virtuous. It must be allowed, though, that he felt in himself this want of purpose, and characteristically had become more devious than ever in seeking to provoke some direct action. The anonymous or pseudonymous letter was the improbable yet perfectly exact resultant of a number of opposed forces within his soul, which was full of that mysterious, romantic fever which does not die, as it is said to do, after adolescence (which does not really die either), but merely sleeps until it is once again aroused by boredom.

The most dangerous thing about his state of mind, in the first place, was that his present ambitions to infidelity began in a negative and entirely theoretical manner, not with the image of a particular other woman whom he desired, but with the idea only of being unfaithful. This idea, which is inductively the concomitant of marriage after perhaps the first year, had fastened on Julian's thoughts with ferocity and persistence; as is usual with abstract notions, it had spread throughout his thought like a contagion, affecting everything; just as, according to the philosophers, jaundice makes us see everything in the world as a mere function of jaundice, so the idea of infidelity cast its somewhat lurid light over the entire contents of Julian's mind, and possibly by now its meaning had no longer very much to do with sex *per se*, if sex can ever be said to be *per se*.

17

A situation of trust had always obtained, and so far as he was aware still obtained, up to this very moment — he was thoughtfully replacing the letter in its envelope — between Julian and Sylvia. They had trusted each other first out of love and later out of indifference or forgetfulness. Of course, there had been theoretical discussions between them on this subject. Flirtations at parties, a quite common thing in the class with which they were associated, were perfectly all right, they could agree on that — beyond, if not beneath, notice. But there would not, there must not be, anything *serious*.

"If you ever did," Sylvia once said in the course of such a theoretical conversation, "I should kill her. And perhaps you as well," she added, while Julian sat there wondering: With what? Sometimes, alone, he would take this remark out and examine it for minutes at a time. Detached from the earnest, rather humorous tone of her voice, it seemed melodramatic and improbable, Julian could not believe she really felt that way. More likely, he thought, she employed this fiction as a means of supporting the emptiness she too must feel — for after all, the world was full of people being compelled to accept it, however grudgingly, on stingy terms, and doing, or refraining from doing, this thing that thing and the other thing for no better reason than that it was or was not done; how should they not dramatize as strikingly as they could this sorry condition?

But the situation of trust existed, and to break that trust, of course, was more attractive by far to Julian than any merely sexual motive: to do evil, as though just to show that one could. For it was evil, that was his opinion, his final opinion against all those who would have said deprecatingly that it was merely natural. It was evil, darkness, corruption, Julian believed that about the sexual act itself, he shared to this negative and repressive extent in religion, that although pleasure was to be derived from sleeping with a woman, that pleasure was itself bitter, angry, committed beyond its means — as marriage itself would witness. In this he resembled those early Christians, some of them martyrs and saints, who engaged in all manner of whoredom and beastliness for the reason that after the initial unchastity of marriage nothing else remained to matter.

The major motive behind all this was nothing more ardent or in itself erotic than curiosity, a trait which killed the cat, invented arts and sciences, and belonged in the first instance to woman.

Out of this complex of circumstances came the inspiration for the letter, which satisfied a deep moral necessity for Julian by that device which psychologists, like the alchemists of old, call *projection*. It afforded, or seemed to, pretext and justification; above all, it had the indispensable appearance of coming from outside, of being a message from the world and thus of making an objective situation which was, however, perfectly fictional.

The composition had cost him a couple of hours and a good deal of trouble, brief as it was. How were these things done? The form of the phrases — that second "sir" in particular, and the sneering repetition of "alone" — now seemed to Julian transparently theatrical, and in such a way, moreover, that anyone who knew him at all well must immediately also know him for the author. Imaginative persons suffer in committing a crime for just this reason, that they are compelled to witness their action from inside and outside simultaneously, and cannot understand how others can possibly overlook their practically candid and exposed guilt. So it is, perhaps, that imaginative persons can commit their crimes only under some special, sustaining inspiration which has the appearance of entering the head altogether from the outside, from the world,

19

with no inward complicity at all. The letter, for Julian, had been such an inspiration, which came to him with an immediacy, wholeness and unexpectedness that prevented him altogether from being horrified at the time. Now, at breakfast, he was in truth a little horrified.

As for the name Federigo: that was a special inspiration, too. Twice during the past few months Julian had been mistaken for a person called Federigo; once on the street, once at a party. This in itself would not have been so striking, such mistakes are made all the time. But the strange thing was that on each occasion the other person had clearly refused to believe Julian's disclaimer. The haggard young man on the street had sneered disagreeably, saying as he turned away, "I don't want to force myself on you, you know. There's no need to *lie*." And the quite charming girl at the party had smiled at him archly as she said, "I won't tell anyone if you don't want me to." On this occasion Julian was quick enough to ask, before she could get away, "Who is this Federigo?"

"Don't be ridiculous," the girl had replied. "I've promised not to tell anyone."

From these circumstances Julian had gathered that there must be an extraordinary resemblance between this Federigo and himself; also that Federigo was a man accustomed to going about incognito — in this day and age! — and in a position to make his acquaintances respect the fact. This last seemed to Julian almighty impressive, and he began privately to call himself Federigo. The name had a charming, operatic flavor which fitted very well with the secret identity Julian often wished he could have. So, when he was pasting together the anonymous letter — which he did very clumsily — and about to subscribe it simply and tritely "A Friend," he all at once remembered Federigo, which seemed to him at the time to be the final deep and witty touch to the whole affair. Right now, as I say, he was a little horrified, not least because he was wondering if possibly he had not used this pet name for himself thoughtlessly in Sylvia's hearing, or perhaps even said it in his sleep. In that case . . .

"What has happened?" she asked. "You are looking very strange."

Julian realized he had been holding the envelope rigidly before him for perhaps a minute. This would have fitted in splendidly with his plan, which made it necessary to arouse by some such means his wife's attention, for ordinarily, so far as he knew, she did not read his mail; but now he hesitated, for a number of reasons, to go through with the scheme. Several disagreeable possibilities, unforeseen in his first infatuation with the idea, rapidly presented themselves. Suppose she confronted him boldly with the fact of her innocence and demanded to know what he was going to do? Suppose she said to him (as Julian thought she very well might): You did this yourself? It also occurred to him that, according to a certain still widely accepted scheme of morality, a husband, on receipt of such a message, would be expected to kill his wife. Would Sylvia expect that? And what would she do? Kill him instead?

"It is nothing," he said, absently achieving just the right tone, the tone in which Othello replies to Iago's "I see, this hath a little dash'd your spirits." Characteristically, his suppositions at this moment did not at all include one which ought perhaps to have come first: that husbands who provoke reality by asking questions about the honesty of their wives may receive replies which they do not altogether like.

If I don't go on now I have got this far, he thought, I shall never get so far again. Also I will always have to reproach myself for losing my nerve.

He placed the letter on the table and covered it with the

newspaper which Sylvia would pick up as soon as he had gone.

"I'll just walk the dogs now," he said, as he did every morning. "Back in ten-fifteen minutes." She responded vaguely and habitually, by a slight lift of her chin, to his kiss.

Viewed from the outside, there was something handsome and prosperous about the spectacle of Julian, an upright man in the prime of life, walking two such aristocratic, long-nosed animals, each attached to him by an elegant silver chain and choker with very small links. Troilus and Cressida were admired, and their owner slightly envied, by the few persons whose business led them to that block so early in the morning: a street cleaner, two doormen on Fifth Avenue, a number of people waiting for the bus on Madison. It was a fine, fresh day, which the sight of what seemed to be a member of the leisured classes, of American aristocracy, intensified in the eyes even of such as felt the slight envy. Even if it was May Day, they had no wish to destroy Julian or his world or the society which had produced him, though they would rather have liked to be him, that is, to replace him in his life with that superior version of himself which they could so easily have supplied simply by taking thought. No doubt one or two concluded their brief reflections on this subject with the idea that he, poor fellow, probably had troubles of his own; for, as everyone knows, money is not happiness.

Julian as a matter of fact was not a person of leisure, and as these things go he did not even have a great deal of money. But appearances impress. They impressed even him, as he coyly passed his image in shop windows on Madison Avenue, to the extent that for a few moments he forgot the situation into which he had busily projected himself.

When he returned to the apartment with the dogs, however,

22

he found his wife reading the paper. The letter remained more or less where it had been; perhaps accidentally moved when she had picked up the paper? Perhaps not moved at all? Julian was unable to decide, and he stood thoughtfully at the edge of the table for a long moment.

"Is there something you wanted to say?" Sylvia asked in a neutral voice. Julian hesitated over the interpretations it was possible to put on this question.

"I thought so," he said at last, being cryptic in his turn, "but I guess I've forgotten what it was. Anyhow, I've got to be off to work now."

He walked casually past the table and picked up the letter. In the involutions of his plot he was already uncertain whether he wanted this action to be noticed or missed by his wife. Such are the problems for the amateur in the realms of darkness.

3

SYLVIA, who had not failed to notice her husband's pre-occupation, opened the letter as soon as he left the house with the dogs. Her first response was a kind of sinking horror such as she might have experienced had a rather expensive shop sent her a bill with the decimal point accidentally moved one place to the right. She very nearly opened the window in order to shout down to her husband on the street below; she was prevented from doing so not only because it would have been ridiculous, but also because she could not think what she would shout.

"It is some sort of joke," she said. "Someone is being funny." She poured herself more coffee, sat down at Julian's place, and began to inspect the letter more closely.

Sir —
    A word to the wise. Your wife, sir,
is too much alone. And not always alone.
                    Your friend,
                        Federigo

For a few moments the impulse to play detective altogether
overcame her more serious considerations, sentiments of indignation and bewilderment. A passion for mystery stories enabled her to go rapidly through all those characteristics of an
anonymous letter which tell the detective nothing: she saw
quite well that the message was composed of letters cut from
magazines and newspapers and pasted together; that the address was typed; that the paper and envelope were "such as
might have been procured from any one of a hundred stores"
— beyond this she saw nothing of any use.
    Then she became angry. The sneering theatricality of "a
word to the wise" — she saw it as accompanied by a wink —
and that nasty foreign name Federigo — by association of
sounds she saw a small man in a green *fedora,* he wore dark
glasses and a little mustache, Sylvia wanted to squash his face
right in — made her tremble with anger, and she was brought
up short before her own absolute helplessness. This was the
most frightening thing about the anonymous letter; it came
from the wide outside, out of the everywhere into the here.
Who was Federigo? and where? and what was he talking
about? But perhaps, and most likely, in fact, there was no
such person, the name came out of the plays of Shakespeare,
or the telephone book, or the racing page of the *Daily Mirror.*
Not only was she helpless in her rage; even worse, her curiosity was balked in its very beginning. You cannot reason with
the anonymous letter, you cannot ask it to elucidate obscure
points, fill in details, be less elliptical. Sylvia could nearly

24

have danced around the room crying "Come out and fight." But there was no way of convincing the anonymous letter of her entire innocence. Moreover, no one is ever entirely innocent, and, as political trials in various countries show quite clearly, particular and present accusations have a way of picking up reinforcements from remote, all but forgotten sins; while broad and general accusations, like this of the letter, are, for sensitive persons, blank checks on a vast accumulated capital of guilt.

"Could it mean my having lunch now and then with Marius?" she wondered. "But, of course, there is nothing in the least wrong with that. Why shouldn't I have lunch with him? Marius, it's true, would be quite pleased to make love to me, but that is all foolishness and I have never encouraged it. Beyond a joke, that is. And besides, who could know about that? I even tell Julian about it, most of the time — 'I had lunch with Marius today' — and he says 'how nice.' No, there's nothing there."

She thought for a few minutes more.

"It is Hugo," she decided. "It is Hugo, who wants to make trouble. But why?"

Sylvia, who was several years younger than her husband, had met him early in the war, and by the time he went overseas they had a quite definite understanding, known to their families and friends though not published as an engagement. This understanding, however, had not prevented Sylvia from being seduced and got with child by another person, though the child had been aborted with the knowledge and pained co-operation of her parents, who had been most kind. Sylvia had very nearly died at that time, and there was some doubt if she could again bear children.

Without her confession of this incident it is doubtful whether Julian, whose knowledge of the world had consider-

25

ably expanded though it had not deepened during the war years, would ever have married her. But that episode gave her, in his eyes, exactly the flavor of sad experience, of tragic possibility, which he would most have wanted to be affected by; she had had, in those days, a dark unhappiness, which had since given way to a kind of severe complacency (she was no longer quite so thin, either). She wore her premarital experience like an unobtrusive talisman, ready to be drawn forth and prayed to in emergencies, believed that the object of marriage (already achieved) was a quiet happiness, occasionally wondered whether or not she was as happy as she believed proper, and used her earlier life as a living witness that happiness consisted in their being always honest with one another. "If I had not told you, I don't think I could have lived," she had sometimes said to him. What she had never told him — and it seems characteristic of this kind of honesty in action — was that her seducer (if that is not too strong a word; but in her confession the whole affair had become more nearly like a rape) had been Julian's good friend and roommate at college, Hugo Alter, who was still, or again, a member of their circle of acquaintance. Sylvia had said, in response to Julian's somewhat hesitant probing of this point, that the man, a stranger and an officer in the Navy, had died in the war: "In the Coral Sea," she said, actually filling her mind at that moment with the pathos of this translucent coral image. In saying this she was moved, perhaps, by a real delicacy of feeling: to have given her fiancé that knowledge in its entirety would have been to give him a difficult and highly ambiguous responsibility; and her having to bear that one piece of information herself, alone, in a lifetime of silence, also appealed to her morally passionate nature as a punishment hardly short of the tragic. Thus she was enabled to entertain privately the most romantic notion of her life without ever

26

running the risk of *having something happen*. Though there was one point about which she remained in doubt; she had never exactly spoken to Hugo Alter about his anonymity to her husband. She had instead, at an early meeting after the war and after her marriage, given him a long, flashing and intently imperious look which she hoped and believed had clearly enjoined silence (a silence which he would have no motive for breaking, would he?) and a silence, moreover, unmarred by any giggle or smirk of recognition. She had been, so far as concerned her own mind, beyond those rapids and on a calm water; at least that was what she firmly maintained in her one glance to that man, her first lover and, so far as first things really come first, her only one.

And now Hugo had broken the silence? Had he? Only one other person knew the whole story of this incident (to which Sylvia now began to give more importance than it really need have had after so many years), and that was Dr. Mirabeau; it had been one of the first things she had told him, last year, when Hugo's wife Alma had persuaded her to undertake psychiatric treatment. Sylvia, however, firmly rejected the notion that Dr. Mirabeau could be Federigo; though she had heard terrible things about crooked alienists, she did not believe them about this very reputable and good man, to whom she had said so much. That was the awful thing about the anonymous letter, it led one to suspicion everywhere.

But no, it must be, it had to be, Hugo Alter. Though she could not in the least think of a good reason why. Yet, even going back as far as the first boy who had kissed her, as a crush on another girl in her freshman year at college, she could think of no other possible occasion for the anonymous letter.

By the time her husband came back with the dogs, Sylvia was full of honest pity for him, though she also felt indignant at the idea of his taking that contemptible letter with any seriousness whatever. She decided against speaking of it to him at this time, in the first place possibly because she never read mail addressed to him. She would first speak to Hugo; or she would tell Mirabeau first, and see what he said. Meanwhile, both her pity for Julian and her indignation against him suggested to her that it would do him good, poor thing, to suffer for a bit. One good thing about this wretched letter, it would make him keenly interested in herself, with an interest she had felt the want of for some time.

It characteristically never crossed her mind that Julian might feel impelled to kill her on the basis of the anonymous letter; she never even reached the point of having to say to herself that "people don't behave that way any more." The amusing possibility of Julian's shooting her in consequence of an honest misapprehension could not have occurred to her, and had it been mentioned by someone else Sylvia would have said: "Shooting me? With what?"

So that on Julian's return the letter was back on the table, where the paper had been before she picked it up. She saw him retrieve the letter and slip it into his pocket in a quick, gliding motion as he walked past the place; and she wondered whether she had been supposed to notice or not to notice this action.

Chapter 2

JULIAN ARRIVED at the office a few minutes before nine, but his employer Mr. Ballou was already closeted with a client; he had left with Miss Duddon, at the switchboard, a note of instruction: Julian was to see, at ten o'clock, a Dr. Thybold, and at twelve-thirty to lunch with a Mr. Archer More at a club called the Round Table. The names of both clients were new to Julian, though he believed he had heard something somewhere about an Archer More, and Mr. Ballou had appended to his message a couple of curt and cryptic orders:

Dr. Thybold. Treat this little bore politely, but with contempt; He must *want* us. Small change, may come to something. Don't repeat DON'T let him know about Olympics.

Olympics was the brand name of a new, king-size cigarette, an account which Mr. Ballou handled personally, and which he was pushing toward the big money on the basis of a complex imagery associating the product not merely with good health but with athletic vigor as well; Julian wondered why this was not to be mentioned to Dr. Thybold, and decided that the doctor might be the purveyor of some small (not king-size) brand of medicated cigarette.

Mr. Archer More. This will sound a silliness, but treat it seriously. Always treat this much money seriously. This is a big chance for you.

With this information, and nearly an hour in which to think it over — but there was very little to think about — Julian went into his office and smoked several cigarettes.

The entire suite of offices was very small — he could even hear Mr. Ballou's voice next door when it rose to some sort of climax, though he could not make the words out — but extremely ornate, with gold wallpaper, indirect lighting, and thick, fitted carpets throughout. "I am being impressive," Mr. Ballou had said when they moved in two years before. "My office has always been under my hat, but now I am being impressive." Indeed, up to that point he had trained Julian, whom he treated not as an employee but as an apprentice and future partner, to do business largely in restaurants and bars, to sketch out schemes rapidly and persuasively on the back of menus, and above all to give the impression of a large and complicated organization full of underlings, busily working away in an office building elsewhere. Such an organization had never existed except in the imagination of clients, the only place, according to Mr. Ballou, where such an organization had any right or reason to exist. "I pray you to remember," Mr. Ballou said to Julian on taking him in, "that our interest here is only in money. It is as simple as that, and if you remember it you will not go far wrong." He added, "That you are here at all comes from my affection for your parents, which will not, however, serve to keep you here unless you give promise of being, in office hours at least, as single-mindedly avaricious, and as efficiently so, as your humble servant." Mr. Ballou frequently and without visible irony referred to himself as "your humble servant." He was a tall, fat, powerfully built man of over fifty, with curly gray hair and features which, in moments of anger or other emotion, emerged decisively and arrogantly from their recesses of folded fat. Particularly since the death of his parents Julian

30

had admired Mr. Ballou and intensely respected him as a father; even better, liked him as he had never been able to like his father. What he cared for most in the older man was perhaps what he himself was most deficient in, a capacity for the forthright, even blatant, expression of feeling, particularly on themes concerning which Julian's own upbringing would have taught him to rejoice or sorrow in silence. Money was one of these themes. Woman was the other. Julian had seen Mr. Ballou kiss a large check, weep over it, then send him out to the bank to have it magically transformed into one-dollar bills which made a stack large enough to cover his bulk to the shoulders as, still weeping, he sat on the floor in his office. And Miss Duddon, whether or not she knew it, was but one in a long sequence of switchboard operators, all of whom, on being interviewed, had been turned around for Julian's inspection by Mr. Ballou, who would pinch their cheeks and slap their behinds, saying: "Look at this, isn't it marvelous? It's marvelous!" Girls who did not take kindly to this treatment, which was for Mr. Ballou not a sexual approach but an innocent and honest admiration for the flesh, were not hired. Julian's sensitive soul had at first been embarrassed and irritated by this behavior; he was incapable at that time of seeing anything innocent about it. Later he came to marvel at, and envy, his employer's ease at this kind of behavior, seeing to his surprise how friendly and pleasant those rather stiff, nervous and absurdly dignified girls became at being treated so. At the same time he became convinced that all this depended, for Mr. Ballou, on a life of the utmost personal probity in such matters; in his naïveté, however, he decided it must be because the old gentleman was "past the age for such things."

There was a peculiar, cryptic joke which Mr. Ballou had taken to using on Miss Duddon almost every morning. He would come in, kiss her on top of her lovely blonde head, and make some such remark as: "The virgin and the sack of gold! The virgin even without the sack of gold! How do you do it, day after day?" to which he would somberly add, "It must be the police force."

The explanation of this performance, which Julian got at the request of Miss Duddon, who was embarrassed to ask for the meaning of a joke at which she had so often laughed, turned out to be proverbial: in the Empire of Genghis Khan, Mr. Ballou explained, it was said that a virgin carrying a sack of gold could walk in perfect safety across the whole of Asia.

"Imagine it," he said, spreading his hands to show this vast extent, "across all Asia. In New York she's lucky to get once around the block."

For no fathomable reason the story struck Julian as an epitome of life in Mr. Ballou's office, where he was on the whole very happy. He and Miss Duddon spoke about their employer behind his back but affectionately as Genghis Khan.

Julian had also, on several occasions, seen Mr. Ballou in his anger, and found it a most disturbing sight. He had not known the literal equivalent for the expression "to dance with rage." The walls shook, pictures came down.

Mr. Ballou had lately several times spoken to Julian about the latter's carrying on the firm's operations "after your humble servant passes on." "Passes on" was the only euphemism Julian had ever heard Mr. Ballou use for any fact of life, and he would not have been surprised to see tears of prospective mourning flow from those shrewd, friendly eyes, which however on such occasions merely glittered at him gaily. He realized, however, that Genghis Khan considered him as a son, and he was touched by it.

As to what were the firm's operations, or more particularly his own part in them — Julian's job at this time was a strange one. He had been removed by Mr. Ballou from commercial advertising, where for some years he had dutifully helped to sell whisky, cigarettes, brassieres, girdles ("foundation garments," as he had learned to call them), soap flakes, perfumes and automobiles, and he had been put to work on a new, experimental project with the general title (for window-dressing) of Private Policy Advertisement, or, as he personally thought of it, in terms picked up during the war, The Line Shooting and Chewing Out Division.

A new development had been creeping up on the advertising world for many years; in simplest form, the idea behind it amounted to this, that in order to advertise you did not need to make anything or distribute anything of a tangible nature that you wished to place before the buying public, you did not need to be, even, in business; it was enough that you had an opinion about something, were unable by talent to publish this opinion in the usual manner, and had money to pay for having your opinion in print. A vast, new market opened up by means of this simple device (or better mousetrap), which, far from having been the original inspiration of American know-how and get-ahead, spread from Mexico, where it had for some time been extremely popular as a means of airing grievances, telling the world what was wrong with the world, putting pressure on government, et cetera. In this country the same practice had been followed in a relatively primitive way at election time, when a citizen or body of citizens might buy space to plug their candidate of choice; but it was now seen that more could be made of the idea than that, much more; it had, without doubt, a great future, and could advertise itself as democracy in action, on the ground of its demonstration that in our country one opinion was just as good as another, if not better.

As a matter of fact, the experiment was working splendidly; only Julian sometimes felt as though he had entered a new, insane world, which was, however, extremely interesting. People came to him out of nowhere, bringing thousands of dollars, because they personally did not like communism, creeping socialism or low necklines; they took advertisements protesting against foreign policy, domestic policy, labor, business, the American Medical Association; or they attacked, within the limits of the laws of libel, such persons as columnists, authors, labor leaders and famous actresses. The idea was beautifully taking hold, it required of the advertiser not one blessed thing more than money and an opinion (if he had no opinion he could buy one of those, too); he did not have to manufacture anything, distribute anything, or even be able to write — Julian's department would produce whatever he needed, in appropriate tones of wrath, plain common sense, honest indignation, pathos, even humor when necessary, on subjects ranging from birth-control to "the ever-increasing death toll on our highways" (Julian had only a few months before brought forth a charming tribute to the one-millionth victim of the automobile, a kind of valedictory and congratulation speech).

The thing in all this which struck Julian as particularly insane was its open and evident altruism. The people who came to him on these errands came straight from the world of profit and loss, of hard cash, the open market and an eye on the main chance — usually the reason for their having this money to (as he thought) *throw away* was that they had bitterly gouged it out of the world in the fierce competition of the market place; yet when they appeared in his office he saw something else about these hard, strong people, not only their narrowness of mind, bitter animus and surpassing belief in their own absolute and utter righteousness, but also and at the same time — without, it seemed, any contradiction *they*

34

were aware of — a kind of not unattractive shyness. In some way, he dimly perceived, they had something to sell, and a prospective customer for it, too; they were purveying their own good opinion of themselves, and trying (by the only means they knew, advertising) to make themselves buy it; there was perhaps something a little sinister in the circuitous objectivity with which they went about this thankless and no doubt frequently impossible task.

"Dr. Thybold," said Julian cordially, rising to his feet as the doctor was introduced by Miss Duddon.

"Thybold," said the doctor. "As in 'thy,' not as in 'thigh.' Please."

"Dr. Thybold," Julian corrected himself. The two men shook hands and sat down. The doctor put a briefcase on the table between them. Julian waited.

"Nice place you have here," the doctor began. "Kind of small, though." Julian remembered Mr. Ballou's instruction.

"We find it suitable," he said.

"I thought there was more to your kind of work," Dr. Thybold continued. "Writers, artists, models, photographers . . ." He looked around as though possibly these services might be concealed in the walls.

"That is all done elsewhere," Julian said with a spacious wave of the hand.

"Yes, of course," said the doctor doubtfully. Decisively hitching forward his chair he began to come to the point.

"I represent," he said, "I represent a small, independent — you're rather young, aren't you, for so responsible a position?"

"No," Julian said, "as a matter of fact, I'm not."

"Oh," said Dr. Thybold, visibly embarrassed. "No offense."

"None at all." The doctor, a thin, middle-aged man of somewhat gray complexion, appeared to Julian to be extremely nervous; in an ecstasy of unexpressed self-importance his hands kept playing with the latch and handle of the briefcase which lay before him.

"My associates and I," he began again, "that is, we have decided to place in your hands — " he broke off once more. "You must realize," he said, "that I am a scientist, I am not used to — the noise and bustle of the business world."

"It is not noisy here," Julian said.

"No, it is not, is it?"

"And no one is bustling." Julian was becoming bored with this performance, however, and thinking to put the doctor at his ease extended a pack of cigarettes.

"Smoke?"

Dr. Thybold drew himself up and glared indignantly at Julian.

"No!" he cried, with a forbidding gesture of the hand, and added, as Julian began to take a cigarette himself, "young man, if you knew what you were doing, you would throw that wicked, wicked package out the window."

"The window?" Julian stopped in the act of striking a match; the unlighted cigarette dangled from his mouth.

"If I could show you," Dr. Thybold went on, "if you could only see a photograph, a color photograph, of the tissues of your lungs at this moment, you would throw that cigarette away and swear off as of now." Whatever difficulty the doctor had experienced in getting started was at an end. He quickly unlocked the briefcase and rummaged in it. "Wait," he cried, "perhaps I have a photograph with me, yes — no, that's not it — here it is!" He pushed across the desk a large, glossy print showing a circular area generally red and yellow in color, spotted heavily with black.

36

"That is the portrait," he said impressively, "of what you can expect your own lungs to be like in twenty years."

Julian had a moment's horrified vision of himself in twenty years. He would be fifty-six. This vision did not, however, include the state of his lungs.

"And the person," he said, "from whom this picture was taken — ?"

"Dead," said Dr. Thybold, not without a trace of satisfaction. "A hale, hearty man — "

"But dead."

"A hale, hearty man of little more than fifty summers, sir," Dr. Thybold swept imperturbably on. "Dead, you might say, in the prime. And all for what, do you suppose?"

"For smoking?"

"Naturally for smoking. Lung cancer, young man. Wait, let me show you some diagrams and charts which my associates and I have prepared from our researches." The doctor plunged back into the briefcase. Julian would very much have liked to light his cigarette just then, but thought it best to wait until the first fury of the attack had expended itself.

For fifteen minutes, more or less, the doctor explained to Julian a number of graphs and statistical summaries which he laid in a row across the desk like a solitaire. So far as Julian could take it all in, it appeared that the incidence of cancer of the lungs, which was greater anyhow in men than in women, rose quite steeply, past the age of forty, for a group of people who smoked more than twenty-five cigarettes a day; a comparable group of nonsmokers at the same age remained relatively, though not entirely, free of this particular disease.

"Very interesting," Julian observed when the doctor seemed about at the end of his demonstration. "Of course, there are so many things one might die of in the meantime. . . ."

37

"Please," said the doctor, "this is not a joke."

"If you don't mind," Julian said, "I think I will light my cigarette."

"That," said Dr. Thybold sharply, "is merely the voice of despair. It is not too late, young man. Take my case, for instance, or that of my associates. Why, as soon as we even suspected where our researches were tending, what conclusions we should be forced to come to, why, we simply gave it up, all of us together. It is not so hard to do, really. Let me tell you how we did it."

At this moment Julian lit his cigarette. The doctor glared at him, and continued.

"What we did was, each of us bought a fresh carton of his favorite brand. We got together right there in the laboratory, we made a little ritual of it, you see, and we burned every last one of those cartons. If you do it all together, like that, say with a Bunsen burner, it's much easier, you see."

"I see," Julian said.

"Besides," added Dr. Thybold, "it helps more than you'd believe to put a little investment of money, like that, into giving it up. Once you've burned a carton of cigarettes you paid out your good money for, why, you've a real stake in not smoking. And another thing — " he smiled thinly in reminiscence — "what an orgy it was, tobacco fumes everywhere for weeks."

"And this incident took place," Julian inquired, "how long ago?"

"Four or five weeks," said Dr. Thybold with a marked decrease in enthusiasm. "I feel like a new man already, you wouldn't believe it."

"Well, no," Julian said. "At least, I wouldn't have thought of it by myself." He blew a large cloud of smoke across the desk.

38

"Please," said Dr. Thybold, blowing and ineffectually pushing the cloud away.

"Sorry," said Julian.

"One must expect to suffer for what one believes," said Dr. Thybold.

"Yes, I suppose so," Julian said. The two men sat in silence for a moment or so, the one elaborately blowing smoke away from the other.

"Perhaps you can tell me now," said Julian, "what you had in mind to do about all this?"

"It was our idea," answered Dr. Thybold, "to enlist your aid in putting our message across the — across to the public. We haven't a great deal of money, of course, only what was left over from the research grant made by the Hobugger Foundation. But we want to use that money in the most effective way possible."

"You know, I suppose," said Julian, "that the Hobugger Foundation comes from a fortune originally made in Cellophane packaging, and that it is allied by marriage to one of our largest cigarette families?"

"I know," said Dr. Thybold.

"It may not have occurred to you that under the circumstances — "

"Poetic justice," said the doctor.

"Oh," said Julian. Then he asked, "Just what do you hope to achieve by this plan?"

"Very simply," Dr. Thybold replied, "to stop people from smoking cigarettes." Delivered of their message at last, his large, nervous hands folded themselves respectfully on the briefcase.

Julian was taken aback by the enormity of the idea.

"We want to scare 'em half to death," said the doctor. "That's where we need your help."

"I don't know if you've got any very good selling points here," said Julian doubtfully, indicating the graphs, charts, etc. "Or, rather, unselling points." He tried a smile. "After all, you can't expect people to give up cigarettes just because they are going to die."

"Young man," Dr. Thybold said earnestly, "your cynicism doesn't convince me at all, not at all. I suppose it is a mask you find useful in your business, but deep down, believe me, I know and you know right from wrong. Understand," he added, "it is not my generation, or even your generation, that concerns us, my associates and myself. It is already too late for us, probably too late for you. We live in a world of blackened lungs. But it is the children, my friend, the children. Do we want them to make the same mistake we made, do you want them blindly to pursue the course of action which is killing their fathers? I don't see how any man in his right senses could sit there and tell me he was willing to see his children destroyed by cigarette smoke."

Julian, with contemptible bravado, lit a fresh cigarette from the one he had finished.

"If we can't shame the parents into swearing off," said Dr. Thybold, "we want to shame them into stopping their children from ever contracting the filthy habit."

"Just there," Julian said, "you may have a possible line of attack; that might have a tremendous appeal. I have noticed frequently that the more people smoke the more anxious they are for their children not to. You might work up some sort of direct mail campaign, possibly form clubs, a national society — "

"Exactly so," Dr. Thybold interrupted. "That's the sort of thing we have in mind. Since all we can do on our own, with relatively little money, is initiate the drive, we must recruit people to help, they themselves must — " he hesitated

40

— "pick up the ball and carry it across the goal line. For let me tell you," he went on in a rather hushed voice, "the end we envision, what we are working toward, is the passage of legislation, federal legislation — "

"To prevent smoking?"

"More than that. To make it a crime to grow, cure, or be in possession of tobacco. Public health officers will be sent out to burn this weed just as they would do now if it were marijuana."

"One question, doctor," said Julian. "What do you get out of all this? What is your motive?"

The doctor assumed a weary smile only very faintly tinged with indignation.

"Is there nothing in your world but money and self-interest?" he asked. "Will you, can you possibly, understand me if I say that my friends and I are motivated by an altruism which is both morally and scientifically as pure as can be? by the simple and sufficient idea of playing our part in building a healthier America? Look: it is as simple as this: cigarette smoking is an evil, science tells us so. Very well, we will stamp out cigarette smoking just as we would communism, prostitution, syphilis, or any one of a host of evils."

"Well," said Julian, "perhaps we can work something out. But we're going to have to scare people plenty."

"Nothing vulgar, of course," said Dr. Thybold, "but no shilly-shallying, either. Just — you know — back the hearse up to the front door."

Julian and Dr. Thybold spent the next hour or so in drawing up a budget and the major lines of the proposed campaign. They became quite friendly once the principle of the thing had been made clear, and toward the end of the interview Julian scored one minor triumph. He had been smoking continuously, and in an absent-minded moment he extended the

41

pack to Dr. Thybold, who with equal absence of mind accepted a cigarette and a light. When Julian called this to his notice he first got angry, but then smiled.

"It just shows you how a habit gets under your skin," he said. "Still, I guess one more won't hurt."

Julian had never dined at the Round Table, which he had heard of as extremely expensive and really rather a club than a restaurant. Arrived there, he was looked at with some suspicion until he mentioned the name of Archer More, after which everyone was at once smiling respectfully. A clerical-looking man in black, who took reservations, led him through the dining room to a small table in the corner. On the way, they passed the Round Table from which the establishment took its name. There were a dozen or so seats, about half of them occupied by gentlemen of middle age who were, it was evident, drunk.

After a few moments Mr. Archer More turned up. He seemed not in good health, and was piloted across the room by a young waiter, on whose arm he leaned heavily; he stopped nevertheless to exchange greetings with the gentlemen at the Round Table, who seemed from what Julian could hear to be making jokes at his expense. For the rest, Mr. More was a very small man, wearing a neat gray suit; his starched collar was drawn up tightly enough to make the chin and jowls bulge over it, and there flowered from this focus a broad, stiff bow tie of blue with white dots. He was smiling as though automatically, and to Julian he resembled a frog in a fairy story. The waiter assisted him into place on the banquette along the wall, and brought pillows which he arranged with what amounted to medical attention under the arms on both sides. Thus propped, Mr. More turned to Julian with an intensified smile, and introduced himself.

42

"Though I'm afraid you must have heard of me already," he added, and giggled.

Julian, embarrassed, was about to deny this, when suddenly he recalled that he had indeed heard of Mr. Archer More; the process of his thoughts must have been clearly visible on his face, for Mr. More giggled with added vigor, saying: "Yes, I am *that* Archie More." Then, with a kind of collapse into the seriousness of an aged schoolboy, "I realize it is nothing to be proud of."

A waiter just now brought them, without any consultation, two large martinis; Mr. More took his glass, with which he made a sort of perfunctory duellist's salute to Julian, and drank off his drink as though he had come in from the desert. Julian, drinking more slowly, thought that he could literally observe the gin coursing through the myriad small veins of Mr. Archer More's face, restoring its character, firming its texture, tinging it to a healthier color — doing, in fact, all that embalming fluid would have done had Mr. More been dead.

This somewhat haughty and holier-than-thou similitude crossed Julian's mind because he had just identified this man as the Archer More who had become something of a culture hero to his generation by reason of his having married, legally and in succession, some ten, possibly eleven, women, to all but the latest of whom, after divorces attended by scandalous publicity, he doled out fractions of an enormous, inherited fortune. He was a man, in other words, very easy to be holier-than or haughty about; perhaps, in fact, too easy, as Julian now began to believe. For, after all, the stern moralist may compare himself favorably to a man once or twice divorced and not everyone, at any rate, will laugh; but when it came to a man with ten divorces to his credit, or under his belt, or however you put it — a man who, had these been enemy

43

aircraft instead of women, would be an ace twice over — the comparison simply fell over on its face, the moralist began to seem petty and niggling before this huge demonstration of what morality was and what it might be. So Julian, after his first impulsive reaction of distaste, looked at Mr. More — who had already been served a second martini — with admiration and incredulity; thinking, just as he might have thought on meeting a celebrated artist or statesman, "Why, he is only a man, and not even a very big one."

"Well, you know my history, no need to go into that," Mr. More was saying. "You'll want to know why I called you in." He beamed at Julian over the top of his glass. "I have already discussed it with Mr. Ballou; in principle, that is. He is a very *good* person, Mr. Ballou, don't you think so? I have experience, and I can always tell real goodness in a human being — if he doesn't happen to be a woman, that is. And I can tell you this much, too, my boy — that Mr. Ballou has a deep respect and affection for you. Never you let him down, young fellow, for he holds you in very high esteem indeed. I might tell you a number of things he said to me about your work, your character — don't want to swell your head, though. Just remember one thing: goodness in human beings is not something you meet up with very often, and that Ballou has goodness." Archer More looked Julian straight in the eyes; Julian, speechless as a child, could only nod his assent to all this. "And so have you," Mr. More concluded. "I can size people up *like that*." He snapped his fingers unsuccessfully, giggled again, and once again became owlishly serious.

The waiter brought more martinis, Julian's second and Mr. More's third.

"As you've probably read in the papers," began Mr. More with a great air of getting down to business, "I'm breaking up

44

camp again. Lois is the eleventh try for me, and as God is my witness" — he raised his right hand solemnly, with the martini glass — "all I ever wanted out of those eleven girls was *love*. Did I want money? Did I want power?" He glared at Julian.

"No," Julian said.

"No," said Mr. More. "I wanted love, that's all. When I saw romance, I went after it. The fountain of youth, that's what I was looking for, and each time I thought I'd found it at last. I really mean that. Perfect sincerity at all times, that's my rule."

Julian nodded as though his head were on a string.

"So when the romance faded out — you know how it happens, my boy — are you married?"

"Yes," Julian said.

"How many?"

"One," said Julian, rightly taking it that Mr. More meant wives and not children.

"Marvelous," said Archer More, pressing Julian's hand in a gesture of dignified affection. "I respect you for it, son. You stick with the little woman and you'll never go through the hell I've gone through. I'd envy you, if it weren't against my principles.

"But to get back to business," he went on, releasing Julian's hand, "when I saw that Lois was going just where the others went, I finally started to do some thinking. Archie, I said, maybe you've been looking for happiness the wrong way — you've been trusting in the strange woman all this time, she with the attire of a harlot and subtle of heart, as it says in the Book. You couldn't take it, I said, that Adam learned the lesson for all of us, once and for all — oh, no, you had to go ahead and learn it eleven times, like the dumbest kid in the school."

45

The waiter, without being asked, brought another round of martinis. Julian wondered when they would order lunch.

"Even then, you know," Mr. More continued, "I was fooling with the idea of trying just once again. I said to myself, Archie, why not make it a round dozen and then stop? After all, you've got a reputation for it now, wouldn't it sort of be letting people down? Sometimes, you know, you have to do what people expect, in this world," he added, emphasizing this general point by prodding Julian in the ribs. "But I saw through that," he went on. "That business of *just one more,* that's what the Devil always says. Besides, if I had yielded just for the sake of reputation and made it a round dozen — only for the world record, say — what would that have been?"

Julian, prodded again in the ribs, did not know what that would have been.

"Pride, spiritual pride," said Mr. More. "Just like taking another drink when you don't need one and don't really even want one." The making of this somewhat obscure connection caused him to look at and then empty his glass. After a moment the waiter replaced it with a full one. Julian began to perceive that they were not going to order lunch, but that this in fact was lunch.

"Well, I don't want to bore you by making a long story of it," said Mr. More, "but I can tell you this, in strictest confidence — I don't want it to break in the papers until I'm ready for it — once I've finished with Lois, I'm finished, for good, no more, *finis,* period. Now, of course, you're asking yourself, 'What will the poor old bugger do instead?' "

Julian, who had by no means been asking himself anything of the sort, nodded seriously.

"Well, I'll tell you, son," Mr. More said slowly and solemnly, "the Lord God has come back into my life, and blessed glad I am to be able to say it. When you're my age, young

46

fellow, I hope you'll know that light which shines from above and says it's never too late to mend. I know I've lived badly, I know I stopped going to church many years ago — and I can see now it was because I'd have been ashamed to be seen in the house of God, being the man I was. But that's all over now, and I'm going to make it up to Him the best way I can. Son, I know that my Redeemer liveth, and my heart overfloweth with gladness." Mr. More put down his glass and seized himself with both hands in the region of the heart; for a moment Julian feared he was actually having an attack.

"Give up all that you have and follow Me," said Mr. More earnestly. "That was the word that did it to me, Give up all that you have and follow Me. I said to myself, you old potbellied drunk, you lecher, I said, what have you got that you can give up? You haven't got happiness, you haven't got friends, you haven't got honor, all you've got is money. Well, you're going to give up that money, lad, and be happy in the Lord."

Mr. More giggled, hiccuped, and motioned to the waiter, who was already bringing him another martini.

"Don't you think if we ordered now — ?" Julian began to ask with desperate diffidence.

"Time for just one more," declared Mr. More, "till I finish what I've got to say." He leaned closer to Julian. "What I'm going to do is, I'm going to advertise the love of God." Dramatically settling back, he allowed a silence to descend upon this statement.

Julian nodded with an air of dazed thoughtfulness.

"Full page ads, *Times, Tribune, Life,* the whole works, as long as the money holds out," said Mr. More with a gambler's gesture of hurling his chips on the table.

"And then?" Julian asked.

"Consider the lilies of the field, son," said Mr. More. He

47

raised his glass. "To the lilies of the field," he said, and they both drank.

"What I want, to start with," he continued, "is simplicity, simplicity and size. I want people to know what I know. It could start this way: I AM THE LIGHT OF THE WORLD, in block caps maybe two three inches high, and under that in little letters the place in the Book that comes from. Then, son, you go on from there. Just go to the Book for your inspiration, you're a writer, you know what I mean, you can phrase it better than I could. Just tell people straight, without any fancy verbiage, how they can save themselves and make this world a better place for all of us to live in, if they'll only believe on the Lord. You might even just scare 'em a little," he added reflectively. "Hell, and all that. But not much, go easy on the brimstone and so forth.

"I tell you what," he concluded, "I want you to sketch out, say, about half a dozen full-page spreads like that. I don't want to begin and then just peter out, you know; there's got to be enough for a real series without scraping the bottom of the barrel. And I want it to rise, you see what I mean? A crescendo. I want it to be a work of art."

"A crescendo," Julian said, "beginning with I AM THE LIGHT OF THE WORLD."

"Don't worry, son," said Mr. More, "you'll figure something out, you've got a head on your shoulders. Consider the lilies of the field. Waiter!"

The waiter brought another round of martinis, and Archer More made Julian solemnly drink with him to the success of this odd enterprise. A silence followed. Julian was horrified and impressed, also somewhat drunk, and his stomach ached with hunger. It was hard to believe the little man could be serious, except that he patently was so; and Julian recalled Mr. Ballou's injunction: always take this much money seri-

48

ously. There was no doubt about the money's really being there, and Julian supposed no one could prevent a man from hurling his own wealth in whatever direction he chose. Practically speaking, a steady course in the Casino at Monte Carlo (or across the river in New Jersey, for that matter) would very likely have the same result, and who could say that Mr. More's chosen course was not the more satisfactory of the two just as it was quite possibly the more amusing?

Julian realized that the silence had continued for an unduly long time. He turned to Mr. More with the idea of saying something about ordering their food, and saw that his host had quietly and without making a disturbance relapsed into unconsciousness. Owing to the pillows, whose meaning now became clear, he had not fallen over; Julian was once again reminded of the embalmer's art.

Lunch was over.

2

SYLVIA's relation with Dr. Mirabeau began perhaps more as a matter of fashion than anything else. Hugo Alter's wife Alma was going to him at that time, and Alma spoke very convincingly about psychotherapy, of which the value, she said, was preventive. "Besides, it is the most fascinating thing in the world. You learn so much about yourself." Sylvia, who occasionally suffered from asthmatic attacks which Alma declared were the result of a want of affection in childhood, allowed herself to be convinced because she was bored and, at the same time, curious. This step had been easy, like the famous descent into Avernus; Dr. Mirabeau was charming, courteous, intelligent, though it is true that he was also expensive. The proposition that all illness — and everything else, health included — was psychical in origin Sylvia found extremely attractive; she quickly learned a certain quantity of the profession's cant-terms, which she discovered helped her never very exciting or witty conversation a good deal; she and Alma, in particular, were able to carry on brief critical exchanges in public about almost everything that was said, with the double assurance of being always listened to and seldom understood.

On the other hand, one did not so readily get out of Dr. Mirabeau's softly tenacious grasp when once one had got in. After the first few meetings, when Sylvia had become established as a patient, the doctor formed the disconcerting habit of treating whatever she said rather as evidence than as rational discourse. After six months, for example, Sylvia became bored, and said to him several times that, after all, there was nothing *really* wrong with her, and that she thought (in a casual voice, referring to it just in passing) she might just as well stop. Dr. Mirabeau, to her bewilderment and, presently, indignation, did not seem to hear these remarks, which at first Sylvia would simply interpolate in the course of her reminiscences and associations as she lay back on the quite comfortable couch which was the doctor's operating table. Finally, though, she faced him across the desk as she was leaving after a session, and said straight out that she had had enough. The doctor folded his hands and smiled gently at her. He was personally, by the way, a most comforting and comfortable person, fat, somewhat soft, with large, liquid brown eyes which were imitated, lower down, in the pattern of beautiful foulard ties he had made for him to his own design.

"Of course," he said, "you are a mature, rational being, you must make your own choices, I quite understand that. And I quite understand, moreover, the sense of desperation which makes it necessary for you, particularly at this moment,

50

to be decisive. You have been feeling as though too much depended on me, as though your own will were somehow being betrayed. That is quite natural — at this stage."

Though she was frightened by the words "at this stage" Sylvia would nevertheless have left for good. But the doctor simply and quietly went on talking.

"As a mature, rational being," he said, "you naturally want to have a full understanding of the causes underlying your decision. You believe, of course, that this is a free decision, rationally arrived at. . . ."

As Sylvia did not leave at this point, the result was that she did not leave at all. Dr. Mirabeau with admirable logic convinced her in a few minutes that it was not Sylvia, that free and rational being, who wished to discontinue the treatment, but Sylvia's illness which like an independent entity — "like one of those demons which primitive psychology, under the guise of religion, saw as taking possession of the soul and speaking through it" — thus realized its own deepest wish to hide from the dry, rational light of diagnosis.

The demon, or illness, had a particularly good excuse *at this stage*, the doctor continued, because *at this stage* certain superficial and symptomatic anxieties appeared to have vanished, or at least abated: no asthmatic attacks during the past several weeks, fewer worries in general, a better *tone* (tone was one of his favorite words, which he accompanied by an expressive gesture of the hand). Sylvia might of course take her chance, these symptoms *might* never return, they *might* not even be replaced by others. He, Dr. Mirabeau, could not exactly say that he was satisfied; he hoped that she would not, even with the best intentions, even to praise him, tell others that she had really — *seriously* — been a patient of his; but of course he could not prevent her from quitting if that was what she felt compelled to do.

51

Six months after that, it was a question of money, the consequence of an argument with Julian, who had demanded to know how long "all this" was to go on. "It is not doing much for you so far as I can see," he had said. "You behave exactly the same as always."

"Yes," Dr. Mirabeau had said, giving her a smile of friendly complicity. "We often have this trouble with the family, with friends — people on the outside, in general. Their want of comprehension is troublesome, but one can understand it. On the other hand" — and he looked at Sylvia keenly — "we very frequently also find the patient hiding behind these so-rational, so-sensible complaints about money, which we may sometimes suspect the patient has even led his family on to make, not so?"

Sylvia objected that she had certainly not made her husband say what he had said.

"Not consciously," the doctor continued. "Of course not. But you are willing enough, are you not, to use such a complaint as a way out? The demon speaks again.

"Let us look at it this way. The therapy is expensive, that is perfectly true. Why? Well, you will say, because the doctor must be highly and expensively trained, he can take but a few patients at a time, he must make a living. . . . That is all part of it, certainly, but not by any means the most important part.

"It is expensive because it is good for the patient, it is necessary for the patient, that it be expensive. You see, my dear Sylvia, if I treated this objection to the cost as rational I should have to agree with you. I do agree, it is abominably expensive. But money, after all, is one of the deepest motives of the mind, the strongest resistances are intimately connected with spending money — which is after all but a surrogate image for *giving oneself*, and therefore admirably fitted for expressing sexual tensions — so that we know, when in the course of our analysis we reach this typical argument about how much it all costs, we *know* then that we are reaching the heart of the matter, where the strongest psychical repugnances have set up their defenses. You can see, then, that the therapy must cost a substantial sum, because it must cost a sum which shall be meaningful to the patient, which shall represent a real investment in health. Otherwise, the larger investment remains on the side of the illness and nothing can really be accomplished, it would be like gambling with stakes too small to bother the players."

The fact that the cost of the therapy must, under the circumstances, be more meaningful to Julian than to his wife was evaded by both parties to this discussion. But just lately a far more horrifying thing had come up, which was Alma Alter's going mad, insane, or, if not mad or insane, then something rather shockingly close to it. Sylvia could not help the feeling that the analysis itself was the disease, or induced it, and that it would have been better, had it not now been too late, to bear those evils that we have than fly to others that we know not of. But, concerning this, it was difficult to get Dr. Mirabeau to speak at all, much less commit himself to any unequivocal statement. "Madness," he said, "a frightening word, true. But after all, what is normal? It is a matter of degree."

This matter of degree had put Alma into what was called a *rest home*, an expression of which Sylvia had her doubts, and which seemed to her to conceal nameless and terrible excesses under the guise of treatment.

Nevertheless, perhaps as a matter of necessity, she trusted Dr. Mirabeau, with whom her relation at this time was, in every respect but the carnal, more intimate than what she had with her husband; and this morning she arrived at his office full of excited indignation over the anonymous letter. It was typical of Dr. Mirabeau, however, that he would not let her discuss this matter across the desk in a friendly and sensible way, but insisted on her first lying down as usual.

"Calm yourself," he said, "and collect your thoughts. There is plenty of time. Take a few deep breaths, try to relax. Feel yourself relaxing. There. And now?"

It was very difficult for Sylvia, lying down, to put the proper passion into her recital; even to herself, she sounded as though she were describing what there had been for breakfast.

"How interesting this is," Dr. Mirabeau said. "Again, please." He frequently made her repeat things, and Sylvia told the story, which after all was not long, a second time.

"You have a copy of this letter with you?"

"No," she replied. "I told you — he came back and put it in his pocket."

"I see," said Dr. Mirabeau, and was silent for a few moments. "Then you had this letter in your possession," he said, "for how long?"

"A few minutes, maybe ten minutes," Sylvia said.

"But you remember the contents exactly?"

"Yes, of course. Just as I told you."

"And there is, now, no reality whatever to the accusation?"

"None at all that I can think of."

" 'None at all that I can think of' — does that not imply some reservation? That if you thought for a moment more — ?"

"No," said Sylvia quite sharply.

"Don't be indignant," the doctor said. "You know you have nothing to fear from me. In this office the ordinary rules of

54

morality do not exist. Let us try in our usual way; associate to this letter, please."

"But this is a perfectly real letter," Sylvia rather plaintively said. "It is not a dream, it came in the morning mail."

"Of course," the doctor said. "I don't say you are wrong, but please realize that it would in any case seem so to you. From where I sit," he added, "you can see that it does not look altogether convincing."

Sylvia became speechless with indignation. She sputtered for a moment, and sat up.

"Please," said Dr. Mirabeau, waving her back. "Let us look at it rationally for a moment, you and I together.

"It is early morning, you have very recently come from the world of sleep, you have only just emerged from that great ocean, or even not quite emerged altogether. You have made coffee, you are sitting there over a hot cup of coffee, thinking — about what were you thinking?"

Sylvia did not remember. Perhaps, she said finally, she had been thinking what she would find to say to the doctor himself, later in the morning. It had rather embarrassed her, she now recalled, that she did not remember any dream from the previous night.

"Ah," said Dr. Mirabeau. "Now your husband comes in, he sits down, he too has coffee, you do not talk much."

"No, not very much."

"You do not break the mood of revery, of quiet, diffused feeling. Your husband has breakfast, he goes out to walk the dogs, all is as usual. While he is gone you continue to sit at the table."

"I moved over to his place and picked up the paper."

"Exactly. And you saw this letter on the table."

"Which I had seen my husband was concerned about."

"Yes. And you read the letter, and of course experienced a certain number of thoughts about its contents: first it was a joke, then you became indignant, then a little frightened, et cetera."

"Yes."

"Then you determined that your husband must not know you had read the letter, so you put it back where it had been."

"Yes."

"He returns. His entrance, with the dogs, breaks the mood abruptly. And when he leaves for the second time, there is no more letter." Sylvia felt rather than saw that the doctor, above and behind her head, spread wide his hands in the magician's gesture which says *quod erat demonstrandum.*

"But I saw him pick up the letter and put it in his pocket," she insisted.

"Of course. Secondary elaboration, which the dream supplied to terminate itself in a satisfactory and coherent manner."

"The dream!" Sylvia sat up once again. "But I saw it happen, this all took place not in bed but at breakfast. It was broad daylight."

"Sylvia," said Dr. Mirabeau, with a soothing sternness, "you may be right. Please remember that I have no means of judging except on the evidence as you present it. The thing may have happened exactly as you say. But try for a moment to look at it objectively, and at least admit to yourself the strength of the evidence against it.

"First, it was early in the morning, you acknowledge that you were still sleepy. Second, the letter exists within a closed circle of evidence, there is no objective witness to its being there at all — unless, of course, your husband should confirm your story by producing the letter; but until or unless he does we have only your version to go by. Then, third, the extreme unlikeliness of the letter; you yourself say that its charge has no basis in fact — and, really, Sylvia, in this day and age, and especially in your class of society, people very seldom send such communications, they have many vices but anonymity is not one of them. Then, finally, and most convincing, at any rate to me, there is the extreme vividness of the text of the letter as against the relative vagueness of everything else in the story; in short, not only does a critical look at the circumstances suggest you dreamed it, but the letter itself, in addition, has all the appearance of being a product of dream. And, as you confess, you had just been wishing you had a dream to present to me this morning."

Sylvia could say nothing, at first. She felt trapped. But at the same time she began to feel that Dr. Mirabeau was right, though her reasoning differed somewhat from his: in the first place, she argued, it would be so much nicer if the anonymous letter did not exist. As a matter of fact, she could not recapture the reality of the situation; it did have, undeniably, a dreamlike air, and she admitted as much to Dr. Mirabeau.

"Possibly you are right. I would certainly prefer to believe that horrible letter was unreal. But it all seemed so vivid — "

"Ah ah," interrupted Dr. Mirabeau warningly. "Not unreal, my dear. What you mean is, if I may be a little pedantic, that the letter did not have the kind of *waking reality* which we are accustomed to dignify by calling it, exclusively, 'real.'"

"But it did," Sylvia faintly pleaded. "That was what was so horrifying about it, that it seemed so real."

"We know by now, you and I, what a character actor the dreamwork can be," said Dr. Mirabeau cheerfully. "The thing we have now to discover is, just what *is* the reality in this anonymous communication from the realms of night."

"Do you think," Sylvia nervously asked, "that it means I want to be unfaithful to my husband, and that in the note I punish myself for this wish?"

"Ah, now," said Dr. Mirabeau with the air of a connoisseur, "that's just a trifle glib, don't you think? Remember always that the note is part of the dreamwork, and the dreamwork in itself means nothing, it certainly never means what it says. Let us start instead in our usual manner, not with the whole but with its elements. Now, just what, in the whole experience, strikes you immediately as having the most significance, as standing out from the rest?"

"Federigo," Sylvia unhesitatingly replied. "I remember thinking there was something extra loathsome about that name."

"Yes," said the doctor. "Go on."

"I don't think I dislike foreigners," Sylvia said. "Not consciously, that is."

"I think you will find," the doctor said with a certain jovial coyness, "that there lurks behind the name no foreigner but someone very close to home, very close indeed."

"My husband?" asked Sylvia doubtfully.

"No, no, think again," said Dr. Mirabeau gently. "Think slowly and carefully. Associate to the name Federigo, please."

"A fedora hat," Sylvia said, "and dark glasses. There's some idea of disguise, I think . . ."

"Yes, yes, go on."

A moment later it came to her.

"Ego!" she cried, almost gaily. "Myself! It is right in the name, plain as day."

"Of course," said Dr. Mirabeau in a kind voice. "Now we begin to get somewhere. Continue, please."

58

Sylvia lay back and shut her eyes. It was quite plain, she deeply hated herself. For the first time that morning she found she was able to relax.

When Sylvia emerged from the darkness of Dr. Mirabeau's office, she was always refreshed by the brilliant reality of the daylight; sometimes she even ascribed this intense feeling for the beauty of the world to the therapy itself, like the man who hit himself on the head with a hammer because it felt so good when he stopped. But perhaps the cycle of her days was more complicated than that. Dr. Mirabeau canceled out her anxieties of the previous days and nights, then the bright sunlight canceled out Dr. Mirabeau and the anxieties generated by the analytic session itself; life seemed to begin again, and had for the first few hours at least a feeling of buoyant freedom. It ought to be allowed, though, that perhaps a part of this feeling was caused by Mr. Marius Rathlin, who had formed the habit of meeting her once or twice a week for lunch; this morning he awaited her on the sidewalk when she came up the steps of the brownstone building in the basement of which Dr. Mirabeau had his office.

"You look splendid," said Marius, "like Aphrodite emerging from her first communion."

Sylvia smiled graciously to this; she felt splendid too. The fine May weather, the hard, keen visibility of the buildings in this quiet side street, and her own appearance, all seemed to go brilliantly together, like a page in *Vogue*; she wished she had brought the dogs along.

"Where shall we go?" she asked, with perhaps a greater display of spirit than absolutely necessary.

"I thought that if you were not altogether starved," said Marius, "we might walk in the Park. Then to Mme. Modera, where the sole is said to be quite fair. You, of course, may prefer something else." Marius's references to his being a Catholic were frequent, but usually rather remotely allusive than direct; it was as though he had taken this means of reminding Sylvia not of his religion but of the fact that it was Friday.

As they began to walk Sylvia took his arm, as she usually did, for no better reason than that he seemed to expect it; in such things Marius was very much a gentleman, so much more so than people whom Sylvia really believed were gentlemen as to be somewhat embarrassing. The elegance of his small manners, his extreme formality in dress, his witty but somewhat oratorical conversation which had so much a way of being a monologue — all these things were at once pleasant and disturbing. A walk in the Park with Marius went like the recitative to a first-rate musical comedy, probably more learned and exclusively witty than anything one would see on Broadway, but having about the same connection with common reality. Even his poverty, and Sylvia believed it was perfectly true, what she had often heard said, that he was the poorest person of their acquaintance — even his poverty seemed disguised in such a way as to make sure of shining through his elegance; as in a theater, again, where the audience is supposed to know at once that the young man is poor, and, a moment later, that he is bravely concealing the fact. After they had lunched together a few times Marius had gravely, with the air of admitting her to a new stage in friendship, asked her advice about the proper way of turning his shirt-collar, which was frayed; Sylvia, who took a motherly but amateurish interest in his problem, could not conceal that he knew far more about how it was done than she did, since Julian, of course, would simply have bought another shirt.

Even now she had no idea what Marius did, if he did anything. He referred to himself as a scholar, or as a student, a title he could very reasonably claim from a large if somewhat disordered store of knowledge relating mainly to customs and manners, but he discouraged very bluntly Sylvia's inference from this that he was writing a book. "I am a dilettante," he told her. "The fact that, nowadays, all dilettanti write books should not be taken for a definition of the species in its true, primitive state. I like knowledge, therefore I study; I respect knowledge, therefore I write no book." And again: "To know something, and then not to write it down in a book — that is original virtue. And in the fullness of time, at the last great Book-Burning, I may perhaps have the privilege of standing with the elect, and joining in their blessed laughter." All this simply confirmed Sylvia in the belief that Marius was writing a book, and inspired her to think that this book, when finished, would be a wonderful achievement. She sometimes secretly thought that he might dedicate this work to herself; their friendship, of a young man for an older woman — she was some four or five years older than he — was of exactly the sort to make such a thing possible, it was romantic, light, *spirituel* (a word she had taken from Marius himself), and, above all, perfectly honest. Sylvia was a woman who could permit herself the most intense spiritual excesses in what she believed was utter innocence, simply on the ground that "nothing really happened." The troubadorlike courtship of the young man flattered her intelligence, and her age (which for this purpose she slightly exaggerated, as if she had been his aunt), with no peril to her chastity — an object which she unconsciously regarded as equivalent to her self-respect, her position in the world, her comfortable apartment and, objectively considered, excellent husband. It also seemed to her that she was preserved from danger in this regard by Marius's religion, which he took so seriously — this too was unfashionable and exotic in him — that he must certainly impose upon himself the most rigorous prohibitions with respect to love. The fact that his conversation, while always polite, and unmarred by those four-letter words which men and women used so frequently in each other's presence these days, was extraordinarily free, seemed to her a paradoxical guarantee of the same security. The immodest proposals which he frequently put to her were, in her opinion, part of the tender and witty joke which formed their friendship and permitted their freedom: "At half-past five this evening," he would say, "you will desert your husband and steal his car. We will drive to a small motel on the shore of Lake Erie, and there pass a week of delicious indulgence. Then you will return as if nothing whatever had happened." "Can't we find something less plebeian than Lake Erie?" Sylvia would ask, joining a trifle heavily in the fun.

This morning, however, Sylvia found difficulty in keying herself to Marius's mood. The anonymous letter, now Dr. Mirabeau had convinced her it was a dream, began to trouble her again, as much as or more than it did when it had been a reality. Now that she was out of the doctor's office, out of that comfortable darkness, so like that of a movie theater, where one projected one's private vision into a kind of temporary and provisional being, she began once again to doubt. The letter had seemed so real. . . . But of course that effect could be duplicated by the dream, people constantly said of their dreams that they were more real than reality. The letter was unlikely, and if it had been real it remained unlikely that Hugo would have done such a thing; what profit would there be for Hugo, what did he stand to gain? Hugo had trouble enough right now, with Alma, with preparations for the divorce, with this new girl he wanted to marry.

While they walked along, while Marius was amusing about the grass, the trees, the children, Sylvia tried to tabulate the consequences of the anonymous letter considered first as a dream, then as a reality. No matter which it was, she now saw, Marius was the point at issue. Supposing there really had been a letter, well, it was very likely that some *friend* (how horrifying!) had seen them at lunch together and put this nasty interpretation on it and felt impelled to stick his nose into other people's business by writing to Julian. But if it should have been a dream, that was nearly as bad; she saw now how her friendship with Marius was open to misconstruction — how open it must be, in fact, if she herself had so misconstrued it in a dream which had the air of being a prophecy and a secret warning. Perfectly true, after all, though she had not until now paid it much attention — perhaps even tried to conceal it from herself — that Marius had a certain reputation for being dangerous to women. It was very unlikely, she admitted to herself with some bitterness, that she was the only one upon whom he exercised his charm; no doubt there were others, even at the same time, with whom the rewards were at least more immediately satisfying. Sylvia experienced that shadowy disillusion which comes over people when they barely begin to suspect they have been foolish. "What can he see in me?" she asked herself. "I am older than he is, he must know so many more attractive girls. . . . And he knows, of course, that I would never really sleep with him."

"You are a bit subdued," said Marius. "Has your shaman read disaster from your dreams? a coffin among the tea-leaves? Or perhaps you are merely depressed with Central Park, which would be understandable: it brings back the most disagreeable recollections of one's grubby childhood."

"It is nothing," Sylvia said. "I was only thinking."

"That is a certain sign of dejection in beautiful women," said Marius. "It probably means you are hungry." And he led her out of the Park by the nearest exit, where he got a taxi.

At the Café Modera they both had the sole, Sylvia perhaps because to do something so specifically Catholic had about it a romantic and very nearly a sinful atmosphere. She was not altogether happy, even so, and during the meal kept looking about to see if they were being observed by anyone she knew, but saw no one. The coffee was strong, black and bitter, with a slice of lemon in it; over the second cup she said:

"I don't think we ought to meet again like this." At once, but too late, she regretted this statement, which seemed to commit her to a more serious view of having lunch with Marius than she would have believed proper.

"What a very charming thing to say," said Marius, smiling. "I don't know if you realize how I will cherish that remark."

"Please," she protested, "I really do mean it. I mean, we know, don't we, that we are not going any further with this? I've enjoyed it, I've enjoyed it a great deal. But I can't believe, Marius, that you can be serious about it, and if you were it would be my duty to stop you. It simply would not be fair to you."

"The last refuge of the wounded ego," he observed, "is altruism."

"Please be serious for a moment," said Sylvia with a light asperity, out of her deep belief that it was impossible to be serious while being intelligent.

"I merely meant," he replied, "that I might be allowed to judge what is fair to me."

"My dear," she said, with an intention of keeping the tone light, as Marius did seem slightly offended, "kindly remember that I am an old married woman."

"You've no cause to say I haven't kept it steadily in mind."

"Don't be angry, Marius, you know that's not what I meant."

64

"You meant, then, what?"

Sylvia paused, and, to give a kind of dramatic countenance to this pause, put her hand gently on his. She felt very ashamed of having to say next, and truthfully, that she was afraid of what people might say, so she did not say this but instead let herself be led to a new concession which she believed to be harmless because she did not mean it.

"I'm afraid this might become too important," she said in a low voice, not looking at him, "to me."

"Dear Sylvia," Marius said, "I have hoped it would."

"So we must stop, that's all," she said with a new energy, disengaging her hand. "It has been fun, Marius, a great deal of fun. But there are limits."

"So it seems," he said, with some bitterness. "No, don't go just yet, there is something I must say to you."

Sylvia, who had been putting on her gloves merely out of nervousness, and not because she had been ready to leave, settled back in her chair with a slight sigh to indicate unwillingness. She was governed in this, as she hoped he was too, by the conventions of a final interview, which imposed on the parties concerned not only certain appropriate emotions but also a quality of rounded and dramatic finish; because there would be no second chance, everything must be said as well and beautifully as possible right here and now. It is perhaps for this reason that such final interviews are so seldom final. Few people have the strength to resist explaining themselves just once more.

Marius had the waiter bring a fresh pot of coffee.

"I don't flatter myself that I can change your mind," he began. "You are a very strong sort of person, Sylvia. Our friendship has meant a good deal to me, and I hoped it had to you as well."

"It has, it has," she earnestly put in, being not so displeased at the idea that she was a strong sort of person. "But don't make it sound so final, darling. We'll meet again. Why, we'll all be at Hugo's house tonight, won't we?"

"I suppose so," Marius replied. "But that's not the same thing. You were the one, you know, who said there were limits — we may draw them at different places. If I can't see you alone like this, it would be better not to see you at all."

"Marius, you are being very childish now."

"That may be," he said. "Sylvia, didn't you ever think I might be in love with you?"

"Please don't talk like that, it's not fair," she said.

"*Not fair,*" he repeated, somewhat disagreeably. "Organized games."

"It is not fair to Julian, in the first place," Sylvia said. "There are some things one simply doesn't say. And besides, dear, marriage *is* an organized game."

"Sylvia — do you love Julian?"

"I do," she said, with something of the tone of altar or courtroom.

"Are you still in love with him?"

"Marius," she said gravely, "for all your intelligence, you don't really understand much about marriage, do you? Or about life itself, for that matter. Things can't always be in that first pink flush of romance. People quiet down after a number of years, and become more, well, more sensible about living."

"They do?"

"Yes, they do. Julian and I have a very nice life together, which is something you don't understand. If you did, you couldn't even think of trying to break it up in this way."

Sylvia put into this speech more fervor than necessary, perhaps out of a feeling that she was saying more than necessary;

66

she was somewhat chagrined, then, to hear Marius laugh at her with a kind of superior sympathy.

"Poor Sylvia," he said. "I wouldn't have believed you'd thought about infidelity as much as all that. Marriage must be a frightful institution. It is, after all, hardly recommended in the Scriptures — 'better to marry than burn' is not exactly what you would call a testimonial, is it? Here you are, after seven years of it, burning merrily — though in a theoretical way, admitted — and at the least question, up you come like a clerk of canon law, ready to give the reasons why and the reasons why not. Tell me, my dear, supposing I were Olympian Zeus, and could spread a cloud about our love so that no man could see, or spread fear about it so that no man who saw would speak, would you then — notice that even under those circumstances I am not asking you to come to my bed — but would you then, in a whisper, acknowledge what you truly felt for me?"

"That would be very different," Sylvia said, feeling that she retreated with dignity. "You are not Olympian Zeus. This is the real world, remember." She herself remembered at this moment the question of the anonymous letter, and wondered whether it was or was not the real world that she was at this moment sitting in.

"What you call the real world," Marius said, "is continually being manufactured out of dreams like these. Sylvia, I am advising you, now, that I love you."

"I don't hear you," she said, actually putting her fingers in her ears so that it was as from quite far away that she heard him repeat, "I love you." She turned to him decisively.

"Marius, this is becoming a frightening conversation. We've had such good times together, why couldn't you let it finish that way? I'd never have stayed here to listen to you, if it hadn't been that this was the last time."

"Exactly," Marius replied. "If you had not insisted this was the last time I'd not have had the courage to say what I have said."

"Well, then."

"Well, then, if you will promise that this is not the last time, that we can continue to be good friends — Sylvia, all I ask is to be allowed to love you, which is something I can't help."

Just now the waiter presented the check, and remained hovering a few feet away; Sylvia looked around to see that the dining room was nearly empty.

"We really must go now," she said. One of the things which disturbed her was that it had become customary for her to pay for the lunch on these occasions — and it sometimes crossed her mind that a good meal might be, for Marius, at least a strong secondary motive in his friendship — and this way of using her husband's money occasioned her perhaps more anxiety than had anything else, until now, about these luncheon dates; money, as Dr. Mirabeau that very morning had so sagely observed, being a surrogate image for *giving oneself,* and therefore admirably fitted for expressing sexual tensions. At this moment, with the waiter hanging about, Sylvia thought she saw a means of solving this difficulty of conscience and perhaps indirectly discouraging Marius at the same time.

"You must promise to be good, then," she whispered to him, again putting her hand on his, "and if you really mean it, you should begin by paying for my lunch."

Chapter 3

Hungry, and somewhat stupefied, Julian returned to his office and had Miss Duddon send out to the drugstore for sandwiches and a copy of the Bible, which he would need in order to think about Mr. More's campaign. He wished he might discuss this matter with Mr. Ballou, but it was a custom in the office, precisely on account of such luncheon engagements, that from three to five in the afternoon was a period set aside for *thinking*. Julian frequently took a nap at this time, and would have done so today but that some small worry kept nagging at him; he finally remembered that what he absolutely must do before returning home was to compose the second anonymous letter. He sighed, and pulled a sketch pad toward him.

One of the unanticipated difficulties in his scheme, he now began to see, would be a certain lack of content; he sat there like a schoolboy unprepared for his exam. Really, he thought, he did not know very much about Sylvia's way of passing the time, and these anonymous letters could not go on for very long being merely sinister and vague; finally they would have to make some identifiable suggestions. But as soon as they did, once they at all committed themselves to a particular line of attack, they would, would they not, become ridiculous? She would begin to laugh at them; she would, and this would be fatal, discuss them openly with Julian. He wondered whether she had actually read the first one, that morning, and, if so, what she had thought. He tried to imagine himself in her place, receiving such an accusation made in such a manner, but this made him feel acutely what a bad thing it was he had undertaken, his guilt came on him in a physical form like nausea — what a terrible thing to do to anyone! He resolved not to go on with it, and, pushing away the pad, took up the Bible instead.

On the other hand . . .

On the other hand, assuming she had read it — and she must have, for otherwise why would she have asked him, in that curiously neutral tone of voice, whether there was anything he wanted to say? — why did she not speak up at once, why not say something right out instead of simply sitting there? Why had she not proclaimed her innocence and said in a straightforward manner that the letter was ridiculous?

Because she was not innocent?

The appearance of this thought in Julian's head, being as it was sudden, unexpected and, above all, not a product of his own scheme, compelled respect if not immediate belief. With very mixed feelings he began to see himself as the victim of some fatally destructive irony deep in the nature of things.

"Federigo, my friend," he said to himself, "we've done it now."

He did not, at this moment, fully believe in the truth of his new discovery, but its possibility, even its likelihood from certain points of view, dismayed him; there was, however, a quality of amusement even in his dismay.

This quality of amusement, this slight gift for sensing absurdity everywhere, had affected Julian's view of life for as long as he could recall; in college, for example, he had had the ambition of becoming a saint, or, undenominationally, some sort of holy man; and sometimes even now he thought how much easier that would have been than the life which was actually his. This ambition had come less, perhaps, from a sense of sympathy with the sufferings of the world than from a dreamlike sense of the silliness of the world. There had been about him then, what was perfectly proper for an undergraduate, a certain want of commitment to a real world, a world really and intransigently existing, and this slight imperfection, this little hollowness where there should have been belief, still formed, negatively, a part of his character, a kind of abscess. For all his scarcely expressed ambitions to sainthood he had not in his adult life ever quite believed in God, and now and then he put it to himself that that was his trouble; but in reality his trouble was simpler than that — he did not quite believe in the world.

So when Julian began to perceive on his horizon this cloud no bigger than another man, his reaction was to be amused, which he was able to be even while he was being troubled. To put the matter exactly, he did not *really* believe his wife Sylvia had been unfaithful to him, but he began for the first time to imagine how easily possible it was that she might be. He could not be angry, either, for he had no image to be angry about, but he also began to perceive how angry he might, in theory, become. Experimentally, more or less like a chemist, he made in his mind a couple of theoretically possible combinations: Sylvia and Marius, Sylvia and Hugo Alter; and for one instant he achieved the real and painful sense of being laughed at by other people, the sudden appreciation of a world baseless, unstable, fluid, in which all one had thought of as one's *position* turned out instead to be merely motion. But after a moment the energy required to sustain these imaginings proved insufficient; a vision of Hugo's mouth, smiling, simply faded out on him; and he was left once more with the hypothetical notion, the platonic idea, of his wife's possible infidelity, in which, again, he did not *really* believe.

There remained the matter of the anonymous letters, which

71

perfectly expressed Julian's relation with a real world. In this
new light, it scarcely mattered, for the moment, what the next
letter would say, but there must be a next letter, since, as he
now began to perceive, the ultimate object of the game he had
begun — far beyond providing him with an excuse for adultery — was to get the real world to commit itself, which it had
already begun to do. One put to the world a hypothetical question; one received, it would appear, a real answer; it was
with some exhilarated yet anxious sense of this situation that
Julian once again took the pad, and composed the following
message:

> Sir —
> Who is Sylvia, what is she? etc.
>   Federigo

That this "etc." seemed to set no limit to his wife's activities
Julian noted in passing but Federigo made no bones about.

With considerable labor he cut the appropriate letters out
of a copy of *Harper's Bazaar* and assembled them on a page
rather dirtily, getting glue all over his fingers; he waited till
Miss Duddon had gone home, and typed the envelope on her
machine. Then, after washing his hands — but the glue clung
very tenaciously — he rolled up the copy of *Harper's Bazaar*
and left the office, posting the letter in the chute outside while
waiting for the elevator. He thought, seeing the envelope fall
rapidly and irrevocably away, that it would be wiser to mail
these communications from some other postal district; also
that this was probably using the mails to defraud — but who
was being defrauded, and of what, he could not just now decide. The magazine he took along and disposed of in a street-
corner garbage can several blocks away.

*   *   *

For some reason, perhaps as a free expression of his new-found criminal character, Julian was unwilling to walk home by his usual route; instead he decided to go through Central Park, where he had not walked since his boyhood — already, he noted with surprise, a considerable distance away. It occurred to him, for the first time bringing with it a sense of discomfort, that he was growing older and would one day die, and all for what? He would have lived a life after the model of the city itself, regular, rectangular, numbered, any place in which might be readily located by a simple system of coordinates, and as readily forgotten. It might be true also that he had grown up as the city had, and that his parallels and perpendiculars had developed from a crooked maze of random growth, far downtown, but it seemed that little of that remained; people of his sort, people whom he knew, did not go there unless they happened to be artists, or brokers with a seat on the Exchange, whose work for some reason had remained in that weird tangle of streets while the rest of the city spread steadily north. Even the business of the anonymous letters, the stirring of some complicated viciousness against regularity and order, now seemed to him to be a freedom of much the sort suggested by Central Park itself, a limited and provisional disorder frowned upon on four sides by the structures of order, a small oblong of chaos set down in the midst of cosmos; even the chaos gave subtle hints of control, the paths wound and meandered lazily but with purpose, here was a zoo, here a playing field, policemen walked their beats here as elsewhere; uptown, in the mid-region of this chaos, the two museums monumentally confronted one another like emblems of the days of creation, irrevocably dividing the city into Art on the east and Nature on the west.

His slight thought of death and of the implacable passing of time evoked in him bitter, rebellious feelings, and, at the same

73

time, a poignant sense of the beauty and ugliness in things; he looked outside himself as with new eyes.

The weather was excellent, though a trifle too hot. Julian entered the Park at Sixtieth Street and Fifth Avenue, where more than at any other place the walk is lined with benches, and the benches, in such weather as this, crammed with people, making of this section, which leads to the Zoo, a kind of social promenade. Though the occupants of the benches were of many different sorts, it seemed to Julian that there was nevertheless something generally the same about them; the same air of sullen, listless freedom, of open-throated uneasiness in which the idea of being *degagé* and informal had produced a result rather shameful and slovenly. There seemed to be among them a large proportion of insane persons; several times Julian avoided the glance of a man or a woman talking vociferously, often in what seemed a foreign tongue, to no one, or to the pigeons which in this place fluttered and clattered impudently around all heads and hats. The behavior of these birds filled Julian with disgust; their constant nearness to human beings had completely destroyed their natural wild timidity and made them, in his opinion, insolent. The ways they went, their flights between two people sitting together, for example, seemed to him estimated on a nice calculation of human baseness, servility and docile indifference. For his own part, he several times had to duck to keep from being flapped in the face with a wing, and it did not improve his view of the matter that he thought the habitués of this sector must be laughing at the sight. He imagined also that if he lashed out at any pigeon which came too close, and broke (for example) its wing, all these people would rise up in one mob and give him a terrible beating, simply out of human feeling and kindness to animals.

As he looked, rather furtively, at the faces that he passed —

furtively, so as not to be challenged as having issued any invitations (for even the slightest glance at man or woman was likely to get in return an exceedingly bold, questioning look) — it struck him how completely, under circumstances of the slightest informality, people went to pieces in their dress and personal appearance, how their flesh, feeling the least permissive liberation from cloth or strap, began at once to bulge yearningly toward the great openness and horrible freedom of nature. The men who had taken off their hats proved to be shining bald with sweat; when they opened their coats their bellies tended to push aside contemptuously the flimsy sport shirt and peer forth in hairy boldness. With the women it was even worse: straps fell from shoulders, jabots crumpled, skirts rode high over knees spread wide apart, garters like instruments of constricting torture were disclosed cutting deep into the fat which rolled up on either side of them. The still air reeked with smoke as though it were a poolroom, and the walk was thick with cigarette butts, cigar butts, mashed bits of unidentifiable goo (some of it like chocolate, some like blood) and mashed bits of quite identifiable turds, presumably of dog. There were also, chiefly on the grass behind the benches, great quantities of tired-looking newspaper, some of it yellow. The white excrements of the pigeons fell everywhere, stippling the sidewalk, the benches, possibly now and then the people; and through all this ran the confused burble, marked by transient passages of clarity, of what seemed one vast conversation.

Julian was disturbed less by the scene, however, than by his attitude toward it, which appeared to him to be precious and undemocratic. "Would you want people to do without a park altogether?" he asked himself, and saw at once the danger of falling into the opposite heresy, that of pitying people because of their appearance, their behavior, et cetera.

75

Nevertheless, it was a relief to reach, after two blocks, the Zoo. The animals, comparatively neat and orderly, each had individual cages, or there would be two or three in a cage, all members of the one family; this effect of decency, and the comparative coolness of the houses, some of which however smelled bad, made a pleasant impression on Julian, who philosophically compared the calm demeanor of the lions and tigers with the frenzied rushing about of the humans, particularly the children.

"The powerful, the splendid and the cruel," he thought, "are locked up; that is what this world is."

Looking up, he saw a number of balloons, gas-inflated, which had escaped their owners' grubby hands and were now sailing aloft and becoming smaller and vanishing into the hot yellow haze of the sky; a few of these balloons had become lodged in the branches of trees, where they hung like moons over a garden party, and this sight for some reason struck Julian as terribly sad, a real emblem of loss and loneliness, yellow balloons, and green, and orange.

"It is love," he told himself, "which does all this."

The thought came to him as an inexpensive sort of revelation while he stood in the crowd which pressed to the bars of the pool where the sea lions played. The sight of these beasts in the water, and even their disappearance in the water, entranced Julian. Here, he thought, was power and freedom, he could even imagine from this small pool how smoothly, silently, and at what great speed they would travel under the waters of a wild, arctic sea, themselves mysterious, tranquil and assured. Their behavior on land, however, displeased him; when they hauled themselves up into the concrete house that had been built for them, or stretched out on its roof, they seemed domestic and ridiculous; they amused the crowd, he thought disgustedly, by *being human.*

76

But the thought of love, just now, disturbed him a good deal, mainly, in fact, by its absence in himself; he did not seem to love anyone. Whatever it was he felt for his wife Sylvia bore no resemblance to those pale, passionate dreams of adolescence which he did not just now feel for anyone else either, and which he remembered at this moment only to wonder where they might have gone. It was true — though scarcely interesting — he was getting older, he would one day die. There came into his head the faces of women adored, caressed, some of them in reality, long ago; he had no desire to caress these women at present, some of them must be, in fact, well along in years, married, with children of their own who would now, or in a few years at most, be going through the same novelty of passion themselves, wondering why no one in the world had ever experienced the same before. Most frightening of all, one could do nothing to stop this terrible passage of time, which cut down and down on the limitless variety of life until, finally, nothing remained but the narrow grave. Was it now, already, too late? A few, trivial years, and he would be dead; many of these people standing near him would be dead, some of the children, even, would be dead. The thought was like a secret intimacy.

He was standing next to two young men, one black and the other white. The fact that they were companions pleased him; it was democratic, like a poster in the subway. Just in front of them stood a young girl — a young woman, say — whose age he would put about twenty or so; she was blonde, her profile as she intently watched the sea lions seemed to Julian very delicate and pure, also somewhat withdrawn, as though no crowd existed about her at all. He wondered if she were with the two young men, and decided that even if she were not they would soon try to pick her up; he envied them.

As though she felt his eyes on her, the girl turned and

looked at him without disapproval, with a neutral sort of curiosity that finished, as she turned away again, in a demure, rather secretive smile. She seemed to be merely watching the sea lions again, but Julian felt the tension her glance had caused in him; and felt it, too, as though they both had the same senses, so that what he was feeling clearly must be felt by the girl. The strangeness, anonymity, of this relation — for it was already a relation — its secrecy in public, attracted him, and he tried to get up courage to go on, but was prevented by his uncertainty concerning the two lads behind her, who, even if they were not her companions, would surely see what he was up to. The fear that a rejection would make him ridiculous in their eyes made Julian highly conscious of his own appearance, his being well-dressed, and, for this place and this season, very formally dressed. Nevertheless, while he half watched the seals, he affected a vague smile, so that if she turned round again she would see him smiling and yet not irretrievably smiling at herself; the expression might be interpreted just as she chose.

She did turn, she smiled more openly. Then by a piece of luck the two young men moved away, out of the crowd, so that no one remained between them. Julian edged forward and to one side in such a random and apparently unconscious manner as to suggest that the people behind were pushing him forward to the railing at which she stood. His hand, on this railing, was touching hers, which she moved slightly away; but at the same time she smiled once again.

"Hello," he said.

"Hello," said she.

They stood together and watched the sea lions for a few moments; the ease with which this had been accomplished somewhat frightened Julian even while it attracted him; his mind, racing on with the flickering speed of an old film, saw this girl already his mistress, saw the guilt, the inevitable discovery, shame, ruin. . . .

"Do you come here often?" she asked him, and, when he replied, "I thought I hadn't seen you here. I come to watch the seals, they look so cool. You must be very warm in that heavy jacket," she added.

"Would you like something to drink?" Julian politely asked, and she took his arm as they left. Julian was embarrassed, however, to see those two young men, the black and white, standing a little distance away, and hoped they had not noticed. "Though, after all," he asked himself, not without a certain pride, "what difference would that make?"

At the café on the terrace Julian had a beer and the girl, who said she did not drink, a coke. This dispelled somewhat the strangeness of their meeting, and Julian began to be a little bored. The girl was very pretty, however, though coarser of feature in full face than in profile.

"What is your name?" she asked, and he replied: "Federigo."

"Mine is Bianca," she offered in return. Evidently the convention belonging to such meetings was to be satisfied with first names. "What a lovely ring," she said, taking his hand for a closer look. "Is it your family crest?"

"Well," said Federigo, embarrassed, "it used to be, long ago."

"My family is very poor," she said. "Both my parents are dead."

He could not think of anything to say to this, and so they were silent for a moment; then he asked, "Do you usually let strangers speak to you like this?"

"If I think they're nice," Bianca said. "I do pretty much as I please."

"Don't you have to work?" he asked.

79

"Sometimes I do modeling," she replied, and added, "I live with my uncle and aunt. If they ever knew I spoke to strange men — oh, lordie." She looked at him boldly, with a keen curiosity.

"You're married, aren't you?" she rather announced than asked. "Oh, it's not hard to tell, you have that heavy sort of look about you."

"Are you married?" asked Federigo.

"Lord, no," Bianca said gaily. "I was, once, but my uncle had it annulled. My uncle is very strict."

After their drink, they walked; at first she took his arm, later they went along hand in hand. It occurred to Federigo, horrifyingly, that they might meet some acquaintance of his; but he decided it was unlikely, in the midst of the Park, and made it a point of honor to keep hold of her hand.

Bianca was fairly tall, and slender; she walked in a free, rather dawdling manner which allowed her body now and then to lean for a moment against his. She wore a perfume which he thought crudely alluring; there was about it a pathos of poverty which set a kind of debased and romantic tone to their being together. So far as Federigo was concerned, they were getting on splendidly; Julian also, for his part, felt a sweet, wild, yet strangely innocent pleasure in all this, as though Central Park were a kind of Eden within whose bounds nothing that happened could really be wrong. They did not talk much, finally; before parting, they sat together on a bench in a relatively lonely walk among trees, and smoked a cigarette.

"I like you, Bianca," he said, savoring the bittersweet of duplicity in the aroma of her hair.

"I like you, Federigo," she replied.

"We might meet again," he suggested, "we might go out together some evening."

80

"This is so sudden," she said, with a little laugh. "What about your wife?"

"Never mind about her," he said, feeling the most delicate twinge in the conscience. "Let me call you up."

"Oh, I couldn't do that," she said. "If my uncle ever got to know . . ."

"Let's meet somewhere, then. We can arrange it now."

"You are persistent, aren't you?" Bianca laughed again. "Sometimes, not every night, but sometimes, I go for a walk in the Park. I like to go into the Zoo at night and look at the seals."

"Tonight, then?"

"It could be," she replied. "About eleven?"

"You couldn't make it midnight, could you?" He had remembered Hugo's party. "Just at the stroke of midnight, by the seals?"

"It would be awfully late," she said, considering gravely, "but I could try."

She got up, shook his hand rather formally, leaned close to him for a moment in the mere sketch of an embrace, then walked away down the path.

"Midnight, then," he called after her, but she did not look back.

2

SYLVIA and Marius did not part after lunch. As they stood on the sidewalk outside Mme. Modera's, and seemed to have, at least from Marius's end, some trouble in at last saying good-by, Sylvia looked at her watch with a show of efficiency and announced that she must drive out to the rest home and pay a visit to Alma.

81

"I haven't been to see her *once* since this latest trouble," she said. "It's shameful, the way we neglect people when something goes wrong for them. We're afraid of catching it ourselves, I guess."

"You know, I ought to go, too," Marius said. "I'll drive out there with you."

This was not precisely the response Sylvia anticipated, since she had introduced the subject of Alma only in order to make the farewell less lingering; in fact she had not, in her own mind, finally decided whether to visit Alma that afternoon or no. It was such an extremely nice day, she feared that the sight of her friend in doleful circumstances (Sylvia imagined Alma lying naked on straw, in a cell) would depress her dreadfully — and then, what would there be to talk about? On the other hand, though, it would mean a drive into the country, Marius would be pleasant company on the way, and above all he would share the burden of finding something to say to Alma.

"We'll take the dogs along," she said, as though on sudden inspiration. "They need the air, poor things."

They stopped in the apartment to get the dogs, and waited there while the car was brought around from the garage. In the ten minutes or so that this took, Marius attempted to make love to Sylvia, who permitted him to kiss her, not very convincingly, once, then made herself out to be very busy tidying things in the kitchen. Marius followed her about from refrigerator to sink and so forth, but Troilus and Cressida, liberated from their captivity in the bathroom, kept frisking about their mistress so that they got in his way.

"Visit Alma another time," he said, not altogether serious and not altogether as a joke either. "Lock up the dogs and we'll spend the afternoon here."

"Please," Sylvia said, "you're not being funny in the least."

82

The car was a convertible, they had the top down. With the dogs in the back seat, sitting up with their noses in the air, the entire group looking quite aristocratic, they drove across the Triborough Bridge and out on Long Island toward the sea. Once they got on the parkway, Sylvia drove very fast, and Marius, glancing at her face in profile, with the long hair blown back, admired her more than ever and thought of her as Artemis; at the same time the speed made him nervous, and, though he forbade himself to say anything on this point, he sat very tensely and kept pressing with both feet on the floorboard as if it were one large brake.

When Marius said to Sylvia, at lunch, that he loved her, he had not meant it in the least, but was consciously, with the tact of a dramatist, responding to the situation which was forming itself between them. Such dramas had no author, they were the common property of the agonists, a *commedia dell' arte;* there were, however, certain conventional lines of plot and even of dialogue laid down to guide people in their improvisations. It had seemed to him that "the girl" (so he called her now, in his thoughts) wished to crystallize a certain romantic and critical element in their relation, and that she wished to do this, in the first place, for reasons that scarcely had any personal connection with himself at all. He wondered why, and decided — not for the first time — that she must be unhappy; unhappy, probably, in her marriage, but without any guarantee that she would be otherwise without her marriage. He regarded such qualities as, finally, built into people — he himself, for example, was unhappy — and without much prospect of change no matter how they might delude themselves by making local and particular changes in either their circumstances or their habits; as a matter of course, however, he rebuked himself for this somewhat Calvinist tendency in his thought. But at the same time, because he was un-

83

happy, unhappiness powerfully attracted him, and though he did not love Sylvia when he had announced to her that he did, he recognized at least in theory the force of that maxim which would have it that we do not run away because we are afraid, but are afraid because we run away. Almost invariably, in so rational a mind as his, the formulation preceded the sentiment; the mind was spontaneous but the feelings had to be coached.

Among their friends, Sylvia and Julian were considered to have a *very good marriage;* they were supposed, that is, to be happy, and much admired on this account by numbers of people who regarded them as a kind of model which might be proposed for the ideal but which it would therefore be hopeless to try to imitate. Marius alone, it might be, saw this ideal as the last hypocrisy of all; he saw this at first simply out of a gift for paradox, but it seemed now to be demonstrating itself before his eyes. He asked himself, sitting there in the car, how far he was prepared to follow this situation, and correspond in it to the role which Sylvia, no doubt, would devise for him; and he replied that his interest in the situation itself, to say nothing of the attractiveness of the girl, would take him very far indeed; only he doubted that he would be very often prepared to pay for lunch.

Sylvia, meanwhile, was wondering whether she ought to tell Marius about the anonymous letter, and, if she did, whether she had best treat it as a dream or as a real event. Marius was intelligent, and for this reason she doubted he would be helpful. Probably he would laugh, especially if she presented her trouble as having been caused by a dream; his knowledge of psychiatry was, intellectually at least, superior to her own, and allowed him to take, sometimes, a very cynical line about her views of the subject; to which she would insist that all his

84

knowledge, since it was not the product of real experience, did not enable him to understand the first thing about the matter; nevertheless, he would very likely laugh at her.

She had sense enough not to take Marius's declaration of love with any great seriousness; people did that sort of thing, it was a kind of game, the charm one discovered in one's acquaintances depended, in a way, on their doing that sort of thing with the right, the light, emphasis. Being admired was pleasant, of course; but tenable only in connection with the utmost honesty. Sylvia's view of marriage, in this respect, made it out to be an up-to-date zoo, where there are no cages but only moats and deep trenches which from most angles of vision let the animals appear to move in perfect freedom and even to approach the spectators; it was an ideal illusion of nature, the animals seemed to stay where they were out of freedom and a sense of duty which had led them to choose their environment, but the trenches were very wide and deep.

Nevertheless, the letter, whether as dream or reality, had produced in her feelings today a critical moment; not that she had not already, many times, entertained the idea of having an affair (only to dismiss it because she did not really believe such things were done by other women she knew well), but that the letter extended the range of her imagination by suggesting not only that she was already having an affair but also that it was, on the whole, as much amusing as reprehensible. Federigo, whoever he was, was right; she did get left too much alone, and if it happened one day that she took a lover, Julian would be as much to blame as herself. Perhaps not quite so much.

Still, what was virtue, and what did one expect of it? If one were well brought up, and had virtue drilled into one in all sorts of subtle and crude ways for so many years, so that by the time one married one simply *was* virtuous — had taken

85

the iron into one's own soul, so that there need never be any prompting from outside again — one began implicitly, she supposed, to expect some kind of reward for it. One went on for years being virtuous — a negative thing to be, by the way — and slowly began to come to the consciousness that *this*, whatever it was, the way one actually happened to be living, was the sole reward and all the reward one was going to get. One became convinced — or did one? — that *this* must be happiness, if only in contrast to the dreadful unhappiness that lay the other way; an unhappiness of which occasional examples came to her notice, one of which they were at this moment going to visit. There were casualties, undeniably; being married to a man like Hugo Alter, for example. You might even say Alma should be happy to be rid of him, but madness (if that was what it was) would be a considerable price to pay for so dubious a freedom, and even so, it was not the full price, it did not take into account a dozen or so years of marriage, a dozen or so years wasted on an unsuccessful experiment. Wasted? It seemed a sweeping judgment.

"It is dreadful about Alma, isn't it?" she said at this point to Marius, and added, primly, "One hates to see even a bad marriage break up. People should stick together."

"Pour encourager les autres," Marius put in.

"There's that, of course," she said. "But doesn't it seem to you that Hugo is being pretty despicable? I mean, this unseemly rush to get the divorce through while she is in this condition?"

"It seems that if she got much worse there could not be a divorce," Marius said. "And then, too, they had arranged it before she absolutely collapsed."

"I suspect — it's a dreadful thing to say — but I suspect he bribed the doctors to say she was sane. I don't know," she added hastily, "it sounds very melodrama when you say it

86

right out — but I really believe people behave that way sometimes, you know. We don't see them doing it, we only see the
results, but there must be terrible cruelty in so many places."

"I've never had the least doubt of it," Marius replied, "but
I don't really believe he bribed the doctors. I should think
that was not easy to do, really."

"Hugo is extremely rich," she reminded him. "That is
probably why everyone goes along with whatever he does. He
always was conspicuously and publicly unfaithful to her, for
years."

With me, among others, she added to herself; for it was perfectly true that at the time of his brief affair with Sylvia Hugo
had been already married to Alma, though it was true also
(for what it was worth) that Sylvia and Alma had not yet become acquainted. Sylvia found it disturbing to have to recall
this circumstance exactly as she was taking such a stern moral
line. She had always thought of herself as the victim in that
episode, but it now began to seem as though her resistance had
been not altogether what it ought to have been. At any rate,
whether so or no, she had nevertheless played some little part
in developing the situation for which she had just denounced
Hugo.

"I don't excuse any of us," she therefore added. "The way
we behave, it looks as though we don't care — as if nobody
believed in marriage any more. Just as soon as the divorce
comes through, you know, he will marry that girl Louisa —
everyone is quite aware he has been keeping her for at least
one whole year, anyhow. She lived this winter in that old house
of his, somewhere out here on Long Island, by the ocean."

"It must have been cold," Marius said.

"And the odd thing was," Sylvia continued, "her mother
and younger sister were there with her, all perfectly at home,
knowing the whole situation — he used to visit her weekends.

87

It must have been funny," she suddenly added, "with mother sitting out on the porch in the snow."

"Hugo and Alma were as good as separated at that time," Marius said.

"Oh, no. It was when she found out about Louisa and the house on Long Island," Sylvia insisted, "that she broke down, finally. She tried to kill herself, you know."

"No, I hadn't heard that," said Marius, without surprise. "Are you sure?"

"She did. It was really rather ridiculous — how awful of me to laugh! — but it seems she hung herself from the chandelier by her bathrobe string, but it wouldn't hold her weight, she's rather heavy, you know — it pulled out all the plaster in the ceiling and came down on her head. She was quite badly hurt, just physically. Then, when they had her in the hospital, when she seemed to be almost well again, she broke this interne's nose, she kicked him, I believe, and rushed out through the corridors in her nightgown. I hear she got as far as the reception desk before they overpowered her. And now she is in this *rest home,* as they call it" — Sylvia wrinkled up her nose to show she was not deceived about rest homes — "and the doctors, if you please, say she is perfectly sane, only a little depressed." She laughed shortly. "She might well be depressed."

Sylvia turned to Marius, causing the car to swerve violently for a second, and said: "The cynicism of it is what bothers me." Seeing the expression of alarm on his face, she got the car back under control before continuing with: "At least, when people get divorced like that, they oughtn't to be allowed to marry again."

"Maybe they still believe love is possible," said Marius.

"For better or worse, in sickness and health, till death do us part," Sylvia said. "What a mockery!"

"Well, it is an institution," he observed, "and like all institutions it requires an occasional human sacrifice."

Compared with Sylvia's drastic expectations, their visit to Alma was at once a relief and a disappointment. The rest home, in the first place, was a pleasant-looking establishment consisting of a large, old-fashioned country house surrounded at a little distance by white cottages, all tastefully landscaped with trees and shrubbery and flower borders, more or less like an extension of the parkway itself and evidently very expensive. They saw one or two nurses, it is true; otherwise, they might have been in a hotel.

Alma was not even alone, much less in bed (or locked away, as Sylvia had darkly imagined, in a dungeon); she was already entertaining half a dozen men and women whom Sylvia and Marius did not know, and whom she introduced as her friends. She seemed poised, quite pretty, though thin and pale, and unenthusiastically pleased to see the newcomers; she said it was sweet of them to come, and made a nurse bring martinis in a beaker, with medicine glasses. She herself did not drink anything, but kept rolling about on the palm of her hand a little pink pellet.

The room, a glass-enclosed porch on the south side of the main building, was filled with conversation and smoke, like a cocktail party, which Sylvia uncomfortably supposed was just what this was. She felt a little ashamed, but also a little angry at Alma.

"What is your little pink pill there?" she asked in a quiet moment, just to have something to say to her friend.

"Darling," said Alma, "that is my escape. A marvelous idea, I wonder why it hasn't become more fashionable than it is. When all you delightful, normal people begin to bore me, when your charm ever so slightly shows signs of failing, I shall pop it in my mouth and take a swallow of water. Then, in ten minutes, no matter how clever you believe you are being, I'll be asleep. One has just to remember to lie down with the limbs decently disposed and clothed, before it takes effect."

They stayed for half an hour; when they left, the party was still going on. Alma thanked them for coming, but did not seem particularly interested in having them do it again.

"You expected, perhaps, a padded cell?" asked Marius, as they drove away.

"No," Sylvia replied, "but I should have expected illness to be treated with more seriousness, more — I don't know — decency, I guess."

"Such as having Alma chained to a wall?"

"Don't be silly, you know what I mean. It seems as though nothing is serious any more."

"You mean," Marius said, "that one's strong feeling about the marriage vows demands a certain demonstrative unhappiness among the ruins. My dear, you would make a good Catholic, of a certain sort, but I am not sure it would be Christian."

"It is damn difficult to sympathize with people, sometimes," she said after a while.

"To pity them, you mean," he said. "Sometimes they just won't be pitied, more power to them. Listen, Sylvia, while you drive I'll tell you a story I read the other day; it will afford you," he added sententiously, "moral satisfaction."

"Yes?"

"Here it is. You know, don't you, that many primitive peoples have curious beliefs about the power of the dead? There's one tribe I recall, in the South Seas, where the people are very gentle and loving with one another — no wars, no violence — but when they die, the belief is that they become bitter enemies of the living. There's a parable, too, but that's not the story I mean to tell. This story is about the tribe of the Halmahera,

90

very fierce and brave in battle because they have strong spiritual help. The way they get this strong spiritual help is, they capture a young boy from an enemy tribe and bury him up to his neck in the earth; then they torture him dreadfully, all the time telling him that the torture will stop as soon as he swears an oath to be forever on their side in battle, and always be loyal to them, the Halmahera, until now his enemies. Finally the boy can't stand the torture, and he swears the oath. At that moment, a man behind him, who has been stirring molten lead in a caldron, pulls his head back by the hair, forces open his mouth, and pours the molten lead down his throat."

"How frightful," Sylvia said.

"They regard it," said Marius, "as a certain guarantee he will not break his vow."

Chapter 4

Few things, perhaps, have so little formality and stiffness about them as a modern party, where people appear to be blown together by a cyclone for a few hours of arduous merriment which most of them will later think of as having been a mistake; nevertheless, ancient and ceremonial purposes occasionally show through. The party at Hugo Alter's house would be in effect, though implicitly and without any announcements, the celebration of his engagement to Louisa Leonard; also, in a sense, her formal introduction to his society, the people with whom he habitually associated; thus, by remote parody, her debut. The old, traditionary forms, by which were asserted the solidarity of the tribe, persisted, although the tribe itself, now called *society*, no longer had any easily discoverable identity or meaning, and although the forms themselves, because Hugo was not yet as a matter of fact divorced, had to express themselves more by intention than by ceremony. Still, it was a public acknowledgment, as everyone concerned was assumed by everyone else concerned to know and recognize; that this was so afforded great satisfaction particularly to Mrs. Leonard, Louisa's mother and Elaine's, who felt that she had brought her troops through a long, difficult campaign to a victory which was honorable because it was victorious, and which would retrospectively supply, therefore, any loss of honor possibly sustained during the conflict.

Mrs. Leonard was a gaunt, austere lady of very old family, with manners and a tone which gave to a mere want of money the appearance of colonial simplicity. The idea that in allowing her daughter to receive the attentions of a married man she had behaved substantially like a madam would have been received by her — had anyone dared to present it — rather with surprise than indignation, as quite out of the range of notions with which a lady might be supposed to be familiar. *Her* intentions — she might have said, in the improbable circumstance of her getting into a conversation on the subject — her intentions had been honorable from the first: marriage, and nothing less, being the object. Of course there had been difficulties, there always were, times (she would have supposed) had changed, and such an extraordinary procedure as the winter just past, in the house on Long Island, would certainly never have been permitted when *she* was a girl — but times had changed. People were always getting divorced, these days, and no one seemed to mind; it was in the papers every day. The romance between Louisa and Mr. Alter had gone on, so far as a mother was concerned, in the most honorable manner possible under the circumstances — he had never concealed the unhappy fact of his marriage, and proclaimed, from the first time she had brought up the subject, his intention of doing the right thing. Any moral discomfort involved in the winter on Long Island, in Hugo's visits to the house during that time, had been quite swallowed up in the physical discomfort of the experience — it was really intended, that place, for a summer cottage, and a primitive one, at that — and in some remote corner of her mind Mrs. Leonard compared this period of nervous suspense to Washington's winter at Valley Forge.

As for the marriage itself, it was certainly very fortunate; but she did not consider that all its benefits flowed in one direction. The wealth on one side was amply compensated, in her opinion, by lineage, breeding, beauty, on the other; Mr. Alter — for after all, what was an Alter? — must surely realize how his position was being improved.

Hugo, as a matter of fact, had thought of no such thing. He was in love again, intensely, and with a faint consciousness of becoming, possibly, an object of ridicule; he was, after all, fifteen years older than the girl, and while that was not precisely November marrying May, nevertheless the phrase which kept occurring to him about his condition — "in the prime of life" — uncomfortably suggested hair-dye and a truss. But his heart, a rather boyish and earnest heart to begin with, was singing with the recovery of feelings he had been afraid might never be his again. So far as he thought of his prospective mother-in-law at all, it was with slight horror at her complaisance, which he considered did not show a sufficient care of her daughter's name. Hugo took both love and marriage most seriously; that he himself was as it were constitutionally incapable of fidelity to one woman did not seem to him especially relevant, because, really, he was a person altogether without pride, and convinced of being in this respect a poor sinner much as he might have been convinced on proper medical testimony of his having diabetes.

"It is just the way I am," he had once said to Julian. "Believe me, I'd be happier if I were like you." And he added, with an earnestness which quite canceled out anything epigrammatic in the remark, "They talk about *free love,* but, believe me, it is not even inexpensive." He was always somewhat out of date; Julian could not remember hearing anyone use the phrase *free love* since they were in college.

Hugo was a tall but stout person, whose round face, light complexion and blond hair gave him an appearance of perpetual youth; as his hair was now thinning noticeably, this

94

appearance had become exaggerated, he looked less like a youth and more like a little boy; the concentrated center of that large, round face showed the wistful, petulant innocence of childhood. He was always wonderfully well dressed in a somewhat old-fashioned and countrified style, of which the most conspicuous elements were a Norfolk jacket and a vest and square-toed shoes with very thick soles. His manners were beautiful, he was amiable and very generous in a lordly way which was sometimes resented; he tended to press things on people whether they wanted these things or not: "Here, use my car if you like." "Why not stay here whenever you're in town?" "If you're free this weekend, you must take over my place on Long Island." This easy behavior gained him, beyond the resentment of some, a number of followers who, Julian thought, imposed on him; but Hugo was wealthy enough, it seemed, or possibly insensitive enough, on this one point, not to notice.

There was perhaps one element in his nature which led to viciousness; he had an extreme love, amounting almost to religious veneration, for happiness. Hugo liked to be happy himself, and found that it conduced to his happiness to be surrounded by happy people, or by people, at least, who had the manners to give that impression whatever might be their inward feelings; so that, while he was generous to a fault where there was no need, and often exercised his generosity so as to anticipate request, he made what could be called a moral point of refusing his aid where the need for it was made depressingly obvious, and he had majestically turned off friends of long standing for being, over any length of time, gloomy in his presence.

This trait had something to do, in Julian's opinion, with his friend's behavior to Alma in the recent crisis. For Alma had endured Hugo's affairs, over a dozen years, with a patience

more than exemplary and somewhat resembling, to an unprej-
udiced view, co-operation: "Our Lady of Perpetual Forgiveness," as one person had called her. She had suffered not
only his women, but — perhaps more important to her — the
money they cost him; she had suffered not only the money,
but — and this must certainly have been more painful — Hugo's periodic collapses, apologies, resolutions and struggles of
conscience, when nothing would do but he must confess all,
not without detail, and beg her forgiveness. Theirs had never
seemed, exactly, a marriage designed to last, but it had come
to seem, finally, a marriage more or less accidentally fallen
into such a pattern as allowed survival. The precise sequence
of events leading to its final collapse had never become quite
clear to anyone; people told tales around the fringes and were
silent at the center. But Julian saw, or thought he saw, that one
person could not go on indefinitely eating another's sins without some reciprocal motion; whatever Alma had got out of
the arrangement, and it must have been something, to have
lasted her a dozen years, had in the end proved insufficient to
her needs. It was difficult to say which had come first, the decision to divorce Alma, the idea of marrying Louisa, or Alma's
falling ill, but Julian presumed on his knowledge of Hugo
that it was the last of the three, and that the mainspring of
the entire action was Hugo's intimate, possessive relation with
the idea of happiness.

Julian frequently compared his own character with that of
his friend, but never arrived at any finally satisfactory ratio.
Sometimes it seemed to him that his own rather rigidly moral
nature won the victory — it was better, after all, to live with
one woman and keep out of trouble; nor did it escape him
that Hugo's infidelities were budgeted on a scale which Julian
himself could never afford. At other times, at times such as
the present, when it had become with him more or less a point

of honor to commit an act of infidelity (to have, as he put it, a secret life), he saw Hugo as royally courageous and himself as guilty of moral cowardice. Whatever Hugo did, Julian now thought, Hugo would never address to himself pseudonymous letters designed to color his actions and make them plausible; he might seek to excuse himself to others, though not often, but he would never begin by deceiving himself.

But perhaps, on the other hand, Hugo had simply not got enough imagination for anything so circuitous; and perhaps, again, the moral deviousness with which the business was conducted would be, for Julian, as it would not be for Hugo, the essential note, and the adultery, carnally regarded, of quite a lot less importance. After all, he now thought, it seemed very doubtful that Hugo really had the happiness by which he set such store; the very fact of his continually looking after strange women suggested a deficiency; very likely he was incapable of enjoying his many actual affairs to the extreme degree that Julian, with nervous ardor, would enjoy even one, even, perhaps, an imaginary one.

Julian and Sylvia, when they came home that afternoon, had both been uneasy in their own minds to the degree that they failed to notice each other's uneasiness. While getting ready to go to Hugo's party, they engaged in the most animated and objective conversation they had had for some time, each with the idea of showing the other that all went along as usual; consequently they quite enjoyed each other's company, and gained a fresh idea of their happiness together.

Sylvia told Julian very circumstantially what it had been like to visit Alma, and how the dogs had enjoyed the outing; Julian gave Sylvia a witty account of his lunch with Mr. Archer More, adding as an afterthought that he had walked home through the Park, liked it quite well, and planned to do so more often during the good weather. Sylvia, because Julian's animation in describing his day seemed to her both natural and charming, felt certain that the anonymous letter was a product of dream, just as Dr. Mirabeau had said; Julian, on his part, became convinced by his wife's gaiety and the nice way in which she laughed at his jokes, that she could not have seen the anonymous letter that morning, and he thought complacently how, if all continued to go well, he would simply intercept and destroy the next one, so that, after all, nothing decisive would have happened, the position would be as before. He reminded himself with some severity that this was, however, not a definite decision; he promised to *think about it* before morning.

Sylvia kept telling herself that she need not feel guilty about Marius; only if she mentioned him at all she would be drawn on into explaining that she had spent most of the day in his company, that he had been in the apartment that afternoon, et cetera, all of which would be inconvenient; also it would mar the light tone of the conversation, which was raising her spirits and making her look forward to the party with pleasure. She would talk with Marius, she resolved, neither more nor less than with others, and she would keep out of those intimate conversations in dark corners which parties so frequently seemed to lead to.

It was nonsensical, Julian thought, to suppose that he really would meet that girl in Central Park at midnight. No doubt she was attractive, in a way, not a way he cared very much about, however; but what mattered was, chiefly, his not being the sort of person who did such things, which were suitable, after all, for college boys. To pick up a girl in the Park, of course, was amusing; it was, even, a flattering thing to think that one could, to have proved that one easily could. Even while he felt somewhat uneasy about it, he also felt rather proud of it. The action of that afternoon had about it a kind of criminal secrecy and gutter romanticism which was pleasing to consider: the prince and the flower girl. But of course it was the sort of thing that went no further; even if he did plan, on a suitable occasion, to take a mistress, she would not be the first one presented to his eyes by chance, and she would be — though this thought discomforted somewhat his liberal views — of his own class, or, better, his own *sort*.

Altogether, Julian and Sylvia, for these reasons and none better, pleased one another so much, their conversation and glances became so teasing and erotic while they were dressing for the party, that at last they felt impelled to spend a quarter of an hour together on the bed before going out. Julian was delighted to take his wife in such perfumed and silken circumstances — she was already almost dressed, and looking very fine — which suggested something romantic and clandestine; while Sylvia, too, was pleased with this sudden storm. Consequently they appeared at the party rather late, and in that rather smug, fat mood of good cheer which is often the result of such activities when legitimately engaged in, with the approval of church and state. It must be said, though, that as the erotic tension between them was thus relaxed, they charmed each other somewhat less than they had a few moments before; but that is natural enough, and each was privately willing to accept, for the time being, this compromise in which satisfaction was taken for love. This private and reserved area of experience, too, this little secret, did much to establish for each of them a benevolent superiority to the world in general and to the people at the party especially. It was like having money in the bank, Julian mused as they walked over to Hugo's house, and he wondered if one's pleasures past really could be added up into a substantial balance, or whether, once they were over, they simply and irretrievably vanished.

The party was large and gay and noisy. Hugo's apartment took up the whole top story of an old, graystone building, and had a terrace which overlooked the Park. When Julian and Sylvia came in, Hugo pushed his way toward them, bringing martinis.

"You already know Louisa," he said proudly, bringing her forward. "Here is Mrs. Leonard, Louisa's mother, and her sister, Elaine. You know everyone else."

It was always the fiction, at Hugo's parties, that everyone knew everyone else; Julian never failed to be amazed, however, at the extent of his friend's acquaintance; on a quick first look around he saw almost no one whom he knew. The invitation had been for cocktails, and read "five to eight o'clock," but the host typically in such a case provided an enormous buffet, and most likely no one who counted himself at all Hugo's friend had taken seriously the stipulation as to time, or provided himself with any other entertainment during the whole evening.

Louisa was slender-waisted and handsome, with very large, black eyes, and long, black hair falling free over her shoulders; a girl who wore massive, crude bracelets of hammered silver, and somewhat suggested a goddess of battles. When Julian had met her before, in less public circumstances, she had seemed subdued and rather maidenly, but now a certain wild emanation of power possibly without control frightened more than it charmed him, and he gathered that she was already a little drunk. He envied Hugo his girl's youth — it was perhaps typical of Julian in his present state of mind to think of this marriage as in effect a transfusion of blood — while at the same time, youth or no youth, and through all the fine

100

ripeness of complexion, sparkle of eyes and freedom of movement, he thought dourly that one detected already in the elder Miss Leonard the possibility and even the probability of Mrs. Leonard, with her pinched elegance and blue-gray hair, who was just now saying that Hugo had spoken so often about Sylvia and Julian, she had been longing to meet them. Now that she had met them, however, there seemed to be little more to be done about it, and Mrs. Leonard stood stiffly before them for a moment, then lunged away to the left with her cocktail glass extended. Hugo took Louisa suddenly away to be introduced to new guests, Sylvia too turned aside, rather because of the unwritten rule that one did not hang about one's husband than because she particularly wanted to talk to anyone else, and Julian was left in a little clear space with Elaine Leonard.

This girl was smaller than her sister, she came about to Julian's shoulder, and, in his opinion, which he gave himself as a connoisseur, quite pretty; the combination of black hair, cut short, and blue eyes, with intensely white skin and teeth, was pleasing, it had an extraordinary delicacy delightfully set off by a smile which was slightly crooked and eccentric, and which appeared and disappeared on her face with great suddenness, as though, behind the young lady which she of course was, there now and then looked forth another creature of *gamine* artlessness and honesty and, perhaps, impudence. All this Julian perceived with great objectivity, with aesthetic distance, and would perhaps have had no further interest in Elaine, whom he considered *too young*, had she not at once said something quite arresting to him.

"Do you know who you look like, very much?" And, as Julian winced slightly, "You must have heard this a hundred times before — you look exactly like Federigo Schwartz."

So, then, his name was Schwartz? With a certain superior

irony Julian patted the right-hand pocket of his coat, and felt through the material the envelope of the first of Federigo's letters, which had been there since the morning.

"How do you know I'm not?" he asked, with a teasing smile. The girl looked at him steadily for a moment before replying.

"Oh, there are differences," she said. "You don't look as strict as Federigo, and your eyes — I think — are lighter."

"My eyes are quite dark," said Julian, a little piqued.

"But Federigo's are black, absolutely black. And anyhow, I don't believe you could be Federigo, because, you see, he's supposed to be off on a world cruise."

"Supposed to be — ?"

"I mean, it's hard to know exactly, with Federigo," Elaine said seriously. "He is a secretive sort of person, and he'd as soon lie to you as not. Anyhow, about the world cruise, I didn't hear it from him, you know. Someone just said the other day that he had sailed. He has his own boat."

"Do you know him well, this Federigo?"

"Oh, no, I've just met him a few times. But you must know him, surely," she added, "he's your double, after all."

"It's a large city," said Julian. "I have heard of him but never met him."

"Probably," Elaine said, "he goes around pretending to be you, and getting you into trouble. It must be marvelous to have someone who looks exactly like you," she added.

Julian considered this statement with some care.

"Well," he said, "he hasn't signed my name to any checks, at least not so far."

"And have you signed his name to any?" asked Elaine.

The course of the party would imitate in little the growth and decay of civilizations, thought Marius as he stood on the edge of this one. In the beginning, a few isolated pairs and groups regarded one another suspiciously, like peoples whose sacred books tell them they alone were made by the gods, and who now have to account for the Ammonites and Edomites who surround them. Presently, a little commerce developed, assisted by the co-operations of hostility — for war was better than peace for the marriage of cultures — and larger groups began to form, with migrations from one part of the room to another. Then, as if on a signal, everyone began to co-operate on building the Tower of Babel; all conversations became one, and all conversations became unintelligible, often quite literally in a number of different languages. There would follow a dispersion of the nations from this Plain of Shinar, and for a while all would be flux and chaos; the person with whom one believed oneself to be talking would suddenly no longer be there, would be replaced in mid-sentence by another or by several others, but all this would seem scarcely to matter, one ear being as good as the next. Then, slowly, more permanent arrangements and alignments would develop; as the weak fell by the way, the nations whose name was History began to form the true, the intimate and mystical body of the party, from whose behavior general laws might be deduced; and it was at that time — still, for this particular party, a little way in the future — that the polyhistors, the great talkers and consecutive, traditionary thinkers, of whose number Marius accounted himself one, would step in to make continuity and a certain amount of sense of the business before an enthralled auditory. And then, once that great age had run its course, not without a further defection of the drunk and lecherous, would follow the *modern period* of arrogance, quarrels, fights (often enough) and rather pathetic, careless libertinism; until at last the pitiful remnant perceived itself to be huddled in isolation and silence among the

103

ashes and cigar butts and the ruined glasses. Then — in the gray, cold light — everyone would go home, and that was a metaphor, thought Marius, for, quite literally, The Lord Knew What.

He made his way through the crowd to Julian Ghent and Elaine Leonard, who were now standing together as if they did not know why, in silence; to them he repeated the substance of what he had just thought concerning parties and world history. It fell quite flat. They smiled politely but without great interest, and Marius concluded they could not have heard all he said, the clamor around them was terrific. Still, the silence at the center of it, where they stood, became noticeable, and to make conversation Marius said: "I suppose Sylvia told you, Julian, we had a quite amusing afternoon driving out to see Alma." He turned to Elaine and added, "Mrs. Alter as is," to which Elaine replied, "I know." This little exchange gave Julian time to compose his face, which nevertheless looked a trifle grim.

"Yes, Sylvia said," he drawled with such ease and assurance that Marius at once perceived Sylvia had said nothing of the sort. The idiot, he thought, she wants to dramatize everything. He smiled boldly up at Julian, who was taller than he.

"Let me get us some more to drink," Julian said, taking their glasses, and he edged away through the crowd toward the bar.

"And you are the sister of the bride-to-be," said Marius, with calm and deliberative rudeness, to Elaine.

"I gather," she replied, "you are one of Hugo's loyal friends who believe he is making a dreadful mistake?"

"Oh, no," he said. "I don't make judgments."

"What do you do, then?"

"I watch," said Marius with great gravity. "I watch the comedy go by."

104

Elaine thought him an oddly pompous person, but at the same time felt some sort of alliance with him, perhaps because they were both younger than the general run of people there; also, of course, they were single, which in that gathering was not the usual thing to be. She could think of him as a boy, which of course was impossible with Hugo and Mr. Ghent and people like that.

"You wouldn't by any chance be one of the clowns yourself?" she asked, smiling her crooked and charming smile.

"You see through my disguise," he said, giving a little bow. "Underneath my breaking heart I have a wonderful time." What a delightful girl, he thought, and considered the likelihood of his falling in love with her there and then — for that smile alone, if for nothing else.

Julian now returned with the drinks. He was furious with Sylvia, also secretly pleased. There were secrets after all, then. Federigo, he told himself, was real. At the same time, looking at Marius rather carefully, he did not believe that this young man made love to Sylvia. A litle pipsqueak intellectual, he thought, and poor at that. It was ridiculous. Nevertheless, Sylvia had kept it secret. Julian experienced a certain pride of power in the advantage he seemed to gain by knowing this small fact; he personally became the irony of fate, and felt, as he handed Marius a martini, as though the pearl onion in its depths had been poisoned.

Oh, dear, Marius thought as he accepted the drink, smiling again at Julian, is he going to become obstreperous? He determined to avoid Sylvia during the whole evening, not caring in the least whether this would allay her husband's suspicions or intensify them, but simply to punish her for this piece of what he called *romanticism*.

"Here's to us all," said Elaine, raising her glass and smiling impartially at both of them.

It was all very well, thought Sylvia with some annoyance, to decide that one would treat Marius with exactly the consideration one gave to others, not more and not less, but it was disturbing to have no opportunity whatever to put this excellent plan into effect. It was getting late, everyone had already eaten, and Marius, who by now had formed about himself a small cohort of people, out on the terrace, to whom he was being witty, had at most nodded twice to her across the room. She resented this rudeness on his part, and considered that if he valued her friendship, to mention nothing more, he had best be somewhat more demonstrative.

Sylvia, for all her recently developed line of psychiatric chat, was not a very light or easy person in society. She was rather slow, and did not like conversations which quickly broke off, or groups which constantly changed their composition while one thought what to say next. She preferred that stage, rather late in a party, at which it was possible to have a long, serious talk with some one agreeable person, a program which had only the one difficulty attached to it, that the gentlemen who most readily settled down to such a long, serious talk were also those most likely to want to take her off in some dark corner or down the hall to a bedroom.

For these reasons she had not, so far, been enjoying herself at all; she felt bored and very self-conscious, as though everyone would notice how much she stood alone. She was also drinking more than usual, perhaps for no better reason than that, where she was standing, there was no place to put down the glass, which accordingly she raised to her lips nervously every few seconds.

Hugo came over to her, and put his arm round her shoulder in a friendly way; she felt humbly grateful, and smiled up at him. Hugo was rather drunk, and leaned on her heavily.

"Having a good time, darling?"

106

"It's a lovely party, Hugo," she replied.

"It is, isn't it? Everyone happy, having a good time. No harm in that, is there?" he demanded sternly.

Sylvia was reflecting, rather vaguely, that this was the man, this one with his arm carelessly flung about her, who had first known her body. Here they were, eight years older, or nine years. It seemed horrible, and yet as though it visibly proved nothing ever mattered; she felt slightly faint, and as if she and Hugo were withdrawn into a space of silence amid the noise, a perceptible isolation. Something of this feeling must have transmitted itself to Hugo.

"We've never talked about that time," he said, somewhat aggressively.

"No," she said.

"You see, I knew what you were thinking," he said, though Sylvia considered this to be no great achievement; what else would she be thinking? But Hugo became very serious.

"I never would have forgiven myself," he said heavily, "if anything had happened to you then."

"Do you think that was nothing?" she bitterly asked him, thinking how odd it was that she and this large body next to her had together made a child, which of course could not be allowed to be born, much less to live, grow up, die — the wretched thing, whatever it was, and nameless at that, had not even had time enough to die. Likely enough she could never have another. Hugo thought that was nothing.

"I mean," he largely explained, with a gesture of the hand, as though this party itself were one of the results of their union, "it's all worked out, hasn't it? You and Jay, my dearest friends — you treat that Julian right, now," he admonished her. "He's a good man. And you're a good girl, Sylvia. Sometimes I think you two are the only really happy people I know. I hope it will be like that with Louisa and me."

"And Alma," Sylvia could not resist adding.

Hugo took his arm away and turned to face her.

"I know," he said mournfully. "You needn't push it. You couldn't make me feel more of a failure than I do already. Believe me, Sylvia, I know I'm to blame — but what can I do, what can I do about it now?" He looked down at her with an expression of pathetic and childish helplessness. "I just *am* that way," he pleaded, adding, with some smug satisfaction, "but my Louisa will keep me in line — look at her over there." He pointed out on the terrace, to the group around Marius Rathlin. "She's got strength enough for two, I count on that," said Hugo.

Sylvia watched Louisa drain the remains of her drink and hand the glass to a young man with a crew-cut who made off toward the bar. She was glad that Hugo could see this as a demonstration of strength of character.

"Tell me, seriously, Sylvia," Hugo said, "does Jay know what happened with us?"

"He has never known you were involved," she replied. "Of course, he had to know about the child — and I presume," she added with an angry smile, "he may have deduced some prior sexual activity from that."

"Don't joke, darling," Hugo said. "I've always felt badly about that. Sometimes I think I owe it to Julian to let him know, and you do, too. This way, it's like holding a dirty joke over his head — if you see what I mean."

"I really don't see what would be the point," Sylvia said, "now. They say," she added, "that every cell in one's body is replaced in a matter of seven years. The people we were then must be outlawed by the statute of limitations, or something."

"Believe me, Sylvia," Hugo said, "I've always been attracted to you. If I weren't a reformed character — " He broke off, laughing, and took her arm. "Let's go out on the terrace,"

108

he said, "and listen to Marius being witty, if that is what Marius is being."

"I'd really be just as pleased, Hugo," said Sylvia, "if you could control your sudden access of conscience to the point of not confessing to Julian. A wife's job is difficult enough without that."

They strolled together out on the terrace.

2

At eleven-thirty Julian abruptly left the party. He spoke to no one, and it did not seem likely that anyone had seen him go. If anyone had, that did not much matter either, for it was characteristic of Hugo's larger parties to proliferate, late in the evening, half over town; people went to nightclubs, for rides in automobiles, to other parties; then, sometimes, they came back.

Doubtless his lust for the strange girl Bianca had been developing unconsciously in him almost from the moment he had left his wife's arms several hours before. But this simple motive would not by itself have been strong enough to overcome the guilt it evoked, and therefore employed those hours in allying itself with consciousness and reason, and building a complex structure of rationale whereby the act itself might be supported. By the time he left, this rationale, for all practical purposes, had replaced in his mind the motive of lust; to the extent that he told himself, in the elevator, that he was merely going to walk once or twice around the block, and not until he found he was walking rapidly down Fifth Avenue, on the Park side, did he fully acknowledge again what it was that he had set out to do.

In the first place . . . But there was no orderly arrange-

109

ment of reasons, they tumbled extravagantly one over the other like the explanations of a guilty schoolboy who does not see that one excuse is infinitely better than two. What it all came down to, though, was that he was angry (Sylvia), drunk (himself) and bored (the party).

He had been one of the group surrounding Marius Rathlin on the terrace. It was true that Marius talked brilliantly and was amusing, particularly when he became a little drunk. But what was all this, thought Julian disgustedly, but talk talk talk? What had it to do with anything that mattered? Sylvia had lied to him by failing to mention Marius; this caused Julian a bitter satisfaction, it represented an opportunity, the world implied so tenuously and delicately in the anonymous letter began to exist. Here was Marius, now, talking (as though that world did not exist) about religion. Marius was wearing his lecturer's voice; thin, high-pitched, with a reedy intensity that further annoyed Julian, who moved a little away from the group and stood by the railing of the terrace, where he abstractedly entertained for a moment the idea of throwing himself down on the street.

Beyond lay in silence Central Park, a darkness thinly laced with lights; while he watched, a traffic light changed from red to green out there in the black space. Bianca would be walking, perhaps, toward the Zoo, toward the pool, where he imagined the seals, silent and unwatched now, plunging swiftly through the opacity of the waters.

He was bored. Out there, somehow, in the silent spaces of the Park — where he had played as a child, and how far away that was! — lay life, impulse, secrecy; while up here on Hugo's fine terrace there was talk. Marius was praising Catholicism now on aesthetic and — of all things — *hygienic* grounds; he developed the paradox that it was the most satisfactory religion "for a gentleman" because it was the most

110

pagan of religions. Mythology, animism, "the nasty practices of the heathen," Catholicism did not deny these things but rather sanctified them, drew them up into grace; it gave the believer a wide and living world. Thus Marius. But Julian considered that all these fine ladies and gentlemen gathered here, listening to the fine talk, kept in their hearts the secret of lust, that their inmost thoughts were concentrated on sex, that madness thinly veiled possessed them all, the madness which all the forces of society seemed designed at once to provoke and restrain but never to allay.

"Therefore," he said to himself, "we live in hypocrisy. I am not alone, but I am merely bitten by the same great louse which crawls in the night from bed to bed." But this acknowledgment made him feel more alone than ever.

He was drunk, though only to that point at which he had a magnified view of his own powers and of what was possible. Because his thoughts were secret, he felt secrecy around him like a shroud, and he left the house.

Julian was fifteen minutes beforehand at the rendezvous; this annoyed him. Like a schoolboy, he thought. The loneliness of the Zoo frightened him somewhat; what seemed the laughter of beasts in distant cages intensified the silence which appeared to him to belong to his own moral isolation. Bright green leaves whispered and waved about the globe of a nearby lamp, and the sidewalk beneath reflected a million particles of gray, stone light; it might have been a landscape on the moon.

The dark waters of the seal pool rolled uneasily, the oily surface caught occasional ripples of light. A seal barked loudly close at hand, and Julian jumped. A policeman passed under the street lamp across the pool and seemed to be eying Julian closely, but said nothing and went on, the metal plates of his heels striking the pavement in a measured beat.

111

Perhaps she would not come? At this moment Julian hoped she would not. He allowed himself five minutes more, then he would take a taxi and in another five minutes appear at the party as though he had never left it. In the darkness behind him animals groaned and chuckled as though in uneasy sleep. Bianca came from the shadows and took his arm. She was wearing a white dress, sleeveless and loosely cut. Julian found his heart beating very rapidly, and he imposed upon himself feelings of desperate gaiety. At one instant he thought: no one will ever know. At the next instant he thought that it would always be possible to kill himself afterward.

"Where shall we go?" he asked, noticing that his voice shook in the attempt to keep its tone light and casual.

"I know a place," she replied almost in a whisper, and he allowed himself to be led away. They walked westward, out of the Zoo, through a tunnel smelling of urine, up a dark path. Julian put his arm around Bianca's waist, his hand slipped down to rest on the curve of her backside, which hardened and softened agreeably with the rhythm of her walking; he observed that she seemed to have nothing on under her dress, and he confirmed this observation by sliding his hand up to touch her breast, at which she leaned closer to him and rested her head on his neck so that he smelled again, in some excitement, the strong, raw perfume with which she seemed almost drenched. Julian's heart was pounding, his mind was shaken by a feeling of wild freedom in which nothing, not the most horrifying or perverse imaginings from dreams, would be forbidden him. The strange thought came into his head that he wished Bianca would resist so that he might rape her. Possibly he would kill her afterwards.

Presently, in a place of darkness, she led him aside from the path. They clambered hand in hand up fairly steep slopes of rock, then into a grove of young trees. She turned to face him, and for a moment they stood apart.

"All right. Now," he heard her say in a new, sharp voice, and almost at the same moment felt himself seized from behind by an arm around his throat, while something else, harder than a fist, came at him from in front and smashed against his nose and mouth. He was thrown heavily to the ground and kicked once or twice, more with contempt, perhaps, than to hurt.

"Go over him good," the girl said. "The bastard's married, too." Great indignation in her voice, thought Julian, who did not altogether lose consciousness under several more blows in the face. He felt his coat wrenched around under him, the lining tore out. Someone with a flashlight looked into his wallet; an inadvertent motion of the light disclosed the two young men, the black and the white, who had been standing behind Bianca that afternoon at the Zoo. One of them, in darkness again, knelt and took Julian's wrist watch. Bianca whispered to them to hurry, he felt a final kick under the ribs, then there was silence and darkness.

After a few moments Julian sat up and took a deep breath. He hurt in a number of places, but was able to move all his limbs. The taste of blood was in his mouth, and he felt a trickle down his neck also; the place where he had cut himself shaving had been opened up again.

For all this, he felt strangely light and peaceful, almost amused. The suddenness of the attack had given him no time to be afraid, and the entire affair had been over very quickly. Of course, it was disagreeable to lose one's wallet and watch and be beaten up at the same time, but Julian's sense of a merited punishment, and one which, moreover, had both anticipated and prevented the crime it punished, gave him an

113

odd feeling of relief. With his clothing torn, blood on his face and collar, he thought gratefully that he had done nothing wrong, that the situation had not changed, that inwardly, by the preservation of grace, he was still the man he had been.

A disagreeable thought struck him: would this assault be followed by blackmail? The wallet of course contained, in addition to some forty dollars, his name, address, et cetera. Suddenly he remembered the anonymous letter; to his great relief this was still in the side pocket of his coat. Probably, he decided, such people did not go in for blackmail; criminals, he had heard, usually stuck to one line of work; and perhaps these little wretches could not even write. This educated thought a little restored his confidence.

Just now Julian realized, in a moment of quiet terror, that he was not alone. Someone, a white jacket faintly glimmering, sat beside him on the ground. Out of the darkness a voice spoke.

"Poor dear," it said. "Poor lamb, you have had a bad time, haven't you?"

The voice — a man's voice — was gentle, caressing, faintly ironic at the same time. The expressions it employed seemed to Julian faintly effeminate, and suggestive of the character of a male nurse.

Now a hand with a handkerchief began to mop at his face. The handkerchief was wet, but smelled slightly also of some sort of toilet water. Julian pushed it away.

"I'm perfectly all right," he said severely, but discovered on trying to stand up that this statement was an exaggeration. The stranger gently and firmly helped him to his feet and supported him with an arm around his waist.

"Here, try to walk a step or so," the voice advised him. "I'll hold you."

With the stranger's assistance Julian was able to get on,

114

limping slightly, and even to get down the rocks to the path. They walked on together.

"You must feel an awfully foolish boy," the voice said out of darkness, its tone both soothing and distantly amused. "You ought to have someone to take care of you."

"I appreciate your help," said Julian, "but, if you don't object, we won't discuss the matter."

"Embarrassment, oh, dear," said the stranger, and clucked with his tongue several times, most disagreeably to Julian. "You've made a positive ass of yourself, and you're afraid I know it." There followed on this a loud, rather too musical laugh. Then they came into the light of a street lamp. Julian, turning, looked into his own face, his own eyes. The stranger — if he could be called that — met his gaze steadily and coldly, with a smile which Julian was unable to return and which caused him finally to drop his eyes.

"Yes," said the other with an air of quiet self-satisfaction, as though it explained everything. "Yes."

For reasons which he could not fathom, Julian was not even surprised.

"You are Federigo," he rather muttered than said, his eyes still on the ground.

"Come, keep walking," the other said. "I think it's time we had a little talk, you and I, and I don't want to be forever about it. Besides, we must get you cleaned up and presentable."

Julian let himself be escorted, Federigo's arm linked in his, for some distance, to a paved stone circle in the center of which stood a fountain. The waters fell from a pitcher held aloft by three stone women closely grouped, and splashed into a surrounding trough, on the edge of which they now sat down. The entire area was dimly lit by street lamps placed around the outer edges, and Julian recognized the place as

115

one where he had once gone roller-skating, around and around the fountain. He looked down into the waters, which were filthy with shredding cigarette butts, matches, candy wrappers, then at Federigo, who was dipping his handkerchief and wringing it out.

"Your intentions," said Federigo, "have doubtless been of the best all along. But you are, you know, a dreadful innocent. Here, hold still," and he began washing Julian's face and throat with the handkerchief.

"They said you were on a world cruise," Julian managed to say through the rather rough scrubbing he received. "But you don't surprise me, you know, I'm not surprised at all. It is quite surprising that I'm not, when you come to think of it." He felt that he was babbling most stupidly, but could not stop. "Did you know that I took your name in vain?" He giggled. "On a letter, it was, a ridiculous letter, though I don't know if it was so ridiculous after all, do you see?"

"Please hold still and be quiet," said Federigo.

He continued to scrub Julian's face vigorously, then rearranged as neatly as possible his shirt and tie, buttoned up his coat.

"A little awkward," he said, "but not too bad. If people do notice, you can always put on a haughty expression and tell them you'd rather not discuss the matter. Your haughty expression does really frighten people, you know; even if they see it is mere childishness, and laugh about it behind your back, they are afraid to say anything to you. Of course, they talk about it among themselves. . . . It's funny, isn't it, what a great deal of such hocus-pocus goes to making up a character, a personality, something that really, in the world's eyes, exists? *Pulvis et umbra*, darling, and yet — there it is, big as life, moving around, putting out pseudopodia in the direction of what it thinks it wants. How dramatic and really entertain-

116

ing it all is! Which reminds me, my friend, what do you think of your little performance this evening?"

"I was an idiot," Julian said in a low voice; he felt as if he were back in grade school, and looked cautiously at Federigo to see if he had answered aright.

"Oh, as to that — it is not absolutely certain," said Federigo. "On the one hand, yes. And, on the other hand — hardly. So the phrase goes, among eminent educators, statesmen and divines. Operationally, it is hard to deny you've been a fool; yet, as I said, your intentions were sound."

"I don't know what it was I wanted," Julian said sadly.

Federigo, for answer, took Julian's hand, closed it into a fist, and rapped the knuckles painfully against the stone rim of the basin where they sat.

"That's your trouble," he said. "You don't really believe it's there till it draws blood. Of course you know what you want, only you're ashamed to say so. You want to know the worst."

Julian considered this statement in silence, looking at the slight cut on the knuckle of his middle finger.

"Yes, blood," said Federigo. "From your own private stock and individual blood bank. You have, I believe, some five quarts of it crawling around in you at approximately a mile an hour top speed, and only slightly faster than that in the heat — as you might call it — of passion." He smeared his own finger on the cut and daintily licked the blood from it. "Salt as sea water," he said, "which is very nearly what it is. It has built up that wall of skin and bone and brain which keeps you from being the All. All that a boy is he owes to his mother, it's a wise child, and so forth." He laughed, and put his arm around Julian. "Put it another way," he continued. "Did you ever stop to think, years ago, when you came out here to play — you roller-skated right around here a number of times — well, did you ever believe you would be here tonight?"

Julian tried to disengage himself from the encircling arm without openly using force, but found it impossible.

"You think you know everything, don't you?" he sneered childishly. "How could I have thought of any such thing?"

"How, indeed?" concurred Federigo, as though this explained everything. "And yet, you know, time is not the whole business. How many times, already, do you suppose you have walked over the very place where you will die?"

"This is ridiculous," Julian said, trying to get up but being heavily restrained by his own feeling of weakness as well as by the arm across his back. "I don't know you, and I don't believe I want to."

"Oh, now, I should scarcely say that," Federigo objected. "Who signed whose name to a letter — or two letters? Besides, I only want to help you to what you want. I'm not here for my own pleasure, you know.

"Look, let us consider it this way," he continued briskly. "As two men of the world, let us agree on one thing, that whatever it is you want, it is not simply to seduce one or two little girls, or for that matter a thousand and three little girls. Very likely one little girl is much like another, when it comes to that last dreadful scene on the bed — don't deny it, dear boy, you do think it's dreadful, I know you do. You are perfectly aware, are you not, that if it was your ambition to go to bed with this one and that one — if it was truly your ambition — it could be arranged quite easily, without this fuss over anonymous letters and strangers in the Park? That little creature, by the way, had clap anyhow, so you are better off than you realize. Or perhaps a touch of clap, a mild dose, is included among your secret desires? Perhaps that would have pleased your mighty righteousness very nearly as well as being beaten about the chops with a flashlight and robbed of your money? Who knows? I merely offer the possibility for your consideration.

"Oh, dear Julian, I've known so many of your sort in my time, you cold Rover Boys of the spirit. Perhaps you think you are the only man in the world who has had the idea of sending himself anonymous letters about his wife? You got the idea you were a pretty wicked lad, did you not? You were in a real tizzy of fright and delight. And yet the thing is done every day, a hundred times a day, the innocent postman — if even he is innocent, which I doubt — trudges along with fallen arches precisely from the weight of such communications, the world is full of people spying on themselves in this manner. Their typical weapon is the boomerang, and they almost never remember to duck when it returns; one suspects they do not even want to duck, it is themselves they have been aiming at right along, and they have tribally adopted the boomerang as their armament because it is the only thing one can hurl at oneself."

"But what does one do instead?" asked Julian, who had to admit to himself the disagreeable cogency of some of his companion's remarks.

"Instead? Instead? Why, look at it. The world is all before you, perfectly real, it all exists, stones, trees, running water, minutes, hours, bugs, mirrors — get out of yourself, and smell the bracing air of reality. That's what to do instead."

"Now you sound like a scoutmaster," said Julian.

"It all exists," said Federigo impressively, "and not only that, but — may it set your mind at rest — *nothing else does.*"

"Nothing?"

"Nothing whatever, a little dust, a little smoke, maybe. When you think that is God watching you, my dear, it isn't."

"Who, then?"

119

"It's only me from over the sea, said Barnacle Bill the sailor," sang Federigo, suddenly breaking forth in a loud voice, raucously gay, as he stood up. "Come, let us walk out of the Park."

As they went along, however, Federigo continued to expound to Julian his curious notions.

"It only takes a mite of courage," he said, "audacity enough to put on the point of a pin. You've lived a sheltered life, you were educated at the best schools, you know theoretically that bad things happen — so of course you can't believe in happiness, and you're perfectly correct. Happiness doesn't really exist, it is only the absence of everything you are looking for; you know, *reality:* filth. But you don't altogether want to find it, do you? Not that you don't look hard enough, but that you make sure every time of looking in the wrong place. You are like the man the policeman found searching for his watch under a street lamp. 'Where did you lose it?' asks the policeman. 'Over there,' the man replies, pointing out in the darkness, 'I'm looking here because the light's better.' " Federigo laughed with unnecessary vigor at his own joke.

"I was in the war," said Julian rather primly.

"Of course, of course, that's what you always tell yourself, you were in the war. You went out there and killed the enemy, didn't you — *out there?* But you hated the sergeant, the captain, the people on your own team? Of course you did! What did you think the war was trying to say, what does it ever try to say? Be your age!

"And that brings me to another thing. Age. You're not dead yet, you know, you have a number of years to stagger through. Well, don't pride yourself so much on your *maturity*. For whenever you do, you'll merely make an ass of yourself, as you did tonight. People don't really grow up, you know, they

120

merely revolve. When you are mature you will realize it by noticing that somewhere along the steep gradient of moral effort you have died. In short, I advise you, my friend, to stop festering, and take a little honest pride in what goes on around you. Do you want love? Go right ahead, fall in love with the first little girl you meet. What's so terrible in that? And even if it were terrible — could it be worse than the way you are going on now?"

They had come out of the Park while Federigo was talking, and now stood on a street corner.

"We'll say good night now," Federigo said. "Don't resent it if I lecture you, I wouldn't do it if I didn't think it necessary. There, go ahead, live, be happy, you can do it. And remember, I'll be around if you want me."

Julian began to say something, but Federigo, squeezing his arm, swung him around facing the other way and sent him off with a coy yet forceful slap on the behind.

"Get on with you," he cried gaily, and Julian heard him laugh. He saw that he was standing at the entrance to Hugo's building. When he turned to survey the darkness outside the doorway there was no sign of his recent companion. The stone frame of the entrance, the glass in the door, the bronze handle, all seemed brilliantly real, the lights in the hallway nearly blinded him by their brightness; he felt like a tired swimmer coming up the beach out of the undertow of the last wave reaching after him.

There was a mirror in the elevator. He looked pale and fairly presentable, though there was a patch of blood which could not be concealed on his shirt collar. It was perfectly true, he decided, that Federigo's eyes were somewhat darker than his own.

3

THE party was still going on, in a subdued way; it had considerably thinned out. The door of the apartment stood open, and Julian crossed the threshold just in time to meet Elaine Leonard coming from the kitchen. She stopped, they looked at one another for a moment, just long enough, as it happened, for Julian to fall in love with this girl, and for her to realize that he had. The glance between them wavered and changed its character several times during that moment; all Julian's free-floating speculation about the secrecy of the world, all his diffused lust, became concentrated upon Elaine's eyes; also, all the disgust, for himself and for others, which had been as it were held over from the episode of Bianca and scarcely allowed entrance into his feelings until now. Elaine, not knowing the how or the why of all this, nevertheless felt and responded slightly, tentatively, and with some unease, to the fact of its being so.

Just how this happened, how such things ever happen, would not be easy to say. She, coming from the kitchen and carrying two drinks, paused in his path and gave him, in the first place, a look intended to go with what she was about to say, namely that his absence had been noticed, not altogether with pleasure; she raised her eyebrows slightly.

He, in part because she knew, or knew of, Federigo, interpreted this glance as somehow involving them together in a conspiracy of undetermined object. He looked back at her with a gravity in which was also something ironical, and his eyebrows went up, too.

She took this as some sort of admission of his being caught, for some reason, red-handed, but with a gaiety attached to it that reckoned informally on her knowing how these things

122

were; she noticed at the same time the blood on his shirt, and that his lower lip was somewhat puffed out. This last gave him an expression at once sardonically defiant and indescribably stupid. She replied by the merest hint of a smile — that smile so full of crooked honesty — intending friendly sympathy touched with sarcasm. This sarcasm, in her, seldom meant hatred or bitterness, but was the expression by which she seemed to understand quite well what she did not in fact understand.

"You've been missed," she said, with a nod of her head toward the further room, meaning to indicate at least that she was not the one who had missed him.

"Oh?" said Julian, and then, "Is one of those drinks for me?" Elaine gravely handed him one. "I was — just out," he said. "What happened?"

"I'm afraid your wife," she replied, "became, you might say, indisposed."

"Drunk?"

"You might say."

"Oh, dear," muttered Julian, summoning resolution. "Where is she?"

"Oh, she was taken home a while ago. Marius took her. There was some fuss over where you were while all this was taking place."

"I had a little trouble," Julian said, "in a bar."

Elaine smiled at him somewhat more broadly, meaning to say again that she understood with a superior sympathy touched to irony by her extensive knowledge of the world and its ways. This smile did not exactly, as the saying is, catch at Julian's heart; rather, it tore at his nerves. This girl of nineteen or so (and she knew Federigo) seemed to see him with a penetrative innocence, the calm of knowledge in her eyes. He felt sentimentally ashamed of himself, as though his

123

presence at this moment visibly corrupted her, and she standing there like a martyr shot full of feathered arrows, taking it as easily as in an Italian painting. He saw himself now in her eyes as some kind of beast, a beast endowed with reason in order that it might make a fool of itself. Please understand, he wanted to say to her, I am not like this, really. I am unhappy. Of course, he could not say any such thing, and he instead gazed intently at her, as though he could make his eyes speak for him: forgive me, they would have said if they could — more like a beast than ever.

She however misinterpreted his long look to mean that he pitied her for being a young girl who did not understand as yet what this world was; accordingly her smile became more crookedly satirical and her eyes quite severe, as she said to him:

"I don't mean to mix in your affairs," with a slight emphasis on the final word. The strictness of her look, the kindness and scorn, both it seemed altogether objective, in her tone of voice, broke Julian down. He wanted to reach out and stroke her hair, thus coming, by a process of varied misinterpretations on both sides, to an expression and glance which Elaine, as she had been fallen in love with before, could quite well understand, as she showed by turning away, after a last smile of conspiratorial kindness which cost her nothing, and walking down the hall to the dimly lit room beyond.

Julian stood irresolutely in the narrow hall, and stared into his drink. He ought to go home, and it was the last thing in the world he wanted to do. He did not in the least believe he would discover his wife Sylvia in bed with Marius Rathlin, though he recognized, too, that he did not believe it only because his experience had not equipped him to believe any such thing, and for no more substantial reason. He did not want to go home to a discussion of Marius, a discussion of

124

Sylvia, a discussion above all else, of himself. It was to be presumed, of course, that Sylvia, having been ("you might say") drunk, would be asleep. That made matters, almost, worse, since he would have to wait for morning with the threat of *explanations* pending; and he could sense already how dreadful, with a hangover added to everything else, he would feel in the morning. He desperately did not want to be told (being quite capable of telling himself, a dozen times a minute) that his behavior had been at least irresponsible, and probably something a good deal worse than that.

Some people can do it, he reflected, and others can't. Why was that? And how horribly unfair. Some people doubtless made a habit of leaving parties to visit a woman; they came back, no one had noticed, or those who did notice were such as would merely smile to themselves. *He* left a party — once! — and the world looked ready to fall on his head. The worst of it was that he blamed himself more than anyone else could — though it seemed likely that Sylvia, when she recovered, would at least compete with him in that line.

If he should be, for example, drunk — in a certain high and authoritative mood which drink at one stage induced — he had no doubt of his ability to explain everything, make everything all right . . . simply, of course, by lying, or by (let us say) dramatizing. With this in mind he drank off the drink Elaine had given him, and went into the kitchen to get another.

But it was impossible, for in the nature of things he would not be drunk at the time of explanation, for just the reason that while he was drunk he would feel no need to explain anything whatever; when he sobered up, though, and he supposed he must, sooner or later, the prospect of feeling guilty, the necessity of saying something to Sylvia, extended itself before him. Then again, how in the world was one to explain, even to

125

oneself, Federigo? who seemed to Julian far more important, at this moment, than anything else which had happened during that time in the Park — not so much a time, it began to appear, as an abscess in time, a darkness, a vivid dream with irrevocable consequences still to be faced in waking.

Then there was Elaine Leonard, and for an instant he beheld his self-contempt reflected from her eyes, his corruption gaining pathos from her purity. The tenderness and abasement he felt swelled in him to a romantic, ardent sadness, and he had a maudlin wish to be nineteen again, with the open world of choice before him. Love, passionate and bitterly exclusive, love for this one girl, he saw, would redeem everything: Bianca, Federigo, everything, the anonymous letters, might be absorbed into the realm of intense feeling and converted, from casual lust and rage, into honesty again — if he loved Elaine.

In a flash he saw before him the dreadful scenes, the quarrels, the cold arrangement with lawyers, the divorce court, freedom . . . a vision of Sylvia, who looked more surprised than anything else. But, of course, Elaine must love him in return, or what would all this mean or matter?

"Julian!" It was Hugo's voice, loud and somewhat peremptory; his footsteps could be heard in the hall. "Julian!" He came round the corner into the kitchen. "There you are," he said, as though his friend had simply been misplaced, like a collar button. "I want to talk to you, Jay," he said earnestly. "Let's fix a drink, and we can talk right here."

Hugo fixed two drinks and handed Julian one, quite disregarding the fact that Julian already had one; his manner seemed to say that this would prevent their being interrupted. It was like the final conversation with an alcoholic — his friends give him one last round of his favorite drink, sit him down, talk to him seriously and more in sorrow than in anger . . . Hugo sat himself down on the drainboard, Julian

126

leaned against the refrigerator facing him. Hugo was quite drunk and in a magisterial mood, nevertheless he seemed somewhat embarrassed to begin.

"Understand," he said after a space of silence, "I don't know, and I don't want to know, where you've been all this time. That's your business. But the things that happened while you were gone, here in my house — ah, Jay, I'm not going to lecture you, you know that. But you are my oldest and best friend, and I hope I'm yours — and just to prove it's still so, I want to ask you to be best man at my wedding. Will you do that?"

"Yes," Julian said almost inaudibly.

"Thank you," said Hugo with a kind of judicial satisfaction. "Now — about this other thing. There's something wrong between you and Sylvia? There must be. She's drinking a great deal. I've never seen her do that before tonight, Sylvia's not that kind of girl. But that in itself wasn't anything, only — if you see what I mean — you weren't there just when you were needed."

Oh, dear God, Julian thought with dreadful anticipations. It must have been far worse than anything he had thought.

"If she had only got drunk and passed out quietly, you know," Hugo said, "that would not have been so terrible. We could have put her in a cab with someone, Louisa could have taken her home — she could have slept here, for that matter. But she made a fuss," he said impressively.

"She made a fuss," Julian repeated.

"When she couldn't find you anywhere. She behaved rather foolishly about it, I thought, she got all sorts and conditions of people to look for you, it was like a kind of game for a while — then, she was quite drunk, you must bear that in mind, she started telling everyone, rather loudly, that you hated her, that you believed she was unfaithful to you but

127

that you wouldn't speak to her and wouldn't give her a chance to defend herself. Then she got dreadfully angry and went about saying 'shit' to people, and so forth, you know how it is when people get, well, intense — not very pretty, and she kept on drinking through it all. Then finally she announced to everyone present that she would goddamn well give you something to hate about, and she collapsed on Marius Rathlin — more or less all over him."

"And?"

"And he took her home," Hugo said unhappily. "Oh, I'm not suggesting there was anything sinister about that, he was terribly embarrassed. But you weren't there, and — and, well, you see how it went. Marius was elected. I'm afraid," he added stiffly, "some people tended to make jokes about it."

"Oh," said Julian.

"I don't mean to put all the blame on you," Hugo said. "I'm concerned, that's all. It'd look mighty odd for an ancient lecher like myself to take a high moral tone with you, but there's also manners, discretion, to be considered. I care for you and Sylvia more than any friends I've got. You may not believe it, because I don't ordinarily talk about such things, but your marriage has always been a kind of ideal to me — the way I hope things will be with Louisa and myself. I know you may have made a mistake," Hugo said with earnest heartiness. "My God, who doesn't, sometime or other? And you've been a kind of *preux chevalier* for so many years, haven't you? But if there's something wrong, Jay, for God's sake don't keep it all locked up in there, let me know what it is. I'll help you out, if I possibly can. But what you need is a man you can talk to — I know how that feels. So break down — here, let's fix one more — and tell Uncle Hugo what's gone wrong."

After Hugo had fixed fresh drinks and sat back again on

the drainboard, Julian in a dramatic silence, because there was nothing else to do, handed him the anonymous letter. Hugo opened the envelope and looked at the sheet of paper long enough to read it a number of times.

"I see," he said to himself. "I see, I see." He looked decisively up at his friend. "Do you think this is true?"

"I don't know."

"Well, do you have any idea who would send such a thing?"

"No."

"Federigo, Federigo," Hugo observed. "Kind of a smart-alecky name to pick out. A wise guy." His voice had become very hard, and he clenched his fist suggestively. "Boy, if I were you," he said, "I'd take this kind of thing very seriously, very seriously indeed. There's nothing more rotten, more cowardly, in the whole world, than a man who won't sign his right name to a letter — whether it's true or not," Hugo added angrily.

"No," Julian dully agreed.

"Surely you have some suspicion, some idea?" asked Hugo.

"No, I don't," said Julian.

"Is this the only one of the things you've got so far?"

"Yes, the only one."

"There will be more," Hugo said with satisfaction of a sort. "These people are never content to stop with one. Take it from me, there will be more," he said somewhat smugly, "and sooner or later he'll give himself away. Listen, Julian," he added, "let me help you. What you need is professional work."

"Professional?"

"Detectives, boy, detectives. I'm going to hang on to this letter," putting it away in his pocket, "and I'm going to take you and it to some people I know. On Monday," Hugo added firmly, "we'll go to these people, Pritchard, Ferriter & Magoun is the firm name — why, I shouldn't be at all surprised they could find out right off who sent this thing. They have methods, you know, science."

"I don't think you should go to all that trouble," Julian said feebly. "If you'll just let me have the letter — "

"Don't be silly," Hugo said, "I know you, you'd put it away and worry yourself sick. Jay, you need help. I can't see my old friends made unhappy on account of some wretched son of a bitch somewhere. We'll get this all straightened away together; why, if you like, I'll help you explain to Sylvia." He winked at Julian. "You got upset, you were worried, you left the party and went to some bar on Third Avenue, you got into a scrape with some drunk and he beat you up a little but you ought to see what happened to him — that's all." He winked again. "She has to accept that, don't you see, because after all — there *is* this anonymous letter, and if that doesn't account for a husband's reactions, why, what would?"

Hugo got down off the drainboard and patted Julian on the shoulder.

"Go home and sleep," he said kindly, "your worries are over. Only don't forget," he added, "if you get another of these lousy letters, you let me know right away. And what's more, if Sylvia's a bitch to you tomorrow, and you've got to allow she might be, just tell her it will all be explained in a few days."

Hugo saw Julian out the door.

"I don't mean to throw you out, Jay," he said, "but probably you've had enough party for one night, and anyhow, this one is nearly over. Remember," he concluded, "on Monday — Pritchard, Ferriter, Magoun. I'll call you up in the morning."

The apartment was dark, a little glow of moonlight or streetlight touched a corner of the bedroom. Out in the hall

130

bathroom the dogs stirred slightly, turning over in sleep. Julian listened for a moment to his wife breathing heavily and evenly in sleep. He undressed in silence, letting his clothes fall on the floor. As his eyes became more accustomed to the dimness he saw that Sylvia was fully dressed and lay on the coverlet. He tenderly pulled off her shoes, thinking that here if anywhere was a proof of innocence, also that Marius might have risked so much at least without becoming an adulterer. Sylvia stirred uneasily, emitting a groan or a snore.

Julian got into his own bed and stretched out. There they lay, he reflected, in parallel, like figures on a tomb, or like an advertisement for pyjamas, except that neither of them was wearing pyjamas. Those figures on the tomb, where had they come from?

On their wedding trip, he remembered, that was where. In England, in some ancient abbey or other down in the west country. A knight and a lady lay, with grave and sharpened features, in a bronze silence atop their sarcophagus. Sylvia had said something, her hand entwined in his just as the knight's was with the lady's. What had she said?

"They must have loved each other well."

"For six or seven centuries," Julian had replied.

Fidelity and death, he now thought. There had been another tomb nearby, the product of a somewhat later period, where the sculptured emblem more realistically imitated the contents: a skull of bronze, through the empty eye of which a bronze and gleaming serpent crawled; that was austere, as Julian had remarked with satisfaction at the time, austere and witty.

"Witty?" she had asked, and he had been unable to explain, at least to his bride's satisfaction, just what it was he had meant.

He wondered now whether he would die in this bed, which

rested, as it seemed, rather uneasily under his weight, and he saw this comfortable contraption suddenly for what it was, a waiting, patient animal. Or else it was a marsh, a mire, and he imagined how one day he would feel himself all at once sinking into its soft, yielding depth, stretching out both hands to the woman, the friends, the doctor — faceless, all of them — who stared down on him from above and watched him swallowed up.

And Sylvia? Would she die in the bed next to his? Had all this been arranged, irrevocably, some long time ago, so that there was now nothing anyone could do about it? Julian wondered whether he would be afraid to die. Perhaps he would, and he saw at the last instant Sylvia bending above him with a bitter and cruel smile, as though this — his being terrified to die — were the final secret, the one she would have waited many years, maybe, by that time, to discover and confirm. Or would she be the one, and he the watcher above the bed?

What was beyond? He considered the God in whom he did not believe, and Who was not therefore, it seemed, in the least prevented from existing, just at this moment. The anger of his conscience, which he could not turn away because it began within him, produced in him a vague, objectless terror, or a terror which had everything for its object, and which he could not escape because it caused everything in the world to reflect himself, so that everything in the world became fluid and unstable, there was no solidity anywhere, as in a dream the most trivial object became charged with feelings of despair and fear, while the world began to fall away as in a dream.

Sylvia for her part was not asleep. She pretended to be when her husband came home, out of shame and hatred. She felt him pull off her shoes.

Thank you so very much, she thought angrily, and wanted

132

to giggle. Her head had begun to ache terribly. Perhaps she had been asleep, after all, but now her head ached. If she got up, however, she would have to say something to Julian, which was impossible, so she lay there and added the headache, grain by grain, to everything else which was so hateful.

A blessed, drunken amnesia was not quite strong enough to prevent her from feeling ashamed, or from the knowledge that she had put on some sort of exhibition which it would be better not to know much more about; the details were under a sort of merciful narcosis, though Sylvia thought that if she remembered them her head might possibly stop pounding.

Marius had been, so far as she could recollect, a perfect gentleman. She did not even think he had tried to kiss her except in the taxi (which was all right). Of course, she must have made a splendidly attractive object to kiss, especially after having (she thought she remembered) been sick in the gutter just as they got out of the cab. Her mouth tasted as though she had been sick. Marius, it was to be presumed, then, had gingerly deposited her upon her bed, where she now found herself — not in it, mind — and he had retired, she supposed, upon such a strict observance of the situation as not even to have removed her shoes, which God knew he might have done. Still, a perfect gentleman.

And where had Julian been all this time? She did not know, and just now she did not much care, either; it was enough that he had not been there when it was necessary — if he had been there, it would not have been necessary for him to be there, because she would not have become drunk, so then he might have gone off wherever he liked . . . That seemed to move in a circle, rather. What was all this about? About Julian's having gone off somewhere — she merely wanted him to know she did not usually mind; she wanted him to have a certain freedom at parties and so forth, it was one of the things that kept a marriage going — nothing serious, only a certain light freedom — kissing other people's wives, just as their husbands kissed her. But it was inexcusable for him not to be there when whatever it was had happened.

That dreadful letter. At this moment, with a blinding headache, she could see it so clearly, on the dining room table, a plain white envelope such as might have been purchased in any one of a hundred shops. But it had been a dream. As Dr. Mirabeau said, a certain light freedom between husband and wife had to be allowed, these days. She herself used to be so strict about such things, like a girl in an invisible convent. With the thought of an invisible convent the pain in her head gave a fearful jump. But now she was relaxed, easy-going. That was the way, a little give and take. They had, she believed, a *modern marriage;* this was, however, the expression people typically used some twenty years ago; she had not realized that modern marriages could be as *démodé* as all that. What had the letter said? She could scarcely remember. All that fuss about it in her mind all day long, and now she could remember only that it was signed Federigo, and said something about being alone. It was strange how dreams faded from your mind. It was a plain, white envelope, and it lay on the dining room table, just as clear, as clear, as clear as the dream could make it.

BOOK TWO

But all the storie of the night told ouer,
And all their minds transfigur'd so together,
More witnesseth than fancies images,
And growes to something of great constancie;
But howsoeuer, strange, and admirable.

— SHAKESPEARE

Chapter 5

THE second letter had been mailed late Friday afternoon, and did not appear in the Saturday morning mail; consequently, so far as Julian and Sylvia were concerned, nothing
happened over the weekend. On Saturday they got up very
late, not feeling well; there was not energy enough between
them to begin a discussion of the previous night. Instead, they
politely and distantly sympathized with one another, and recommended aspirins at odd intervals when the silence seemed
to become unbearably intense. At four o'clock they encouraged themselves with cocktails until they could eat a light
supper (Julian with a show of domesticity made an omelet)
and went to the movies, then early to bed. On Sunday they
read the papers thoughtfully for a long time, got out the car
and took themselves and the dogs up into the country; the
trees were a hazy, beginning green, flowers appeared, it began
to rain. It did not rain hard, but steadily. They felt chilled
and gray, and drove back to town. It was late afternoon, and
they went to another movie. When they came out it was still
light, still raining, they got sandwiches and beer from a del-
icatessen, went home, ate, Julian smoked a cigar, Sylvia did
as much of the double-crostic in the *Times* as she could do
without effort, and went to bed.

Nothing happened. . . . It was terrifying. At every moment it seemed something must snap, but nothing did, neither
of them screamed or broke into tears and curses, or suddenly

137

turned on the other with a knife, though each thought of such things constantly. They were both polite, good and, on the whole, kindly persons, who had been taught by their parents and at the best schools not to raise their voices, indulge in tantrums or make scenes; they were reasonable beings. Moreover, they loved one another. Their belief that they loved one another — love, on this view, became a slow-burning unhappiness —was the sacrifice imposed upon both of them equally by pride; even at their worst moments in seven years of marriage they had never allowed to pass their lips that word *divorce*, which would have seemed to them both an admission of moral failure. The dogs, Troilus and Cressida, slept, were fed, moved gracefully around the apartment, and were silently, as possessions have the habit of being in these circumstances, a reproach, as though to say: How can you be unhappy with two such fine dogs? The furniture too rebuked them, entering into the spirit of the silence: the clean-lined, slender legs of the low, modern tables, the alert appearance of the couch with its square corners and straight back, the inquisitive curve of a lamp which bent its bell-head heavily from a corner; all these smart impersonal objects, as coldly reasonable here as they had been in the shops whence they came, all at once achieved the identity of unhappiness: if we thought you would be like this, they seemed to say, we would not have come here. Julian recognized this appearance from distant childhood; it was the critical look the Christmas presents began to have when one became ill-tempered and was punished in their presence.

The movies they saw were both murder mysteries, portraying a world of sinister gestures most of them meaningless, sleights of hand to defer the recognition of the really guilty person; detectives moved in a desert of clues, the camera picked up dramatic contrasts of light and shade everywhere, the characters loved and hated each other by turns on demand of the plot. In both stories the murderer turned out to be the girl who had hired the detective in the first place, and with whom he had been more than half — saving only his keen perception of evil in the heart — in love. To Julian, the reflexive idiocy of this arrangement, so fashionable in the detective novel, betrayed as though accidentally some real and intimate source of guilt; in one of the pictures there were even anonymous letters. He and Sylvia sat in the darkness to witness all these things, occasionally they even held hands, transmitting to one another by slight increases of pressure the most cryptic intimations of feeling. They were like two survivors clutching each other across a piece of floating wreckage in the midst of a silent and wide ocean.

Three or four times during the weekend occurred the following exchange.

"I love you," one would say, bestowing a light kiss on the other.

"I love you too, darling," replied the other, with a little caress.

These words seemed to sink without resonance or reverberation into the wide silence. They sat in the living room, where from above the mantel of the empty fireplace Sylvia's portrait looked down. It had been done five years before, the painter had made Sylvia extravagantly slender (it seemed now) and with a look of wild innocence, in the style of Ophelia — in a white gown, clutching blue flowers with flashes of dark red — of which the intense poeticism disagreeably suggested insanity. Julian felt he wanted to tear this work off the wall and fling it on the floor in front of his wife, but was prevented from doing so in the first place because he did not know exactly what he would say after that. That picture, he thought — its eyes, for all their naïve and startled expression, covered the room like radar — is the most dreadful lie ever perpetrated. Covertly, by brief glances, he compared it with Sylvia, in whose comfortable, handsome body he found no trace of the thin, bitter, erotic ecstasy suggested in the canvas. How could she sit there with that dreadful reproach, that living lie, looking down on her from the past?

Sylvia looked up from the paper.

"What is the name of the disciple who doubted that Christ was risen?" she asked. "Six letters."

Julian did not know, and offered to look it up.

"That's not quite fair," she said, "but still — "

"It was Thomas," he announced after several minutes. "He wouldn't believe till he put his hand in the wound."

"Of course," said Sylvia, "*doubting Thomas.*"

This is what life is, Julian thought. We use the Bible to fill out crossword puzzles. The Word that died upon the Cross. It was a puzzle, certainly. He did not believe in God, yet it was quite true that he typically felt someone watching him, just as Federigo had said. Federigo? Was there any such person? Had he been there, that night in the Park? Julian uncomfortably remembered a few vivid details, the arm about his shoulder, the somewhat coy, bantering tone of sympathetic yet mocking amusement, the "boomerang" — had any of that taken place? And Bianca? He felt a sinking sensation of remorse, as if he were about to be sick to his stomach. It had all happened, it was all perfectly real — to the stomach; only the mind found it vague and unconvincing.

Federigo, he said to himself reasonably and in a convincing way, is either real or a hallucination. But here his mind began to boggle, since neither alternative could possibly be found acceptable.

If he is real, Julian quickly decided, he must be the Devil.

If he is unreal, I am going insane.

The Devil of course did not exist, for if the Devil existed, then God would have to exist — but did that necessarily follow? Or was it the Devil himself — whoever that might be — who alone existed, and alone sponsored, criticized and assessed the belief in a God? So that God was the imagination of the Devil working on the world? This line of speculation impressed Julian as at once ridiculous and too deep to be followed any further, he simply became confused. Besides, considered as a real, objectively existing Devil, Federigo appeared absurd; he did not have enough reality.

Considered, on the other hand, as a subjective impression, he uncomfortably had too much; if Julian tried to think of him that way, it seemed he had unquestionably been *there*, no getting around it. But he was not going insane; he had read somewhere that the very thought one was going insane was one's best guarantee against it; insane people never believed they were. On the other hand, if it was only for that reason he believed he was not going insane, where did that take him? Confusion again.

The thought of insanity, however, fascinated him, it presented a way out. The prisoner pleaded insanity, he had committed his crimes while of unsound mind, therefore they were not his crimes. Of course, as his rigorously brought up mind had gathered from all its experience so far, this was a solution too glib for belief. On exactly the appropriate occasions, when one was ashamed, afraid, hoping somehow to avoid an onerous duty, one generally did not fall sick of consumption, break a leg, go raving mad, or simply explode into a thousand pieces; one faced up, and went on facing up, to whatever was going at the time. If somewhere in this life tragedy existed, this perhaps was where it might be found, in the enduring pain

of responsibility which provided no such symbolic escape —
in duty, shame, guilt, fear, without the alleviation of sickness,
madness, death.

To live a clean, honest life . . . Julian knew quite well,
in theory, that human suffering, misery and degradation were
everywhere around. Civilization, on the other hand, was
organized to the end that these phenomena should not obtrude
themselves, that they should be as much as possible confined
and segregated, and dealt with by people who qualified as
technicians with respect to misery, suffering and degradation
and could, therefore, handle the tabooed objects without fear
and without revulsion. Others, though, would do well to walk
quietly and with their eyes to the front. The blind beggar on
the street, the crippled and drunken Legionnaire in the subway, the woman vomiting in the gutter between two parked
automobiles: to acknowledge such things was to ask for trouble, it was, for a member in good standing in civilization,
slightly subversive, and smacked of *making a fuss* which was
neither necessary nor justifiable; even charity, when it was
unofficial, became a political act.

Julian remembered having once seen a dead man on the
street, a window-cleaner fallen from his ledge. A crowd gathered at a little distance. Women, with faces averted, went carefully around the body on clicking heels and continued on their
ways. It had been beautifully delicate, the expression they
unanimously wore, an expression of pride and the highest
breeding which did not permit them, just at that instant, to
look down. Nor had he himself done anything except feel an
indescribable helplessness and lonely guilt, until a policeman and a doorman came running up, and the latter covered
the body with a rubber mat taken from before the entrance of
a building down the street. He thought now that the policeman
and the doorman had been enabled to do this thing for no bet-

142

ter reason than that they wore uniforms, and it went through his mind that Marius had said something similar about war: "It's splendid, because you can tell the good guys by the color of their hats."

As for Marius, now, did that young man, he wondered, have a real intention of having an affair with Sylvia? Julian reminded himself sharply that it was not impossible; it merely seemed impossible, or, better, very unlikely, because he implicitly tended to take it that Marius saw Sylvia just as objectively as he did himself, and therefore that Marius would not see in Sylvia anything so exclusively attractive, unless — which she was not — she was to be had for the asking. Then, too, apart from her being, so far as he knew, a chaste and modest person, and still a little frightened of pleasure, there was undeniably the fact that courting Sylvia, especially with any degree of secrecy, would be an expensive proposition, even if it meant no more than buying her occasional meals — she liked to dine well, did Sylvia, as her figure began to show — and now and then (Julian supposed) some little present or other. Of course, Marius might personally require a rather motherly type; and Sylvia, for that matter, someone who by his youth combined lover and child. This idea abruptly disgusted Julian, who believed accordingly that what he felt was jealousy. He glanced over at his wife, as though she must have followed his thoughts, but she continued imperturbably to bite the eraser of her pencil as she looked at the puzzle.

It's amazing, he thought, what things can go on in the human head, what battles and betrayals, all in utter, lonely security. He closed his eyes and deliberately began to think of Elaine with tenderness and lust; he discovered sadly that it took deliberation to do so, his mind kept slipping off to other things, her image even at his most intense concentration remained vague except for a rather crude intimation of what

143

her smile was like. They were alone in an unidentifiable room, he put his hands on her shoulders, there was the smile again . . . he pulled the dress down over her arms, the same dress she had been wearing the other night, and then without interruption he ,was thinking of Federigo again, seeing his smile instead of hers. That this should be so provoked him to a slight anger based on the fear that he might be impotent — which is ridiculous, he added. But it bothered him, as though it were morally a reproach, that he could not concentrate even upon what he proposed to himself as supremely desirable; it was so, it seemed, only objectively, and his poor, reasonable mind was like an adult saying to a child, "What do you mean, you won't have chocolate ice cream? You know you *love* chocolate ice cream." It is old age, he thought sadly, I've had my time. Upon this consideration it became to him a point of honor to prove himself upon Elaine — upon her body and her spirit — because the victory would be won not only over her but also over death. Surely, he reflected, that was natural enough, Sylvia herself must understand that.

"I can't do any more, I'm going to bed," Sylvia remarked, standing up.

"I'll just stay here for a little while," he replied.

"You look sad," she said. "Is anything wrong?"

"I'm just thinking," he said with a certain heaviness.

"I thought maybe it was your headache again," she said, bending over to kiss him. "I love you," she whispered in his ear.

"I love you too, darling," he whispered back, raising himself up to kiss her softly behind the ear.

What went on in the human head, Julian decided, went on also, on a slightly larger scale, in the human apartment. Apartment, that is, where people keep apart; he had never thought of that before. Privacy — what it meant was secrecy,

144

hypocrisy. Two people got married, they pooled their possessions — all their possessions — and sat in an apartment, where they were as dragons guarding some dread secret which they themselves could not understand. People came to the apartment to visit, they saw the thick carpets, the good furniture, the color scheme, the well-chosen prints and paintings, they moved over to ask mute questions of a row of books on a shelf — but all these things told them very little, they never saw the apartment at such times as the dragons sat alone, at such times as the secret itself became more terrible and burdensome than any threat to it from without the walls could possibly be. It was this, perhaps, which gave him the constant sensation of being watched, assessed, marked in some secret book — the idea that somewhere there existed a world which exactly replicated the way in which this world ought to go, and with which this world was steadily, point for point, being compared — conscience (he had read somewhere this clever definition) was the still, small, inward voice which told you when someone was watching. But according to Federigo, no such other world — and therefore no such voice — existed; or if it seemed to, it was only Federigo himself, or, more strictly, Barnacle Bill from over the sea. Only?

It seemed to him now that his life was a kind of dramatic performance; all that happened appeared to have a singular quality of being witnessed and made prominent, as though on a stage or a movie screen. The cameras moved quietly, recording everything: *Sylvia, in nightgown, moves across left to kitchen for a glass of water; Julian looks up but says nothing; she returns, blows kiss, exits up right to bedroom.*

Julian was tired, and every time he shut his eyes for an instant the world of sleep, that lay so close behind the eyelids, persisted in throwing up to him its cynical and whirling hints; when he laid back his head against the chair he would at once

145

see (how strange, to see by shutting the eyes!) men with the faces of bulldogs crawling about in snow, or children who were skeletons in dimity dresses; and then someone would throw a snowball at him and he would wake suddenly in horror with that icy lump imbedded in his brain.

I really must go to bed, he thought, and all at once he remembered what he had dreamed the night before.

He had been in bed (a curious place to be, in a dream), it was a warm night (as in fact it was) so that the covers were thrown back and he lay naked on the sheet (just so). Well, on this sheet crawled a reckonable number, say five or six, very little worms, about the size of nail parings (large ones) but dark and corrugated. As Julian watched, their tails, or at least one end of them, they didn't seem to have heads, kind of withered off until detached from the rest, whereupon each tail became another little worm; this began to happen with considerable rapidity, and there was soon a large number of worms. He noticed at the same time that his body was covered with red spots, which in the dream he sensibly took to be worm-bites. And he woke up. The momentary relief he experienced at seeing his body quite free from any red spots was soon replaced by a queer, remote depression which had stayed with him right through the day — different from, more basic than, his secular depression over marriage and life — as though something had gone wrong, either with the dream itself or with its relation to his waking life; as though, he put it to himself, remembering certain remarks made by Federigo on the subject of clap, as though he might in some obscure way have required those red spots to be really — really? — present on his body, for reasons too nefarious to be named.

Gets up from chair; moves away from camera to kitchen; returns with whisky and soda in glass; exits up right to bedroom; camera trucks slowly toward bedroom door.

146

Stimulated by her anxiety, Sylvia's dreams had already presented her with an anonymous letter, which thus gained the status of a recurrent image, a symbol, and would be presented to Dr. Mirabeau for inspection on the morrow. She had carefully copied out what she could remember of the dream:

The letter lies on the dining room table; I try to pick it up, but it seems to be glued down. Anyhow, I know perfectly well what it is. It is from Alma, I say, and suddenly notice a man sitting across the table from me. It is Federigo — I know this although he does not look at all like what I imagined. Instead, he is tall and fair-haired, and smokes a pipe; he says something about a walk in the Park. I know I must not go with him, and then I feel someone pulling my head back by the hair.

Sylvia placed a pencil and pad on the night table before going to bed, so that it would be convenient for her to receive any further revelation which might be granted.

2

MONDAY morning came; the anonymous letter lay on the table; Julian was determined to follow exactly the same procedure with the second as with the first. One must go through with what one begins, he thought, and took care, as he read the letter (with a delicate tremor of the hand) to make a long face and a small mouth.

"What is it?" Sylvia asked.

"It is nothing," Julian replied again, and presently took the dogs out for their morning walk.

Sylvia, who was so convinced of the first letter's being a dream as to have dreamed of it now twice running, stared at

147

the new letter with some consternation; she saw Julian's hand tremble, as he made a long face and a small mouth and put down the letter on the table. She did not believe it, even the similarity of the envelope and the paper — no one she knew would use notepaper like that — failed to convince her, and when her husband departed with the dogs she sat for a couple of minutes without touching the letter. It cannot be, she thought at one instant; and at the next, suppose it mentions Marius, then what? Suppose it says something about Hugo, then what? what?

SIR —
Who is Sylvia, what is she? etc.
FEDERIGO

Though she noticed that her hands were trembling, Sylvia felt on the whole relieved; this was not exactly nothing, but it was nothing *in particular*. Compared with the first, it was even rather genteel; in becoming literary Federigo had sacrificed somewhat of his tone, except perhaps for that sharp, rather sinister "etc." That *all* our swains commend her? It seemed a sweeping statement, and for that reason faintly ridiculous. On a sudden suspicion she rushed over to the bookcase and spent several minutes hunting for the song, which when she found it proved to contain little enough cause for alarm.

"He is literate, this Federigo," she decided in an access of detective-story vigor, "but not sufficiently so, or surely he would have added the one telling line, 'Is she kind as she is fair?' Or perhaps he was hurried?"

But chiefly she thought how, provided with the letter itself, she would triumph over Dr. Mirabeau. "A dream, doctor?

148

Are you quite certain? Then how do you explain this?" she would say, producing the document. And she would of course sweep out of the office then and there and for good. But as a precaution, Sylvia, still holding the letter, pinched herself to be sure she was awake.

After Mirabeau, she decided, Marius must see this letter; he might have some idea as to the identity of the writer, and better even than that it would convince him of the existence of a certain romance and danger in their relation — which of course must be what the letters were about. If he continued after this to claim that he loved her . . . the idea had its perilous charms.

As for Julian, poor thing — what did he imagine was going on, what must he imagine? Still, it was contemptible, it was dishonest of him, to think such things in silence. But would he be silent when he returned this morning? Or would he say to her, Look here, what about this? as any honest man ought to do. Or was that what any honest man could be expected to do? Divorce? Death? Horribly extravagant notions had entered her dining room. Surely husbands did not murder wives over such things these days; even the subtle *décor* of the apartment spoke out rather sharply against the idea.

It now struck Sylvia that Julian's behavior in this business, beyond being contemptible, was also mysterious. On the one hand he might have confronted her with the letters and demanded an accounting; on the other hand he might have kept silence, she would in that case never have seen the letters, and gone secretly about preparing whatever action he proposed to take: detectives, perhaps, with divorce or even death somewhere in the background. But he had done neither of these things, and substituted instead something oddly in between: she was allowed to see the letters, but that was all, there all communication stopped. Whatever this meant, and she had no idea at this moment, it was deep and subtle. Perhaps, in the case of behavior so deep and subtle as this, Julian himself might be quite uncertain as to where he stood, and, if neither player altogether understood the rules of the game, one might succeed as well as the other. Sylvia, imbued at this moment with the spirit of innumerable detective stories, cached the letter in the drawer of the desk where she kept six months' receipted bills and all the checks returned from the bank: a messy pile of papers of all descriptions; it would be like finding one particular leaf in a forest.

Julian came in with the dogs, which he unleashed. Sylvia was sitting over a cup of coffee at the dining room table, the newspaper spread out before her. He stood about uncertainly at his end of the table, looking down at the other three or four letters which had come in the morning mail.

"Is there something the matter?" Sylvia asked, and waited nervously. Julian looked down at her.

"There was another letter here, wasn't there?" he asked.

"I don't know," Sylvia replied. "I haven't looked at the mail yet. Maybe it got under the paper, though." And she made a show of looking under the paper, shaking it out, looking around on the floor. "It's not here," she said indifferently. "Who was it from?"

"That's very odd," said Julian, frowning, and added, "it wasn't important, only an old classmate of mine — I never really knew him well — who is getting married. It took him a long time to make up his mind."

"Who was he?"

"Ah, you didn't know him — as I say, we never really got to be friends."

"And who is the girl?"

"Oh, I've no idea about that," Julian said, "a name I'd

never heard before, Jane somebody, I think. You're sure you haven't seen that letter?"

"Quite sure," she replied, "anyhow, you know I don't read your mail, darling. Probably it'll turn up stuck to the underside of a dish or something." In a burst of co-operative sympathy Sylvia lifted three or four plates. "Anyhow, as it's not important . . . " she said after a moment.

"Still, it is extremely strange," he said, shaking his head. "I mean, I don't have hallucinations, do I? And how could such a thing simply disappear?"

"I don't know why you're making such a fuss, darling," Sylvia said, and added, with a slight edge to her voice, "unless you're implying I have for God knows what reason concealed this trivial document while you were out."

Julian stared at her for a long moment, and Sylvia coldly stared back. There was after all something mean and petulant about his face, she decided, something childish between the eyebrows and in the pouting mouth; it emerged very clearly when he attempted to be ominous without saying so, like a hard type in a movie.

"No, of course not," he finally said. "Of course not. And anyhow, it is not important. Only strange." And with the customary casual kiss he left for the office. Sylvia sat for a long time, while the coffee grew cold. She felt she had clearly won a victory, for in some sense he certainly had backed down, but its meaning remained altogether obscure; what in the world was the battle about? It seemed as though they were engaged in some sort of bitter contest in separate sections of a revolving door; they put out their tongues at one another, and shouted things which the thick glass prevented entirely or made meaningless, and all the time, pushing as hard as they could, they went merrily round and round. Someone, perhaps, would fly out on the street in the end.

151

The office was dark, Sylvia could rather feel than see, above and behind her eyes, the edge of a circle of light which, like a magical precaution, surrounded the doctor and his note pad.

"Any more anonymous letters?" Dr. Mirabeau was jovial this morning. But Sylvia had no intention of playing her high cards off first; she had planned this scene, with dialogue, as carefully as an Elizabethan in a tragedy of revenge.

She humbly reported two dreams, the second of which had come to her only that morning in a delicious five minutes of renewed sleep. This second one was very brief: a strange man presented her with a calling card, which was, however, perfectly blank.

"So, so," said Dr. Mirabeau with satisfaction. "I could have predicted from your behavior last Friday that this image would come up again. Its insistence, by the way, is a very promising sign; certain resistances would seem to be dissolving, the materials of the dream become more pointed. Glued to the table, you said? Glued to the table in the first dream and in the second it is a blank calling card; notice that in both cases you are unable to read any message."

Sylvia noticed.

"I still can't help feeling," she said, "that the first one, the one I reported Friday, was real. Its *tone*" — giving the doctor his very own word — "was different, somehow."

"Can you think of any reason why that should be so?"

"Only," she said in a weak voice, "that it was real, after all, and that *it* started the dreams."

"Ah, Sylvia," said the doctor calmly, "we've been over that. No backsliding, now. You can see, can't you, how it would be to the advantage of the forces behind the dream to convince you of their reality, to get as it were a foothold in your waking life?"

"Then how do you account for this?" cried Sylvia in a

152

somewhat coarser tone of triumph than she had quite bargained for. She sat bolt upright on the edge of the couch and spun the letter to him across the desk. Dr. Mirabeau's eyebrows went up, wrinkled, remained up as he drew forth the sheet and studied it, while Sylvia concentrated with fierce humor on the expression of his face, which otherwise, however, did not change in the least for several moments; then a wise, broad smile began to spread itself out — like sunshine on butter, she thought angrily, and wondered what wonderful thing he thought he had discovered now.

"Well?" she asked impatiently.

"The letters of which it is composed," said Dr. Mirabeau imperturbably, "are from *Harper's Bazaar.* My wife takes it, I was reading it only yesterday. The paper is right, and here, you see, is an initial S at the head of an article, which I particularly noticed because it was so very flowery. From a magazine read chiefly by women, you see," he observed with satisfaction.

"You mean," inquired Sylvia, "Federigo is really a woman?" But of course. Why had she not suspected a woman in the first place? Alma, possibly. To have used a man's name was the most elementary precaution.

"Yes," Dr. Mirabeau said in a strange, rather priestly tone, as though sorrowing over human frailty and at the same time seeing the sad humor of it. "Yes, a woman."

Sylvia began to recover her confidence in Dr. Mirabeau, who she considered was now demonstrating a plain, manly common sense which had taken her in a moment further along the road to a solution than she had thought it possible to get. She might have noticed, herself, about the slick paper, and herself identified the letters from *Harper's Bazaar,* which she read; and of course she might then have drawn the simple yet inevitable conclusion for herself: a woman.

153

"The same woman that wrote the first one," said Dr. Mirabeau, "if there was a first one, which I still beg leave to doubt. Sylvia," he said, with deep patience, "I'm surprised at you, I really am."

Observing her somewhat flabbergasted expression he held up his hand before she could find any words.

"Please," he said authoritatively. "You were tempted, and you fell. Of course. I can understand that, only it is a little late in the therapy — I had thought — for shenanigans of this sort. Am I a dummy, Sylvia? Is your physician a little boy, to be fooled?"

"What in the world do you mean?" she asked with indignation and bewilderment.

"Calm, Sylvia. Listen, I will tell you a little story. When Sigmund Freud first announced to the world his discovery that all dreams — absolutely *all* dreams — represented a wish fulfillment, this news was not received everywhere with screams of pleasure and delight, you know that. Not only psychologists stood up to say he was wrong, but even the unconscious of the patients set to work to denounce his theory. A young lady came to him with a dream in which disgusting but trivial things happened to her. 'Now,' she cried triumphantly, 'tell me if you can what wish is fulfilled in that stupid dream.' The Master merely looked at her, and he said, 'Why, dear lady, of course — the wish to prove that I am wrong.'

"And in the same way, Sylvia," he continued over the beginning of any protest on her part, "in exactly the same way . . . You leave here on Friday, you are still a little angry, it seemed so real to you" — he imitated in passing her pleading tone, adding a rather disagreeable whine — "so: what to do next? Why, of course! Give the poor old dummy a

154

real anonymous letter. He thinks he knows it all, you'll show him he's not so smart. Dream, eh? I'll give him dreams. And you wrote it yourself. Didn't you?" He smiled at her to suggest he was being angry only as a friend, that professionally it was quite all right, was the sort of thing his poor, feeble-minded clientele did to him day in and day out.

"That is the most outrageous and absurd thing I've ever heard in my life," said Sylvia, standing up. "Don't imagine for one moment, doctor, that I am going to put up with this course of — of — nonsense," she sputtered, "for an instant longer. This is the end."

"Just one moment, Sylvia," said Dr. Mirabeau in a grave voice. He rang a buzzer on the desk.

"Nurse," he said as the door opened, "Mrs. Ghent has become a little overexcited, it is nothing much, but we want to see that she calms down before she leaves here."

The door closed; Sylvia heard it being locked.

"How dare you!" she cried.

"Sylvia, please try to get yourself under control; have a cigarette, sit down. You know," he added, "you make me a little concerned. To try to score off the doctor, that is one thing — but to take it in this way, with such vehemence, when you are found out; that doesn't show such a firm grasp on the real nature of things, does it? You seem to have reached a rather perilous degree of detachment. Tell me, apart from these dreams do you sleep well?"

"As well as I ever have," declared Sylvia, "but don't you delude yourself for one instant — "

"Have headaches? More than ordinary fatigue? Eye-strain?"

"Dr. Mirabeau! Just what are you getting at?"

"I am a little disturbed, as I told you. I may as well mention that your friend Alma began behaving in this fashion a few months ago, and I am wondering whether in your case an ounce of prevention might not be the best thing possible. If we could, as it were, isolate this local disturbance over the letter-dreams, let it have a chance to cool off . . ." He seemed now to be addressing himself rather than Sylvia, who accordingly became very frightened.

"Please tell me plainly," she demanded, "what you are trying to say. All this is utter nonsense, as anyone but a psychiatrist would have been convinced long ago — "

"Ah, it is nonsense, then."

"Not the letters, *of course* — but your ridiculous interpretation. And I will not stand for being detained in a locked room by anyone. Medical ethics, doctor — "

"Sylvia, if you do not take yourself in hand at once," he said with asperity, "I shall feel quite convinced that you must have a few weeks of rest and professional care, and as your physician I shall take steps to see you get it."

Sylvia, as much amazed as frightened, collapsed on the couch and began to laugh; her laughter became very nearly hysterical. She saw herself going the way Alma went.

"There, that's a good girl," he said soothingly, "laugh it out or cry it out — one's as good as the other, they're much the same thing, really." He came round the corner of the desk, patted her hair and dropped his handkerchief in her lap. She continued to laugh rather wildly for several minutes, choked, wept a little, and dried her face with the handkerchief. This seemed to her the most improbable thing that had ever happened to her, and she wondered whether she would simply be abducted through the back door and placed in an ambulance. Julian might not know for several weeks. . . .

"Now, that's better," said Dr. Mirabeau. "Maybe now we can talk it over sensibly. Come, tell me, what made you do it?"

156

"All right," Sylvia said, putting on an air which she hoped would be proper to the circumstances, something between sullenness and hilarity. "It was silly of me," she said, "I don't know what I wanted."

"Well, then, that's all I wanted to hear," he said heartily. "No need to apologize to me, you know."

"May I have it back?" she inquired in a small pathetic voice, stretching out her hand.

"Why don't I simply tear it up here?" he asked, "and we'll consider the matter closed."

Sylvia debated whether the letter were close enough to snatch; it was her sanity he was holding there, and about to tear it up, at that.

"I'd like to keep it, if you don't mind," she pleaded. "It will be a reminder to me."

"Very well," he said, relenting, and gave her the letter. "I see no harm in that. And now, you know, I don't think there is any point in going on with the session today. The time is almost up anyhow. And I feel, in an odd way, that despite everything we have gained ground.

"Still," he added, pressing the buzzer which caused the nurse at once to open the door, "I'd like you to think over what I said about an ounce of prevention. If you're feeling some extra pressure these days, why not? What's to prevent your taking a few weeks of quiet in the country? You could join Alma."

"You make it sound positively tempting," Sylvia said as she left, "we could play gin rummy together.

"For weeks and weeks and weeks," she added when she was far enough down the hall to be out of hearing. The letter had become quite precious all of a sudden, and she clutched it very tight in her gloved hand as she emerged from the darkness of Dr. Mirabeau's basement office for, as she hoped, the last time.

157

It had not occurred to Sylvia that just on this morning, when she wished to consult him anyhow, and when as a result of what had just happened she needed someone to whom she might unburden herself, Marius might not be waiting for her. She stood on the sidewalk for a few minutes, looking indecisively up and down the street. Then she went to the drugstore on the corner and called him up.

"My dear," he said — his voice on the telephone was flat and small and brittle — "you must realize that with all the gallantry in the world I simply can't afford to buy your lunch as often as I would wish, unless we eat at the Automat. Accordingly, I offer you the Automat."

"Nonsense," Sylvia said impatiently. "I'll pay for the lunch this time. I want to talk to you."

As it was Monday, many restaurants would be closed; finally Marius mentioned one in the Fifties that they could agree on, and there they met. Sylvia, who was not characterized by any such oriental punctiliousness as would defer business to the end of the meal, showed Marius the letter at once, and gave him a brief history of the situation up to the present time.

"I mean," she said, "I've never been so frightened in my life, I almost thought my mind *was* going."

Marius, looking thoughtfully at the letter, heard her story to the end in silence. As he had no interest whatever in detective stories, no futile deductions from it occurred to him. "How very funny," was what he said when she had finished. "Yet how very serious, too."

"Well, which is it?" she angrily demanded. "Funny or serious? If you're going to be superior about it — "

"I don't see why it should not be both," he replied. "And why do you get so impatient? I am at least accepting, to begin with, your version of the business, and from what you tell

158

me that is more than your witch-doctor did. After all, there are perfectly good motives available for your having written it yourself."

"Such as — ?" she asked in a dangerously haughty tone.

"To be perfectly immodest," he said, "you might be design- ing to develop my interest in you by adding this element of peril and romance. There, there, don't get excited, I don't re- ally think that. But even worse than that," he added, "would be the plausible idea that it was your husband's interest you were trying to attract — which would mean, once you got him to inquire somewhat into what you do all day, that I would be the first person he would come across. Presuming, that is, that there are not a great many others . . . ? All right, all right, I take that back," he said hastily. "But, you see, that is what made me so angry at you the other night — you didn't tell him we were together during the afternoon, in a perfectly in- nocent way through no fault of mine, God knows, so that when he finally found it out he naturally thought it was not innocent — what you keep secret never is, of course — and my telling him must have looked liked bald-faced bravado. For a mo- ment there I thought there might be a small scene — 'I'll thank you, sir, to keep your hands off my wife,' is the way I imag- ined Julian saying it. And when it developed, later on, that Julian was nowhere about and you *devolved*, to say the least, around my neck in the presence of one million witnesses to whom you proclaimed that you were taking off to commit adultery — well, almost proclaimed — and I had to take you home . . . It is true that I got slightly worried, and it went through my mind that for no particular reason we would find Jay waiting for us in the bedroom with — I don't know what. I kept imagining a crossbow, or some other suitably primi- tive weapon such as a kris, somehow I don't see your husband handling a gun, do you? That's why I didn't stop even to take

159

off your shoes, you know. I kept having the odd feeling that he was standing in the closet, so I fled like Joseph at my earliest convenience. Sorry."

"Oh, God," said Sylvia miserably, "was it as terrible as that?"

"It wasn't great," he said. "But never mind. Glad to be of service. And really, I guess, he was not in the closet."

"I'm sorry, Marius. I had no idea. I wish you hadn't told me."

"I hope you're not going to cry in here, Sylvia. They may think it is the food. It is true, though, that embarrassment is the most terrible of the emotions."

"What shall we do?" she asked him plaintively.

"*We?* Oh, dear, I might have known this would finish with me in the middle. The first thing to do, if you'll pay the man, darling, is to leave here. That is my opinion."

As they walked up the block toward Sixth Avenue they passed a record shop, from the open door of which several sorts of music flared out on the street.

"This is where I live," Marius said. "Upstairs. Would you like to see it?"

Sylvia recognized a degree of arrangement in all this, beginning with Marius's proposal of that particular restaurant; nevertheless, she wanted to be in a quiet place for a few minutes.

" 'Where should this music be? In th' air or i' the earth'?" said Marius, giving Sylvia the strong impression that he said this to every girl who climbed these stairs. Indeed, the music — only slightly muted, and with some effect of distance — seemed to come from no particular source and surround them as they stood in the one bare room where Marius lived.

In one corner was a narrow cot covered with an army blanket. Opposite this, a small black desk and chair stood against

160

a wall which was absolutely blank save for the dramatic exception of a large crucifix, a cheap one of black wood with a silver figure of the Saviour drooping artistically on it. In one corner, behind a hanging, was a gas stove and small refrigerator; bathroom and closet completed the arrangements, which struck the girl as beautifully and yet rather pathetically austere.

"I'd expected more books," she said, looking at the small row at the back of the desk.

"Oh, I live in the public library," he said. "The goodness in poverty is not having to own the damn things. Now, Sylvia, if you feel like going to pieces, the house is yours."

Sylvia sat down on the chair at the desk. She did not exactly weep, but she bent her head in her gloved hands and bit her lip nervously. Marius stroked her hair softly, standing beside her. It was a scene of tender emotion, except that neither of them felt anything but rather confused.

"About the letter," he said, "I don't know what one does with such things. I could *think* about it for a bit, if you like."

"What good will thinking do?" asked Sylvia.

"Well, I merely meant that that's practically all I can do," he replied. "I am not a detective, you know." After a moment, he added, "You might simply confront Jay with the thing — here are the letters — what is going on? — that's one way."

"I suppose so," she said dully, "but I just don't want to."

"Why not?"

"There would be some sort of dreadful quarrel," she said. "I'd hate it, I always hate it when the weakness in people comes out, when they suddenly look like children who are going to cry. I just hate it."

"Be the best thing, maybe," Marius said. "Have it out. But maybe you don't want to have it out?"

"What does that mean?" she asked.

161

"Maybe you'd rather have it come true — now the letters have given it a kind of presumptive existence. This Federigo has offered you a suggestion."

"I don't know," Sylvia said. "I don't know what I want."

"You seemed to, the other night when you were drunk," he insisted. "The idea being that if your husband could believe such a thing about you when it was not true, there'd be a certain gaiety in making it come true."

"Don't remind me of the other night," said Sylvia in a small voice. "It will make me wish I was dead."

"Ah, Sylvia," he said. "Darling." He took her hands and drew her to her feet, into a kiss and embrace which lasted awkwardly between tenderness and passion until she found they were standing much closer to the bed than the desk.

"You're a very beautiful girl," he whispered to her. "I do love you, Sylvia, very much."

She permitted, and co-operated in, a number of caresses which rapidly became more ardent. They sat down together on the bed. A march by John Philip Sousa stood out among the medley of musical sounds below.

"No," she whispered as he began to open her blouse. "No, dear. Not here, not now." She was staring at the hanging figure of Christ on the other wall; despite that she was not religious, or perhaps precisely because she was not, she was horrified to think they were desecrating that image.

"Why not?" he urged her, also in a whisper, then, his glance following hers, he saw the crucifix.

"Ah, that," he said brusquely, and going across the room he tore it from the wall and put it in the middle desk drawer, which he slammed. Sylvia was inexpressibly shocked.

"Marius! How can you do that? How can you dare do it?"

He stood facing her with a kind of defiance at once humorous and pathetic.

162

"My dear," he said, "it is my secret. I am not a Catholic at all. I only wish I were. Please don't tell this to anyone, Sylvia."

For her part, she could only stare at him.

"I've always wanted to be," he went on, wringing his hands together. "I think it is the most wonderful thing, I love all of it — the tradition, the ceremony, all the splendor and kindness. But I could never bring myself to join the Church. I just, you know, behave as if I were, I observe Lent, I observe all the feasts, I meditate on the Seven Deadly Sins, the Seven Sacraments, the Seven Penitential Psalms, the Four Last Things, I think constantly of Christ dying on the Cross — "

"But you don't go to church?" Sylvia asked incredulously.

"I did, to learn the rituals," Marius confessed. "I still do, now and then."

"But no confession? No communion?"

"I couldn't," he said. "As St. Augustine tells us, it would be taking hell fire in my mouth."

"Oh, dear," said Sylvia very abruptly.

Marius sat down beside her again.

"You see, I don't believe in God," he explained, putting his arm around her again. But it was no good; he felt vulnerable and victimized, even though extremely tender toward the girl who had received his dreadful secret; while as for Sylvia, she had begun to giggle uncontrollably, she had never been so confused in all her life.

3

JULIAN's conspiracy against the world began to frighten him by the power it had, being itself in its inception unreal, of evoking perfectly real events in its wake. He felt bitterly

ashamed of himself for his demeanor that morning at breakfast, but what else was he to have done? It was impossible for
the letter simply to have disappeared in the brief time he was
out, yet it was impossible too — for him — to say directly to
his wife, What have you done with that letter? Secrecy con-
demned him to silence, silence to a world in which, it seemed,
no objective evidence of anything existed — could he be absolutely certain he had written and mailed the second letter?
He remembered his doubts about doing it, his determination
to do it, remembered that he had sat right here at his desk
and done it — but he could not achieve, try as he might, any
convincing image of his having done it. Possible, after all,
that he had dreamed the whole business? No, it was not possible. There was, in the first place, the first letter; he clearly
had not dreamed that. He reached thoughtfully into his
pocket, which was empty, and recalled in dismay that he no
longer had the first letter either; Hugo had it. And Hugo was
going to call in a company of private detectives.

But that too, if all had been a dream, could have been part
of the dream. Julian did not think it likely, but he had, just
now, sitting like a hermit in the midst of the vast silence, no
way of demonstrating the reality of these events, of Bianca, of
Federigo, of the letters. His face, of course, was still a bit
bruised, though the swelling of his lip had gone down. There
was the cut on his throat, but that originally happened while
shaving, did it not?

The morning mail, when Miss Duddon brought it to him, included a small package which turned out to contain his wallet; there was, of course, no return address. The world, that
greater anonymity, had spoken. Julian was relieved at the return of the wallet, which cut down on the likelihood of his
being blackmailed by those people, and he was strangely
charmed by the tact and courtesy of their having chosen, from

the two addresses on the identity card, the office rather than the home; feebly, he even felt grateful to Bianca; the gesture savored, very faintly it is true, of Robin Hood. At the same time, it meant that everything was real, the existence of this objective communication from the outside inspired conviction also about the letters; it all must have happened.

Then the detectives too would be real. How terrible! One consequence produced another. Could they find out anything? It seemed doubtful, unless, as he suddenly realized, they would include him among the suspects merely as a matter of course. They could check on the office typewriter. But how foolish to think they would suspect him, Julian, the husband, recipient of the letters, and the very person, in the first place, who hired the detectives. And yet, he dismally acknowledged, this was exactly what happened in the movies, where it seemed that the criminal's first action after committing his crime was invariably to hire a private eye to trace himself down and turn himself over to justice. Did things really happen that way? Were people really so filled with guilt as to make such a thing likely — in real life? But real life, as it was called, continually imitated art, so that if the detectives of twenty years ago, say, would not have suspected the husband, these detectives — having been, of course, subjected to the movies — would certainly suspect the husband. And Federigo had told him that for a man to send himself anonymous letters, far from being so extraordinary as to be considered unique, happened with incredible frequency and was perhaps not even unusual. Federigo? There was another problem. Problems were everywhere.

In all this, Elaine proved to be the only agreeable thing to be thought about. Julian called up Elaine. Louisa answered the phone, and he spoke to her in a deeper voice than usual,

165

not quite a disguise, in case she recognized him anyhow, but not quite not a disguise either.

"This is Julian Ghent," he said to Elaine when she got on the phone. "I'd like to talk to you, if I might — about our conversation the other night," he added.

"Yes, go on."

"I mean — if we might get together somewhere?"

"Oh. I see." Her voice was doubtful; a silence followed. Then she said, "I'm very busy."

"It's rather important," Julian said. "How about this afternoon?"

"Oh, I couldn't. I work in the Museum of Art in the afternoons. I paint," she explained.

"You paint," repeated Julian, somewhat put out by the introduction of this new element. "Well, might I come round to the Museum, maybe just before closing time — take you for a drink?"

After another silence, Elaine said, "You might."

"The Metropolitan?"

"Yes."

"Where will I find you?"

"I don't know, exactly," she said. "You'll just have to look around among the paintings. Don't come early, Miss Desmond doesn't like us to be interrupted."

"Miss Desmond?"

"The teacher."

"Oh. I see."

All in all, it was not a very warm or satisfying conversation. And what, actually, did he want to say to the girl when he got there? I love you? It did not seem likely.

To put these thoughts aside for a time, Julian concentrated with great determination, during the rest of the morning, on Dr. Thybold's campaign to rid the world of tobacco. That did

166

not seem likely either, but he managed to devise what amounted to a threatening letter in the name of modern medicine, addressed to "intelligent men and women everywhere," and especially to parents. "Would you," it began, "deliberately inoculate your child with cancer of the lungs?" Julian fancied there might be a small picture for a letterhead, showing a naked babe on an operating table, and a surgeon — or possibly just the surgeon's hand — poised with the needle aimed at the child's breast.

When he had done this, not giving himself time to think of anything else, he drew the Bible to him and began to consider the campaign of Mr. Archer More. I AM THE LIGHT OF THE WORLD, he wrote in block letters across the top of his pad, then spent half an hour searching for the source of this expression, without success. He would have to ask Miss Duddon, or have her look it up in a concordance at the library. Let it go for the present.

With the Bible beside him, Julian began to compose a passage of several paragraphs on the state of the world. He depicted children dying everywhere (not of lung cancer) — some by bombs, some of famine, some on the bayonets of savage troops. It was quite hard, he found, to bring these scenes of carnage into a right relation with Faith; for he felt, personally, that exactly the same thing would be going on if people turned to God in great droves and filled the churches to overflowing at all hours of the day. But on the other hand, the somewhat swollen style demanded by this work — "the I-say-unto-you kind of thing," as he privately named it — came very easily to his pencil, only that it induced a certain self-hatred.

I must try to imagine, he told himself, what it would be like to be Archer More. His mind quailed before this idea.

The whole business, Julian began to believe, Thybold,

More, the art of advertising itself, the entire world of demand
and satisfaction, buying and selling, consisted to a dangerous
degree in the production and communication of anonymous
or pseudonymous letters. He took up the first magazine that
came to hand and looked at the advertisements. Page after
page, all the same. Everywhere people were speaking blan-
dishments and threats, appealing with bitter persistence and
ferocity to fear, shame, desire, guilt, despair — and always
under a pseudonym which gave authority: in the name of science, in the name of God, the name of happiness, the name of
love, the name of honor and the name of freedom from under-
arm perspiration. All this was deemed to be perfectly honorable, also necessary; if it did not go on, the wheels would
stop turning. If the wheels stopped turning, then what?

Julian did not know what. He imagined the stopping of the
wheels, the generators, dynamos, locomotives, the taxis in the
streets below; there followed a confused vision of the gleam of
metal fading, rust on a window frame, the huge city and the
social fact filled with the sight of a soft wind, and silence,
silence, silence.

As for myself, he thought, I have written two anonymous
letters, two. In them I did not speak as though I were God or
the Government of the United States, I did not pretend to be
Health or Morality or Industry or Labor or Management or
Science or Fear of Death or Love or Conscience or any of those
fine and wonderful things. I pretended to be Federigo, and
look what is happening to me.

Hugo did not forget, he came to the office himself during the
afternoon and dragged Julian by main moral force to the offices of Pritchard, Ferriter & Magoun.

"I don't want you to forget it," he said over his friend's protest. "I personally, as your friend, want to see this thing

168

cleared up as much as you do. Or as much as you ought to do."

The detective firm was not far away, on the fifty-fourth floor of a skyscraper.

"This isn't the original Pritchard Ferriter Magoun," Hugo explained as they went up in the elevator. "These young fellows bought the name and the good will — the mailing list, you know. When they came out of the Army, it was. It's Mr. Bilsiter I want you to talk to, he's a good sort of man, he'll know what to do."

Mr. Bilsiter, whose first name turned out to be Chauncey, was a large, soft, fair-haired young man — the hair had also a graceful wave to it — with an egg-shaped face in which huge eyes carried out the egg-motif; there was also a very lofty forehead with some sort of eczema on it. He was on the phone when they were shown into his office.

"But darling," he was saying, "she *knows* already, that's exactly what I'm trying to tell you, she *knows,* and what's more she tore up the prints and laughed in his face and said he could show the negative to whoever he damn pleased. If I were you, Fred, I'd drop the whole thing right away — tell him we don't do business with people like that. There might be violence, anything can happen with that woman. I've met her, darling, *I know.*" Mr. Bilsiter replaced the phone very decisively.

"Hugo!" he cried. "How nice of you to stop in. You haven't had any trouble, have you?" he asked, less cordially.

"No," Hugo replied. "My business has gone along fine, thanks. The decree is being granted this week. Your people did splendidly," he added, with some pompous embarrassment. He then presented Julian, stated succinctly what their business was, and handed Mr. Bilsiter the first letter from Federigo. Julian felt hypnotized, he thought this could hardly be happening to him. At the same time, he was a little less terrified than he had been, for Mr. Bilsiter did not look as though he could detect eggs at Easter. He was now staring owlishly at the letter through a magnifying glass.

"You poor thing, how disagreeable for you," he said to Julian. "Do you know this person Federigo, I mean do you know anyone of that name?"

"No," said Julian.

"Heard the name anywhere — read it in the papers, maybe?"

"No."

"Hmm. Foreign name, eh? Italian."

"I noticed that," Julian allowed himself to say.

"And no one has mentioned such a name in your presence recently?"

"No."

"I ask," said Mr. Bilsiter, "because in these matters, where a person doesn't use his right name, it almost invariably happens that he gives himself away by being clever, he uses a name which bears some allusion to his experience, to what he is doing — he doesn't simply lift one out of the phone book, which would be the sensible way."

"Really," said Julian, "it's not very important, and I don't suppose you can do much on the one letter. I don't like to take up your time — "

"You've received only the one letter?"

"No," said Julian, before he had time to think. Now I've put my foot in it, was what he did think when he got there. Hugo and Mr. Bilsiter were looking at him keenly.

"One came this morning," he confessed. "I'm afraid my wife took it," he added miserably. "At least I couldn't find it anywhere." He explained how he walked the dogs in the morning, and thought as he went along what a ridiculous figure he must be making himself out to be.

170

"So — Sylvia knows, does she?" said Hugo. "What did she say?"

Julian was forced to recount that disgraceful little scene as well.

"I'm afraid," said Mr. Bilsiter, "to be perfectly plain about it, sir, I am afraid you are growing a pair of horns. Or why would she deny it?"

Hugo hastily got up.

"I don't think I need to hear this, Jay," he said kindly. "You can count on Chauncey to help you see it through. I'll call you up to hear about how things are going along." He patted Julian's shoulder with funereal sympathy and took his leave.

"As I see it," Mr. Bilsiter said when he and Julian were alone, "the letters by themselves don't give us much to work on — unless, of course, you get more of them. Oh, we'll check what little we can, but if you've no connection whatever with anyone called Federigo — if the name rings no bell in your mind — we're fairly stuck, you see, to begin with. We must play a waiting game," he said sagely. "On the other hand," he went on, "what we can certainly do is pin down the contents of the letters, establish the truth of the accusation they make — I'm afraid I have no doubt at all it is quite true — and collect the evidence, names, dates, places. . . ."

"Evidence?" asked Julian stupidly.

"For the divorce," Mr. Bilsiter explained. "You won't, I should think, have much trouble at all, it looks like being a perfectly clear case, perfectly lovely. The one thing I don't like, though, is Mrs. Ghent's knowledge that such letters exist. She may lay low for a while, not see the man." He frowned, then said in a brighter tone, "But they seldom do, you know. In my experience it usually turns out they somehow refuse to acknowledge that someone knows, they can't re-

171

sist seeing each other just once more and then once more —
and so it goes, as if they were invisible. You know, just the
way people who pick their noses in public always think no
one has seen them."

"But really," Julian found space to protest, "I don't want
a divorce, I — "

"What you do with the evidence," Mr. Bilsiter said, "is naturally your own business. You may be the old-fashioned sort,
I don't know. I don't want to know. We collect the evidence,
and there our responsibility ends. We do divorce work, Mr.
Ghent, we are not toughs or thugs in this firm. In plain English, if you decide to kill your wife, or, for that matter, yourself, kindly don't tell me about it."

When Julian left the office of Pritchard, Ferriter & Magoun
he had rented the services of a private detective, who was to
report to him upon his wife's actions daily for as long as was
necessary, these reports to be made by mail to Julian's home.
All this Julian did, or allowed to be done, not only because it
was too late to turn down Mr. Bilsiter — it seemed as though
that would be an open admission that Julian himself had
guilty knowledge of the letters (which Hugo would of course
get to know at once) — but also because he had become somewhat bemused and spellbound by the idea. He saw himself sitting at breakfast, over the coffee, reading about Sylvia while
she unsuspectingly sat opposite.

Perhaps there's something in it, after all, he thought as he
left the office. It will do no harm to find out, just as a point of
academic interest, what she does all day long. It's funny how
little I know of her life — or of her, for that matter. What
does she think? What does she think about me? That is something no detective report can tell me, of course. Still, it is interesting simply to let things happen as they will. And
of course I don't need to *do* anything with what I find out;

172

unless, that is, the whole awful dream turns out to be quite true. . . .

"You certainly have started something now," said Federigo, who was walking along beside him. "Detectives and all. Probably bloodhounds next. It's a long boomerang that has no turning."

"I should think I've got enough troubles without you," Julian nearly snarled, as they walked uptown.

"Without me, my dear friend," said Federigo, "you wouldn't have the troubles. Without me," he added, "you'd be dead. Here, let's walk up through the Park." He took Julian's elbow and steered him across Fifth Avenue.

" 'And Peter called to mind the word that Jesus said unto him,' " blithely said Federigo. " 'Before the cock crow twice, thou shalt deny me thrice. And when he thought thereon, he wept.' Very beautiful, that, and so mysterious, don't you think? 'And when he thought thereon, he wept.' Julian, when are you going to weep?"

Julian maintained an angry silence.

"You believe," said Federigo, "that eyes are made for seeing, but I tell you — I say unto you, to give it the proper tone — I say unto you that eyes are made for weeping with."

They walked through the Zoo, Federigo chatting all the while.

"Tell me," Julian said at last, "what must I do to make you leave me alone? Do you want me to apologize for using your name? I'll do it, I'll swear never to think of you in the future, if that is what will make you leave me alone."

"To make me leave you alone," said Federigo, "you must be other than you are."

They walked, after this, up past the pond where children sailed boats, or at least where they had done so when Julian was young. As Federigo pointed out, however, there was now but one vessel in this entire water, its progress followed by two or three elderly men; it was a miniature submarine.

"It would solve all your problems, wouldn't it," Federigo then observed, "if she simply died this week. A natural death, of course."

"Shut up, shut up," cried Julian in a childishly savage voice. "Keep your despicable thoughts to yourself."

"Oh, it hadn't occurred to you? I thought it had. Beg pardon," said Federigo mildly. "Just an idea," he went on, "just an idea. I was thinking chiefly of your freedom, after all, you can't blame me for that. I wonder what your detectives will find out. Will they realize how utterly strange it is for a man to get such letters and then allow his wife to see them, and even to keep one? If they think of that, dear, I shouldn't be surprised if it was all up with you — honor, morality, honesty, the whole works: pouf! And all for what? You haven't even been unfaithful. Ha ha, that started the whole silly treadmill revolving, and here you are, just what you were before, only a few days older. Except in thought, that is. And I say unto you again, whoso looketh after a woman to commit adultery with her, why, he might just as well go right ahead, isn't that so?" Federigo chuckled disagreeably, and pointed ahead up the path.

"There is the Museum of Art," he said. "School's out for today, my friend. Run along to the great masterpieces, let your conscience be your guide." He turned away.

"Stop! Wait!" cried Julian.

"I thought you wanted to get rid of me," Federigo called back over his shoulder; he ran down a small side path and through a tunnel, where Julian followed. On emerging and looking everywhere around he caught no sight of Federigo, but felt, nevertheless, as though that gentleman continued to watch him from a place of hiding.

174

Chapter 6

I⊤ WAS characteristic of Julian, as a morally minded person, to view the world more or less entirely in terms of his own decisions; he implicitly believed that once he had made up his mind to be unfaithful, and had gone so far as to find the right girl to be unfaithful with, and even fall prospectively in love with this girl, she would at once fall into his arms, the way ahead would become clear, there would be easy sailing, et cetera. Things did not of course turn out in exactly this way; he found he had underestimated rather grossly the world's independence of his moral vision; furthermore, courtship took time, money and attention, all of which had to be provided without disturbance, at least in appearance, to the normal distribution of his time, money and attention.

As to time: he was fascinated, his entire sensibility was heightened; instead of a dull succession of moments along which he traveled like a bead on a thread, he began to see time as a house, an immense closed space of many mansions (like the Museum, in a way) with secret passages, hiding-places, alcoves, false partitions behind which whole rooms could be concealed without disturbance to the apparent dimensions as seen from outside. If one shaved fifteen minutes off here and ten there and another ten over here, if moreover one were then twenty minutes late getting home, there was very nearly a whole hour which seemed scarcely to belong to time, which afforded a delightful, cozy, though temporary shelter from the inexorable public succession of moments registered on clocks everywhere around it. In fancy he compared it with that model of an Egyptian tomb in which, on one rainy afternoon in the Museum, he first kissed Elaine; a brightly lit space with cold, smooth, pinkish walls and a sign which said:

TOMB OF PER NEB
*"False door" through which it was believed that the
deceased entered into the bliss of the other-world.*

In order to secure this corner in time, Julian began to take taxis uptown, leaving the office twenty minutes early and saving also the half hour or so it would have taken to walk.

This cost money, and money was more inexorable than time; time, being manufactured, as it were, out of waste materials, out of moments which separately would have meant nothing and been useless but could be thus assembled into a spare hour, need not be regarded as literally being taken from Sylvia and given to Elaine; with money it was otherwise. They had, too, he and Sylvia, a joint checking account — which they could not be said to have, really, as regarded time — and any inordinate withdrawals on his part would be noticed at the end of the month. Julian resolved at first to spend very little on Elaine, transferring in this manner the guilt of his conduct from the moral to the financial realm; but guilt it remained, slice it how he might, with the result that now and then, in an access of disgust and contempt for himself, he would spend a great deal of money on her all of a sudden; which he would then regret. As a solution to both problems at once, of time and money, he devised a series of dentist's appointments — for it was quite true that his teeth needed attention — which out of consideration for his work he placed in the late afternoon, so that he could leave the office at four and

176

attribute all extra expense to the dentist, whom he would claim to be paying in cash (he even went so far as to invent a personality for this dentist, to make him the sort of man who would have to be paid in cash, in case an explanation should become necessary). Then even this began to worry him, for the ridiculous and yet quite disturbing reason that he was spending money on Elaine which ought properly to go to the care of his teeth: images of death and slow decay — "I am killing myself for love" — gave a secret poignancy to his love, the more because their source was too silly to be mentioned or even coherently thought about.

Attention, however, or, more properly, the quantity of love or of feeling generally, disturbed him in quite another way; it did not at all appear to diminish by division as money did and as time would if he spent more of it with Elaine. On the contrary he came from a meeting with Elaine buoyed up and filled with affection, of which Sylvia received the benefit; Julian was more charming with her, more interested in her, and took her out to dinner more, than he had done for months. He recognized his feeling as in part a kind of obscure gratitude to his wife for not noticing anything, or appearing not to notice anything, and this gratitude, as it could have no direct expression, took the form of an increased tenderness and demonstrative pleasure in her company; even in bed, where Julian desperately thought of Elaine at all instants — and thought with terrible remorse that it was she whom he betrayed — it was, after all, Sylvia who received his passionate and treacherous ardor as sheer advantage.

Julian during this time had moments of the most intense wretchedness, but they alternated with moments of great charm — not necessarily, either, the ones spent with Elaine, but chiefly perhaps the moments of imagination; at least life became less dull. He thought longingly about the enchantment of

177

a polygamous society; how easy and delightful it all would be. When he read in the newspapers some story of a man's having successfully led a double life for some years undetected, with two wives in the same town, he was extremely pleased at what he took to be a demonstration: neither woman dissatisfied, each with her own home and her own life and her own husband, and the man doubtless charmed with the essential element of secrecy and darkness in his life, which satisfied what Julian considered to be the basic, neglected element in the male character, the need to be at least two persons; as he named it, the *dramatic need*.

One such story in particular fascinated him. A young man in a Southern city had managed for over a year to be the husband simultaneously not merely of two but of three women — but that is a little too much, thought Julian, imagine the financial arrangements and the struggle to keep those identities fully separate. This situation, however, had a quite amusing finish; the young man finally was caught out over something trivial: he refused to take wife number three to the same double feature he had been forced to see with numbers one and two; the third wife was suspicious, in the first place, for no better reason than that she had wanted particularly to see this bill at the neighborhood theater, she began to think, she asked questions, she set on detectives, and the husband was caught. Before being put away by the iron indignation of an offended society (which nevertheless, according to the tone of the newspaper account, was laughing enviously up its sleeve) this extraordinary man admitted to being somewhat bored with the whole business, and glad it was over.

So affection seemed to expand, with Julian, as required, it rose to its occasions; the more love he needed the more he had. Somberly he recognized, however, that this happy state sufficed only for the beginning of the program; for just so

178

long as love remained spiritual in fact, whatever it might be in intent, no wickedness appeared on the surface. But beneath the surface there waited, quite plainly, the brute sexual fact, where the principle of division obtained exactly as it did with money; shameful as it was to acknowledge, love's incarnation was corrupt while love's spirit was not; what was given to one woman in bed could not be given to another, nor was there here any way, such as an appointment with a dentist who did not exist, of fictitiously extending, so to say, one's capital. This worried Julian, though not, at this time, very much, for the good reason that he could not by any means be certain or even very confident of Elaine's soon becoming his mistress; that existed, if it did exist, at some remote crossroads not quite to be located in ordinary time, and as for the moment he felt borne along on a wave of precarious happiness he did not require himself to think very rigorously about the approaching time of decision.

On the day he first met Elaine in the Museum Julian had walked meditatively and slowly through the galleries; he wished to come upon her, if he did, as though by accident, for he was still full of the sensation of being watched, and even had the faint, absurd suspicion that the eyes of the portraits, which seemed to follow him along, had been slit open to admit in their places the eyes of Federigo.

He found Elaine seated before a huge canvas by Titian containing among other figures a billowy, naked courtesan the size of a taxicab or so, which she was copying, not very well, on her easel. He stood behind the girl for a few minutes in thought and a certain dismay; that she should paint was a sufficiently jarring note, somehow, and that she did it badly was almost intolerable; moreover, in flat heels and a smock she looked like a dreadful little schoolgirl. He very nearly dropped the whole affair at this time, but one thing alone kept

179

him there, and this was the tenuous certainty, something in the straightness of her back, some highly accented concentration on what she was doing, that she was quite aware of his presence behind her. Julian came closer and stood there in a critical posture, his head to one side and hands behind his back. The girl turned slightly.

"There you are," she said. "I'm nearly through. Terrible, isn't it?" she indicated her canvas.

"It is a little, well, lumpy," Julian said, comparing it with the original and noticing at the same time that Elaine had a pretty smudge of white paint on one cheek.

"Mother likes me to do it," Elaine said. "Perhaps she believes it will keep me off the streets. I don't mind, really, though. Oh, Miss Desmond," she said with an air of pleased surprise, "this is Mr. Ghent."

Julian saw a fierce-looking old lady, very small, in oatmeal tweed and thick woolen stockings, who put one hand on the cameo at her breast and sighed flutteringly.

"That's all right, then," she said. "It is so hard to keep people from annoying the girls during the session — this place, you know, is a veritable wolf-haunt, ideal for pick-ups. You know one another, then. That's all right. But I must insist," she went on while shaking hands with Julian, "that you do not disturb Elaine during the hour, I will not have it. Do you paint, Mr. Ghent?" Miss Desmond began edging him slightly away from Elaine.

"No, I'm afraid I don't," Julian politely replied.

"Not at all?" Miss Desmond asked. "Not even a little bit?" She coyly held up finger and thumb close together, as though to show in how slight a degree it would be possible for Julian to paint.

"Not even that much," he said, and drew Miss Desmond further aside to say in a low voice, "I am sorry to interrupt in this way, but there is something important I must say to Elaine. She is my cousin, you know," he added.

"Not bad news, I hope?" Miss Desmond asked. "If you must, then, Elaine," she called, "you had better put away your materials and go with your cousin. But remember," she said severely to Julian, "this is an exception. It must not, must not become the rule."

"Why cousin?" Elaine asked after they had got away. Julian laughed. The success of even this slight deception, in which Elaine had co-operated passively at least, pleased him a good deal.

"Why not?" he asked lightly, taking her arm as they left the Museum. He led her to a bar nearby — there was not much choice in this neighborhood, and it was a disagreeably domestic and ordinary bar — but the waiter would not serve Elaine because she was too young. This amused Julian and accordingly annoyed her. They got into a cab and went downtown to a place on Third Avenue called the Delta Café, where there was not enough light in the booths for the waiter to make out Elaine's age, and where in any case he would not greatly have cared.

"I hope you solved your little difficulties the other night," said Elaine.

"Ah," said Julian neutrally, indicating either that he had, or that no solution was possible and that, in any case, the whole matter was beyond discussion.

"I think you've a lovely wife," Elaine then said without the least malice in her voice. "A perfectly beautiful girl. I wish I looked like that," she said simply.

"Yes," Julian said. "But Sylvia's not entirely well. She goes to a psychiatrist, you know."

"Oh?"

"This is a rather difficult time," he added, "I don't know if we will stay together, Sylvia and I." It was the first time Julian had phrased this idea aloud, and he felt ashamed of it. But there was also a kind of pleasure in this shame, and he thought that now he had begun to betray his wife he would go on to the end, probably a bitter end. "I'd rather not talk about it just now," he said.

"Why did you call me today?" she wanted to know.

"Because I felt lonely," he replied. "I wanted someone I could talk with."

"And you suddenly decided on me?"

"I've thought about you a good deal since we met the other night," he said. "I like the way you smile."

They looked at one another. In the semi-darkness of this place the slightest glance gained a conspiratorial character; they were like two spies, full of suspicion, inquiring for a password. They looked into one another's eyes, saying nothing but what could be said for them by their eyes which were either windows of the soul or mirrors on the world. Julian's glance intended earnestly what he would not say, and hers inquired into its sincerity with a like earnestness in which there was, however, some amusement. The brief dialogue of these eyes ran something like this:

ELAINE: This is very nice, and even exciting. There are reservations, of course.

JULIAN: I do mean it. I know exactly what I am doing, and I know it is wicked.

ELAINE: I am free to do as I like. You, on the other hand —

JULIAN: I can't help myself, you can do with me whatever you please now.

ELAINE: I may please and I may not, but thank you.

"I hope we can be good friends," Julian said, and took her hand. "May I see you often?"

182

"I'm sure we'll be good friends," she said, gently disengaging her hand.

They continued to meet at the Museum. Julian would arrive toward the end of Elaine's painting session, and hang about evading so far as possible the eye of Miss Desmond; then Elaine would put away her equipment, Julian following at some distance, and they would meet almost as though by accident in some quarter of the building where Miss Desmond had no business; among the medieval armor, in the Egyptian collection or far away where the Chinese jade and pottery lived. In this way Julian came to see his friend against a number of exotic and diverse backgrounds, and this effect of variety did not at all diminish her charm for him. He was very happy at this time, though also somewhat apprehensive of being seen by someone he knew. He had a curious double feeling about this; there was, first, the odd self-consciousness whereby he *knew* at every instant that he was being watched, spied upon. At certain moments he had the penetrative knowledge that he himself was doing the watching, that he stood back in a corner of the gallery, slightly shielded by statue or glass case, and saw himself over some little distance taking Elaine's arm, walking with her, heard himself talking to this girl (his voice sounded very odd); at these moments he watched with cynical doubt and a sneer how their heads came close together as they looked at one or another exhibit — came together and casually, whisperingly, drew apart again without a smile, without a glance, with no acknowledgment of what they both knew.

On the other hand he was possessed by a supreme and unfounded confidence in either his discretion or his luck; for the very reason that he felt himself constantly observed by the critical eyes of his own guilt, he did not really believe it was

183

possible for any other person to see him and Elaine together; he told himself that his friends were really not the sort to be found dead in any museum but the Modern Art. Then, too, there was recklessness; supposing anyone should see, what of it?

When, one rainy day about a week after their first meeting, Julian and Elaine entered the Egyptian tomb with the pinkish walls and found it empty and perfectly screened from observation, they were both quite aware of what was going to happen; each was quite aware, also, of the other's awareness, and yet perhaps not altogether certain, so that there existed a fine tension between them as they turned toward one another in the clean, empty tomb which the Museum authorities had illuminated very brightly perhaps against just such a contingency.

Elaine kissed him with amateurish and experimental ferocity, fastening her teeth on his lower lip; it was, for Julian, an uncomfortable business, which he felt she probably considered highly erotic from having read about it in a novel. Nevertheless, it was a clear triumph, and in pride he reminded himself that this was happiness.

After a moment in which they clung together she let him go, pushing him a little away, and stood back as far as the space of the tomb allowed. She laughed, beginning with that out-of-kilter smile which he found so terribly appealing.

"My dear," she said, "this is not a good thing for us to be doing."

"You are absolutely lovely as an Egyptian," Julian said.

But of course this kiss, this moment of clarity which divided so exquisitely the past from the future, entailed as a consequence long discussions; they were two civilized people, yes, that was agreed, but what exactly did being civilized include in such a situation as theirs? Julian said at one point — they had left the tomb and were strolling aimlessly around the mon-

184

uments of Egypt, hand in hand — that they must be absolutely honest.

"We must know what we are doing," he said, and Elaine nodded gravely. They knew what they were doing to such a degree that very soon, having made the circuit of the hall, they found themselves again before the tomb, whereat they smiled at one another — "well, once more," whispered Elaine — and went in. They were unaware that at this time, and again as they emerged a few moments after, they were observed by Marius Rathlin, who was enraged at the sight of them.

It would not have been extraordinary for Marius to visit the Museum at any time in the course of his studies, but as a matter of fact he had come there because Elaine's mother told him on the phone that Elaine was to be found in the Museum. From some little distance, just as he had caught sight of the girl and been about to speak to her, he saw Julian come up and take her arm; Marius had more or less been following them since, with a grim smile of utter indecision on his face.

Marius had not seen Sylvia since the afternoon of his confession; her drastic response had, to say the least, somewhat clarified his feelings about her. After his humiliation he had felt very angry and had a vision in which he seduced Sylvia, there she was lying naked on his bed, and he laughed at her — in the vision he even spat on the floor — and walked out of the room (the vision allowed that he himself was fully clothed). He rated himself most severely for this feeling of vengefulness, which, however, he could not help having, and decided that the best thing would be never to see her again. Surely she must perceive, if she had — which he was not altogether sure she did — any delicacy at all, that he had given into her hands a certain power over himself, perhaps the greatest power one person can have over another in the limits of polite society, the power of making him appear ridiculous.

185

On the other hand, did he not have the same power over her? The situation of the anonymous letters, and the incredible attitude of Dr. Mirabeau, were sufficient subjects for humor. So that it was, for the time being, a stand-off between them, or they would be two blackmailers taking in each other's washing; the figure confused but the meaning clear.

He had decided finally to stand on his dignity; she would have to make the first move. And in keeping with this decision he had not seen her for a week or so. Then he had turned his attention to Elaine, who was, he told himself, younger, more attractive than Sylvia, blessedly unattached, altogether more suitable; he even began to think of marriage.

And now this! It was like moving in a dream down one corridor after another, and finding at the end of each one Julian. Kissing in the tomb! it was horrifying — by which he meant as he honestly acknowledged that he was envious.

He debated whether he should scurry round to the other end of the hall and casually approach them so that they should pass face to face — if he did this, he would with generous irony and the most exact punctiliousness stare at Julian and fail to recognize him, thus in the one gesture combining scrupulous courtesy and sophistication with the cut direct. He did not do it, however, because while he would have loved to embarrass Julian he feared to offend Elaine.

Marius had spoken to this girl but once; she had no idea, could have no idea, of his possibly feeling anything in particular about herself; yet he already imagined himself in love with her, saw his pathetic figure skulking behind Egyptian statues as the rejected suitor, and attributed this chance revelation in the Museum to design, to her conscious cruelty; all this of course increased his sour love.

But if he did not approach them, then there was nothing to be gained by staying in the Museum. He watched them for a

186

moment more, strolling hand in hand away from him just as though their being together were the most honorable and upright thing in the world. Marius hastened away with his secret knowledge, knowing he would use it — somehow, he did not yet know how — and regretting for an instant at the same time that if he used it he must thereby lose the precious detachment which made him the keen observer that he was.

"But that's nothing," he said as he went down the steps outside, "I am a suitor, I am entering the arena, this that is happening to me is love." He walked away in a confusion of feeling. "As for that Julian," he thought grimly, "he is living in a fool's purgatory."

2

ALL IN ALL, Sylvia considered, things were looking up; for nearly a week she had not seen Marius, and during that time there had been no anonymous letters. Could there be, perhaps, some connection? She had also deliberately missed two appointments with Dr. Mirabeau, and was beginning to hope the doctor would simply and without comment of any sort submit his final bill at the end of the month — for of one thing she was very certain, she was not going back to him, not even for so long as it would take to explain that she was not going back. Perhaps it had been Dr. Mirabeau who was really her trouble all that long time? Not that she believed he had sent the letters, no, she would not go so far as to think that even of him — but might it not be true, at least in the odd world of the psyche, not that one went to the doctor because one was sick, but that one was sick because one went to the doctor? It might well be, look what had happened to Alma.

It even seemed to her that her husband was becoming kinder again, more attentive and loving, even erotically interesting, all of a sudden; this too had happened since she left off going to Mirabeau.

Sylvia liked to think that things solved themselves the easy way if given the chance; she began to see the tension between herself and Julian, accordingly, as "one of those times that come up in every marriage," while as for the anonymous letters, though she remained puzzled, she decided at the end of a week without them that this was one of the things it was unprofitable to puzzle about. Something nasty had undoubtedly happened, and been felt, reflected, in her behavior and Julian's; but she would be willing to settle for its being over, even if this meant she never would understand exactly what had happened. Had she known the letters would stop, she reflected a little angrily, she never would have told Dr. Mirabeau and consequently she would not have been subjected to the humiliation of being thought insane. But then — looking on the bright side — she would never have had, either, the nerve to break off the treatment, never would have discovered in a sufficiently convincing way how blind that treatment could be to whatever happened from the outside, how it refused to believe in anything not inwardly provided for. So it was an ill wind which had blown this much good at least. Again, she would not, had she known there would be no more letters, have told Marius of them either; but then neither would she, probably, ever have come to know in return Marius's own delicious (and extremely odd) secret, which put her on even terms with him. She hoped, even so, that Marius was not vastly offended over his confession and her uncontrollable response — surely he must be able to see the enormous humor of it? — and determined, though she would not be the first to break the silence, that when next they met, which would most likely be at Hugo's wedding a few days hence (the divorce-bak'd meats, you might say), she would be very kind to Marius, and say

188

something — she did not know exactly what — which would indicate sympathy and secrecy; and to which he must reply (of course!) with like indications about the confidence she had placed in him. Doubtless the *whole thing,* as Sylvia vaguely phrased it, was going to die down and be forgotten; whatever Julian may have been thinking it was evident that he had now changed his mind — whatever had happened, for example, during Hugo's party, would not now be brought up as a reproach to anyone.

The point was, she now saw, to live a full, busy life; it was only in idleness that one became infected with dreams in which life might be otherwise. One could, of course, continue in the most innocent way to be good friends with a young man like Marius, if that were an arrangement in which he would sensibly co-operate. But anything else, so far as she was concerned, would be out of the question, though perhaps with regrets. Of course it would be nice, in some ways, to have an affair; but things simply were not constituted in that way these days (she had a moment of doubt here; were they not?), and the point about taking marriage seriously meant above all that one did not, absolutely did not and must not, make trouble. She resolved that some time soon she would have a friendly explanation with Marius on this score. "Of course we are tempted," she would say in her new wisdom, "it is part of the game. Ideally, my dear, I should be delighted to go to bed with you, I'm sure we should have a splendid time together — but one simply does not do such things." In imagination she saw Marius nodding gravely and tenderly his assent to this proposition, which combined romantic charm with moral security; and Sylvia believed that if he were any sort of man at all he would care for her more deeply than ever — she would even say as much: "If you are as intelligent and kind and good as I know you are . . ."

Sylvia's full, busy life at this moment centered around the preparations for Hugo's wedding. Exactly what it would center around after that event she had not yet considered. There were numbers of things to be done in a short time, for the date had been set rather suddenly and late on account of the divorce. Sylvia still did not altogether approve of this marriage, it is true; yet she was by nature incapable of remaining apart from "making arrangements." She helped Mrs. Leonard with the invitations, she went with Louisa to give advice about what clothing would be suitable for England at this time of the year; she arranged by herself the catering for the *bon voyage* party in the stateroom.

"You know, suddenly I'm very happy again," she said to Julian one evening.

"Ah, darling," he said, with a kiss, and stroked her hair.

"For a while I thought we were going to have a perfectly furious quarrel," she confessed, "but love wins out again. I hate quarreling, I guess I'm just not the violent type. I'd rather just have everything go along smoothly. Real happiness is kind of quiet, just like this, sitting here with you, not saying much."

"Ah well, every marriage has its ups and downs," Julian replied, his feeling of unredeemable shame mixed with secrecy and triumphant contempt producing, with some effort, a commonplace.

"Those horrible letters — !" Sylvia said boldly. Julian smiled in what seemed to her some physical discomfort, and raised his eyebrows.

"Yes, the letters," he said.

"Darling, you didn't really believe there was anything wrong, did you?"

"I was a little uneasy," he said in a joking tone, "you're a damn' attractive wench, you know. But then I decided I was

190

being silly — you'd be incapable of keeping a secret for twenty minutes, wouldn't you?"

"But who is Federigo?" she asked with a great sense of relief that these cards though face down were finally on the table. "Do you know?"

"I've no idea," Julian replied. "That was the most horrifying thing — that feeling that we were being watched over by some stranger, or even by one of our friends posing as a stranger."

"You haven't got any more of them?" she hesitantly asked, very much wanting not to know.

"No," said Julian. "I guess whoever it was gave it up as a bad job. If I ever catch up with him — " he added significantly, making a fist.

"Well, if you do," said Sylvia sensibly, "I hope he's not bigger than you are."

This was the end of the discussion; they were like two people examining an infected wound and pretending to each other that the hard, inflamed spot which covered it represented the formation of new, healthy skin; they probed very tenderly indeed around the edges, and if the one winced the other pretended not to see. Even Julian began to believe that this was a new life, if not necessarily a more honest one than the old, and that whatever happened with Elaine would at least have no connection with the letters of Federigo, which had served their purpose (along with, perhaps, other, unforeseen purposes) and were definitely at an end. He reminded himself, however, that the activities of the detectives were not at an end; the most recent report let him know how Sylvia had spent Friday: she had gone shopping with Louisa, with whom she then had lunch and went to a movie; the evening she had been with Julian himself, who thus appeared like a stranger (an odd feeling, again as if he were in a play or movie) in the report directed to himself. All this, if dull in the reading, was impeccable domestically. Ah well, he supposed he must keep these bloodhounds on the track — at a rather considerable expense — until Hugo left with Louisa on his honeymoon; then he would tell Mr. Bilsiter it had all been a mistake, or at any rate that he did not want the trailing continued, and the whole matter would be forgotten by the time Hugo returned from England.

There was, meanwhile, one little thing that troubled Sylvia, though she talked of it with no one, and this was the odd feeling which overtook her now and then, wherever she happened to be during the day, that someone had his eye on her; she could sense it, there was a spot on the back of her neck that seemed to be receptive to a stare. But however often and suddenly she turned around, in a crowded restaurant or walking down the street, she was unable to identify her follower, if she had one, which she came finally to believe she had not. "Now this," she told herself, "would be the ideal tale to put before Mirabeau, who would call it entirely subjective — and in this instance he'd be entirely right, too. It is the beginning of a mild form of persecution-feeling; I was worried and guilty over things last week, and this is a kind of psychical hangover from that time. If I simply relax, and realize it is my own conscience which is following me around, everything will be all right." The uncomfortable feeling persisted, however, or at least it returned intermittently during each day, and Sylvia bore it stoically.

One evening, when as it happened Julian was out — it was the second time in the week that he had to work late, for as he told her, his vacation was coming soon, and there was a good deal to clean up before he could leave — Sylvia had a phone call from Hugo, who said he would like to have a talk with her.

192

"Why don't you come over here?" she said, thinking this must have to do with the arrangements for the wedding; and Hugo promised to come.

"Where's Jay?" he asked, and when Sylvia told him that Jay, poor thing, had to work late, Hugo raised his thick eyebrows.

"His vacation is coming soon," she explained on seeing this expression.

"Where do you plan to go?"

"No idea," she said. "We haven't even thought of it yet."

"Ah." Hugo was not a man who could be comfortable in the possession of secret knowledge; his awareness that Sylvia, who was possibly unfaithful to her husband, was being shadowed by detectives which Hugo himself, moreover, had been responsible for hiring, made him feel quite ashamed, for he really did like Sylvia as much as he claimed to do; so he reminded himself that he personally, Hugo, wanted this question of the anonymous letters cleared up, it was all — detectives, that is — for their own good, it was his business to see his friends happy again, which was as a matter of fact the errand he had come here on.

"Look, I have a notion," he exclaimed, as if it had just come to him. "Why don't you just take over my place on Long Island for your vacation? At Lantern Point."

"Oh, Hugo, we couldn't do that," said Sylvia, thinking that this might be very nice indeed.

"And why not? Do you both good to get away from — well, to get away from civilization for a bit. It seems to me you've both been under some strain, these last weeks."

So it had showed? But of course it had, Sylvia reminded herself. How couldn't it have showed, considering her behavior at Hugo's party, Julian's absence . . . ? A moment of anxious doubt overtook her, and she smiled gaily.

"Every marriage has its ups and downs," she said.

"Sylvia," Hugo said earnestly, "I want you to tell me one thing — are you and Jay — are you, that is, breaking up, have you thought of doing that?"

"Darling Hugo," she replied, "you of all people must surely know that married couples *do* now and again think of such things — that's one of the thoughts that keep them going."

"Ah, then it's not serious," he said heavily. "I'm so glad. You two, you know, are just right together, never let anyone tell you otherwise. And if you ever have any little troubles, why, I hope you'd let me know before you do anything, well, anything odd."

"Hugo, what are you trying to say?"

"Sylvia, I hope you haven't been having any — wrong ideas. About Julian the other night."

"Wrong ideas?"

"Such as — well, you know what I mean. I happen to know," Hugo said impressively, "that Jay left that party only because he was unhappy and wanted to be alone for a while. He went to a bar and while he was there he got into a fight with some drunk. So if you've been thinking anything else, Syl, get rid of it right off."

"Hugo, how do you *happen to know* all this?"

"Because, of course, Jay confessed it to me. I can tell when a man like Jay is telling the truth and when he's not, I've known Jay for longer than you have."

"And did he also confess," Sylvia asked, "what he was unhappy about, that he had to leave the party to be alone?"

"Well, I didn't want to push it too far," Hugo said, "but after all, you know, you were giving one or two fairly good reasons, yourself, why he might have been."

194

"Yes," said Sylvia, frowning. "I'm sorry I was a fool at your party, Hugo."

"Oh, that." He waved it away. "Don't think of it. I only wanted to be sure everything was all right between you two."

"We did have a few bad days, you know how it is," Sylvia said, "but everything's fine now — so far as it's your business, darling," she added sweetly, but Hugo was not embarrassed.

"Of course it's my business," he said, "when my friends are unhappy. But whatever it was," he went on after a pause, "I'm delighted you've cleared it up. I've always thought about you two, you know, that there are faithful types and unfaithful types — you and Jay are faithful types, you couldn't do anything out of line if you had to. It would hurt too much. With me," he added reflectively, "it's different. Even now, you know, and I'm terribly in love with Louisa, I can see the time coming when I shall want someone else, it's just my nature. But I suffer for it, Syl, you know that."

"Hugo, I'm sure you do," said Sylvia, "even if," she could not resist adding, "it must be great fun to suffer in just that manner." She softened this remark with a smile, which Hugo returned.

"Now then — what about the place? Say you'll take it, Sylvia, it will give me pleasure to think someone's getting a bit of use of it — Elaine and her mother wouldn't think of going up there again, I don't believe they liked it one bit and I can't say I blame them, in the winter at any rate. It's primitive, you know, I've deliberately kept it that way. Out on this lonely point on the dunes, it looks over the sea — it used to be a smuggler's hide-out, the original house, you can still see the foundations. They used to light bonfires there to deceive ships into wrecking on the shoal, and then they'd plunder the wreck. Mooncussers, they were called, because they hated the full

195

moon that gave them away. There's a wood stove and fire-
places, you'll find plenty of wood left. No electricity, of
course, and you get the water from a well, you pump it up.
I think you and Jay would enjoy it. Be fine for you, too."

"It sounds wonderful," Sylvia said, dubiously imagining
herself drawing water from a well. "I'll think about it, and
talk it over with Julian."

"Nonsense, surprise him," Hugo said. "Look, I've brought
you the key. Just pack him into the car and take off, you'll
both love it. Do say you'll have it."

Sylvia accepted the key, reflecting that they might actually
go up there. To live the simple life, she thought, to get away
from things for a while . . .

Hugo kissed her at the door before leaving. This kiss began as a friendly salute, which he with some force prolonged
and finally attempted to convert into something quite different; Sylvia pushed him away rather angrily.

"There are faithful types and unfaithful types, just as you
say," she reminded him, and he laughed.

"I don't know why I wanted to do that," he said. "For old
times' sake, maybe. We're getting older, darling, we're all
getting older. I could love you again, Syl," he added, "I could
ask you to go to bed with me again just for that, because we're
getting older and, after all, what else is there for people in
this life? Or maybe," he continued, philosophically rubbing
his behind against the edge of the door which was swinging
back and forth, "maybe it's more that I want to betray Louisa
even now, already, or that I just dread getting married again
even if I do love her. There's a lot of hate in love, isn't there,
you get a kind of need to do the dirty on someone just because
you love her. The first time I was unfaithful to Alma, you
know, I kept thinking about her all the time. It was like slap-
ping her face and saying over and over, 'Take that, and that,

196

and that.' Like in the movies." He laughed again. "It was more like sleeping with Alma than sleeping with Alma was."

"Are you saying," Sylvia asked dangerously, "that you felt that way with me?"

"No, this was well before your time, darling," said Hugo, rather delighted with himself; then seemed to see that this was going too far, according to Sylvia's expression. "It's just the kind of rotten no-good I am," he said apologetically.

"That doesn't need much further demonstration," Sylvia said.

"Syl, one more kiss, darling," he said. "For old times' sake, and to say the world's not worn out yet. Another couple of days, you know, and I'm lost forever."

Feeling a certain wry, inward humor in all this — that it would be all right to do very near anything so long as you felt you loved only your own husband — Sylvia accorded Hugo this farewell kiss. She felt herself caressed as from a great distance, a distance of more than seven years, and it seemed not to matter at all. These fumbling hands and squeezing fingers, the soft lips and behind them the hard teeth, what were they searching for in her body? She seemed to be standing back and looking at this body receiving those caresses as though it were the body of another person, for whom she felt both pity and contempt.

"Darling girl," muttered Hugo as she pushed him away. He sounded drunk, though he was not; that was what the body did, the empty body with no one at home inside.

"It would have been fun," he said, recovering himself and smiling down at her.

"Yes, I'm sure it would have been great fun," said Sylvia, and closed the door firmly after him.

THE WEDDING of Hugo Alter and Louisa Leonard took place in church, very solemn and ceremonious; everyone was beautifully dressed and took a serious if not a reverent interest in all that went on. Julian Ghent, being best man, had a close view of the proceedings, and as he did not bow his head more than a little at the appropriate moments, found himself regarding the combed and plastered silver hair of the minister from a distance of only a couple of feet during a considerable part of the service. This ancient and reverend head bowed over its book seemed to focus for Julian agreeable feelings of righteous displeasure which mingled with his conventional wishes for Hugo's (and Louisa's) happiness and with the emotion, not religious in form but connected commonly with all the higher and mightier observations of the passage of time, which he felt no less than most who were present, and which even brought tears to his eyes. He morally resented the authority over love which everyone was compelled to assume in the minister as the witness of church and state; he resented the power which must be really present in the business to bring him close to tears; he resented the rich, golden and vested hypocrisy which in a muted voice sanctified by compulsion. Julian did not weep, but he felt the tears in his eyes and the slight trembling of the chin which had always warned him, in childhood, that he was going to cry. Instead, so as not to, he fiercely concentrated on the bowed, silver hair before him, and wondered whether clergymen were trained to use a special sort of hair-cream, to anoint themselves formally with it, in the hope of achieving just this dull silvery luster which seemed, for himself at least, the quintessence of past time together with the seriousness and sorrow of life. As he handed Hugo the ring Julian was reminded that his grand-father, who died in Julian's childhood, had had just such silver hair, metallically combed and plastered and stiff, thin enough to allow a view of the skin of his head; this grand-father died in the winter, and because he used to winter in Florida the story given to the child Julian was that Grand-father had gone away to Florida. Julian had been sent out to the Park to play, he remembered it was a bitter cold, dark day with which he always associated a sepia picture of Florida on a postcard — a picture of the Everglades, a writhing of rich vegetation and one passage of reflective, shiny water in the foreground, all of it of course in the dark rotogravure brown which was then the fashion. Here, then, in the minister's bowed head, in the firm but thin strands of hair through which the scalp gleamed, this returned to Julian, not flooding suddenly back like a revelation but slowly spreading and sinking like a stream released over soft ground: how the name of death, when he learned it, had taken on that choc-olate brown together with the smell of the postcard itself, which was in turn associated with the characteristic smell of Florida — where he had never gone, perhaps because Florida and the Everglades were the names of death — and which carried with it the forbidding bitterness of that afternoon in Central Park, with the keen wind which had brought the tears to his eyes and numbed his fingers. Standing there beside Hugo and Louisa Julian suddenly felt sorry for his grand-father who was more than a quarter of a century in his grave, alone and unthought of by anyone save, for this instant, Julian himself, who seemed to enter for a moment the cold, bitter Everglades of the mind.

It was strange that the celebration of happiness should bring with it this ancient image and the cloudy thought of death; yet even the celebration of happiness mentioned the name of death, reminded of it and of the provisional nature of the happiness whose relation to time was here being so seriously remarked. Oh, my friends, he thought, I do hope you will be happy. But even the thought carried with it all unlikelihood, and induced in Julian's mind a sophistication quite the reverse of what his inward exclamation sincerely intended; he saw the marriage as mockery, all its implications of virginity and freshness amazed and made the best of by an old gentleman in an odd costume whose silvery hair had the dull gleam of a counterfeit half-dollar, or for that matter a real one.

Louisa was very handsome in a gown of heavy white satin. Hugo looked solemn, imposing, somehow ever so slightly pathetic as he gave the appearance of listening to the words of the service with great attention — as though he might put them down in a notebook and check his daily conduct against these recommendations which smoothly flowed from the minister's mouth.

Mrs. Leonard wept happily and with loud sobs throughout the service and after, in the taxi on the way to the boat, and throughout the nervous, rather dreary party which occupied the two hours or more before sailing time.

On account of the confined space of the cabin — a quite capacious one for ordinary purposes — the party was small and gave the impression of being enormous: "Not more than three hundred most intimate friends," Marius observed to Julian; moreover, pieces of hand-baggage were everywhere, and presents — flowers, baskets of fruit and baskets of bottles of whisky — continued to arrive the whole time. Everyone was standing up, talking, smoking, drinking; for a background, which one became aware of only intermittently, there was the slight, preparatory trembling of the vessel itself, the humming sound that went with it, now and then a huge blast of the horn which caused all the guests to pick up their belongings and look nervously around, and the purposeful rush of all sorts of people, including officials, past the open door of the suite. Through the urgent, loud conviviality could be detected another sort of urgency, as the time of departure brought to the surface people's worst anxieties about a possible failure to get off the boat before it left — an anxiety which punished, Dr. Mirabeau might have said, their dreamlike wish to remain on the boat and sail off forever; there were arguments about the time, and a sentence frequently repeated was: "Don't worry, they'll warn us when it's time to go." All this was very fatiguing to the nerves, not least because prolonged farewells tend to lose their character in a few moments, leaving what remains to betray itself finally as an uncontrollable wish to escape.

At the center of all this, a peculiar force of secret awareness, which might be given very generally the name of love, related several of these people in a network of unequal tensions: the exclusive character of these relations was witnessed by a superficial gaiety spread among them all, which disguised, or at least intended to disguise, isolated and secret communications of some urgency.

Sylvia, for example, was aware as Louisa was not — not in particular, anyhow — of "the kind of person" Hugo was so far as this related to herself; she could even perceive this honeymoon voyage not as a setting forth into the new and the unknown but as an interlude in a possible, highly theoretical relation, not yet by any means over, between herself and Hugo; this thought formed a kind of revenge, very remotely, for the sake of Alma, so that Sylvia could look on the new bride with superior pity, poor thing. This awareness of hers was concealed also from her husband Julian, who did not know either the quality of Sylvia's relation with Marius —

what it had been, what it now was, what it might be — nor the secret of Marius himself for that matter, whose elegant, learned, altogether fictitious affectation of Catholicism made for something esoteric and aristocratic in his presence.

Marius, Sylvia saw, was talking with Elaine, over near the window. Now *that* would be a very fair match, she considered. Of course, Marius would have to give up his rather bohemian ways and take a job, but if he did he and Elaine might make a lovely couple; both quite small, thin, highly bred (all this in appearance, anyhow) and charmingly young. Sylvia imagined herself as the Older Woman, *stepping out of his life* with a gracious smile and the hint of tears, to whom the young people would owe their happiness; all this, of course, as she realized with a slight start, began with the assumption that she had first been the young man's mistress, otherwise it would lack its romantic significance. If Marius had not chosen that moment, the other day, for his confession, if it had not struck her as so ridiculous — if, if, if — who knows what might have happened? It was so easy to make a mistake.

Marius, who would in a few minutes tell Elaine of his love for her — would he tell her of his having seen her with Julian in the Museum? — at this moment savored with delighted detachment the last rewards of irony. He saw Sylvia — looking at her with keen, neutral attention across the stateroom, a tall, serenely beautiful woman in a severely cut suit of navy blue — as eaten inwardly with doubt and self-distrust and unhappiness over the anonymous letters which, with Dr. Mirabeau, had very nearly driven her into adultery with Marius himself; and as invincibly ignorant, at the same time, of the real occasion available for her despair to feed upon; that her husband was deceiving her with Elaine, who looked at this moment the picture of pretty innocence as she smiled at something he, Marius, had just finished saying. As for Julian him-

202

self, whom the anonymous letters must have worried — not quite needlessly, it would seem — about the conduct of his wife, Julian seemed at this moment the ideal victim, being as he must be at once worried and happy, scared of unknown and generalized danger but meanwhile quite foolishly secure in the secrecy of his passion which was not secret. Marius felt as though even the deep trembling of the ship beneath his feet were part of the exultation of his power, and knavishly concluded that if he could at one and the same time make Sylvia and betray Julian to her, this power would have wrought its beautiful utmost; after which — and even through which — he would love only Elaine.

Elaine for her part regarded Sylvia with what is usually called honest pity — a misnomer, since this virtue is almost by definition excluded from the feeling of pity. She felt quite attracted to Julian, and she loved situations of a certain danger; they were, in fact, the only things she did love. Her feelings for Julian were experimental, but boldly so; not unlikely she would go to bed with him, some little time after he asked her to, *if* the adventure could be kept light, casual, charming; there was a regrettable tendency she had noted in Julian, he wanted to *be in love*, with all the serious, irrevocable and somehow disconsolate connotations of the idea. Elaine was quite delighted with what she thought of as her own toughness, a kind of knowingness about the world which should (and did) surprise gentlemen of thirty-five or so in a girl of twenty, and an ability to take excellent care of a self which, whatever else she gave or seemed to give, kept its privacy and sufficiency. Looking over now at her lover's wife, Elaine was like the executioner whose superlative technique can detach the head from the body so suddenly that the victim mercifully will have — so far as human beings can tell — no time in which to feel pain. As for Marius, with whom she was talking at this moment, he was a sweet boy who transparently was going to tell her in a few minutes that he loved her; Elaine had no real objection to his doing so at all, but hoped he would not be pathetic, if only for his own sake, since what she admired happened to be strength and a certain ruthlessness — the thing, perhaps, which attracted her to Julian, whom ordinarily she would not have suspected of strength, was the engaging carelessness he displayed about his poor wife, and this carelessness more than anything else would prevent her from ever getting to know, since it was as a rule, she believed, when people became serious and sad in love that they made fatal errors. Love was most charming when it involved deceit.

As for Julian, he too was possessed at this moment with a delighted awareness of his superior power in having at the same time in the one room his wife and the girl with whom he was in love; it was like seeing two express trains which seemed to be rushing toward one another at a great speed of closing but proved at the last possible instant to be on separate tracks so that they passed one another in perfect safety, with the appearance of accident, of luck, yet with the consent in reality of forethought and plan. And no one knew! He smiled at Elaine, who happened to glance his way, and she smiled back; the secret seemed to shuttle palpably through the smoky and crowded room. Only one thing at this time disturbed Julian's Machiavellian pleasure, and this was the momentary thought of Federigo, who remained to him, it appeared, as a kind of legacy left over from the anonymous letters. He is the Devil, Julian thought, and, simultaneously: I am insane. But both these thoughts, deep in the silence of his body — he felt them, as it were, in his stomach rather than his head — rather increased than diminished his feeling of reckless, arrogant mastery over the nature of things. He smiled at Sylvia, who was not looking at him; this smile might have gone between her ribs and killed her. He was even willing to smile at Marius, that poor, prissy little gentleman, who was talking so earnestly — doubtless wittily as well — to Elaine, not knowing of course that this was Julian's Elaine whom he tried so hard to impress. Marius returned the smile somewhat angrily, he thought, and Julian decided this smile might refer also to Marius's having attempted Sylvia's virtue and found it — as the detective reports would seem negatively at least to show — unassailable; and Marius, unable to make his friend's wife, was unaware of turning now toward his friend's prospective mistress. Julian's feeling of towering, isolated strength increased until it seemed it might topple from an insane height.

Hugo, who was becoming more drunk than anyone present, felt grateful to everyone indiscriminately; everyone seemed to co-operate in making his life charming and happy. He was, in a way, honest with everyone, so that they all must love him for exactly what he was, which he supposed to be something of a minor villain; whatever anyone of his acquaintance did, so far as marriage was concerned, he could always compare himself to his own advantage with Hugo. Therefore people did not want him to change, they needed him just as he was, and it was as if Louisa somehow embodied the expression of their gratitude to him. She was beautiful, and her beauty was enhanced in the light of his own licentiousness; she was not merely married but as it were sacrificed to him. He sought out Julian and tried to express to him something of this feeling of being, as he said, "like a God." Julian nodded rather distantly to all this, and Hugo remembered that his friend had troubles of his own; he inquired about the progress of the detective reports.

"Nothing," said Julian, "perfectly clear."

205

"I knew it," Hugo cried enthusiastically. "What did I tell you — you've nothing to worry about."

"Except, of course," Julian added, "she had a visit from you the other night — you were there for a little over an hour, according to the report." He laughed. "Are you the man, Hugo?" Then he added, "I think probably the best thing to do is drop the whole business. There have not been any more letters. And this Bilsiter is being so absurdly thorough, he called up and asked me how long we'd been married, had there been anything in the past, had I ever been away for any length of time — that sort of thing."

"Oh, really, you don't say?" said Hugo, with an abrupt change of expression.

Marius meanwhile had told Elaine bluntly that he was in love with her, and now sought some means of demonstrating his knowledge without altogether giving it away.

"Do you see much of our friend Ghent these days?"

"No, of course not," Elaine replied, "is there some reason why I should?"

"No reason at all," Marius said with dark significance, "absolutely no reason. I just thought I'd ask," he added. "He's in rather a bad spot, you know, these days."

"Oh, really?"

"Yes, it seems he gets these anonymous letters suggesting his wife is unfaithful to him. Letters signed by someone who calls himself Federigo."

"Why, I know a Federigo," Elaine exclaimed in pleased surprise. "But it couldn't be that one, that's Federigo Schwartz, for he's away on a world cruise and besides, he doesn't know Julian, I don't think. He is Mr. Ghent's double, did you know that? The spit of him, like twins."

"Oh, is he, indeed?" Marius smiled a sinister smile indicative of more understanding than he actually at this moment

206

was in possession of. Here was a strange new piece of information to be deeply considered; there was a Federigo, he was the image of Julian Ghent; what did one make of that, now? He looked very intently at Elaine.

"Is she, do you think," asked Elaine, "unfaithful, I mean?"

"All I mean is," he said to her, "that because of this situation in which our friend Ghent finds himself, his tastes may be a little capricious just now, and one ought not to take very seriously, for example, his interest in Egyptian art."

Elaine beautifully showed no surprise; Marius thought she was wonderful at this moment.

"My dear, don't threaten me," was all she said.

"Are you in love with him?" Marius asked in a low voice.

"Of course not," Elaine replied with a little laugh. "And you mustn't be so serious, yourself, either — if you love me," she added, "you must please me a great deal and make me happy. No romantic sulks, now."

So the party continued for some time; everyone had a secret from someone and for this reason believed himself powerful, sometimes this belief was erroneous. A was victorious over B, B over C, but when it came to the end of the alphabet, A would be found to have been conquered by Z. Finally the visitors were warned that it was time to leave the ship and they collected their belongings and began confusedly straggling out on deck.

Hugo went as far as the gangplank with Julian, holding his arm, in fact. At the last possible moment, drunk, blushing, and speaking very fast in a low voice, he told his friend that he had been the man who, seven years before, had got Julian's wife Sylvia with child.

Julian stopped walking and simply stared at Hugo stupidly.

"I suppose I should tell you to hit me," Hugo said, a helpless expression on his broad, red face. "Go ahead, it's your

207

right," he added, more or less thrusting his face forward to be hit, and helpfully adding, "I won't hit back."

Julian was unable to do anything at all, he stood there as if paralyzed.

"This way, please," an officer cried. The crowd moved, swayed, sifted down the gangplank carrying Julian mercifully along with the others; Hugo himself was very nearly taken off the boat in this manner. There followed a tiresome period during which all Hugo's friends stood on the pier waving their handkerchiefs, though Julian, who had not recovered from the shock he had just received, could not be certain whether he was waving farewell or simply shaking his fist with a handkerchief in it. To be on the safe side, he did a little of both, and hoped that it left Hugo in doubt too.

Chapter 7

JULIAN GHENT, when young and a single man, had been quite unsuccessful with women. He betrayed himself time after time by being evidently too eager when he should have been restrained, a little aloof, or even downright disdainful. Some older and more adept ladies would even tell him about this fault, making an artifice and a convention out of what they were supposed to feel in the course of nature, but even guided by this good advice Julian continued to be too candid in revealing his desire, so that nearly all ladies, however much they liked and even (some of them) loved him, continued to deny the final gift of their favors. For the first axiom in love is that whoever does not despise is despicable; love is, like chess, a contest in which tolerance is impossible, lucky accident unlikely and a draw very infrequent except between grandmasters.

The most poignant thing was that the young Julian had known all this quite well in theory, but was always afraid to put it into practice to the extreme degree that would have been necessary. His love affairs always began well, for when his feelings were not involved beyond admiration and desire he possessed naturally a fine arrogance which made it seem as though the advances were being made from the other side; but as soon as he saw the overwhelming effect he was having on the girl of his choice he would respond helplessly by falling in love (perhaps with the image of himself which he saw reflected in her eyes), and he would say to himself: "All right, then, she loves me, let us drop the pretense." A fatal error, since it was certainly with the pretense that the girl had been in love, and she, her own ambition to servility and degradation thus put off, would take her revenge by a mocking coldness, a light-tempered carelessness, the appearance of perfect freedom from the pains of love as soon as she saw that these pains could be suffered instead by Julian. And this attitude of hers, which he as much as anyone had created, would further inflame in the young man an unhappy passion, or a passion perhaps for unhappiness, which increased as the chances of satisfaction diminished; he would grow bitter and disagreeable, until quite soon even the friendship which was tacitly supposed to replace love would become unendurable to the girl, and all was over.

This flaw in Julian's nature would perhaps never have been overcome by any internal resources; he would be, it was possible to predict, all his life a failure at the edge of success, a perpetually bitter optimist. Yet his weakness — of inveterate pride, vanity, sentimental greed — had oddly been made over into strength by his marriage. Not only did the satisfaction of the immediate desires of the flesh allow him to be less urgent about woman generally, but also the jealousy of his wife, by making an affair with another woman very nearly unthinkable, provided Julian with exactly that aloofness and restraint necessary to let his more attractive qualities shine forth, so that at parties other women were frequently found trying to get him off into corners and sometimes making improper suggestions to him. The dignified coldness of his response humiliated and further inflamed these women, so that Julian perceived now how successful he might have been had circumstances not made success impossible to take hold of.

What he did not perceive was the paradox, that this success he could not take hold of was owing entirely to his wife Sylvia, who thoughtlessly, by the reflection in him of her jealousy and strict views, made her husband attractive to other women. Had his marriage been suddenly annulled, Julian would doubtless next day have relapsed into his weak-willed, pleading ways, and been spurned again by everyone.

These considerations lead to the further thought that it is, after all, virtue which seduces to love. Thus the high price placed on virginity warrants a certain reticence which is lovable because it is in the first place contemptuous of love and can therefore incite the lover to humiliation and hurt. The whole proposition is morally wicked, perhaps econom-ically unsound, but, however, erotically and abysmally virtuous.

Julian's relations with Elaine Leonard developed, accord-ing to the familiar pattern (with certain technical differences on account of his being married), in the direction of un-happiness and began to exchange their original freedom for bondage. The charm of leading a double life, in the first place, began to go sour on him; moreover, he realized it could not be kept up for very long; something was bound to give, one way or another. There was even a danger that Elaine, who was perhaps not so much cruel as young and thoughtless, and who, whatever else she was, happened not to be a coquette or tease, might become bored and consequently explode the whole business herself — for fun, as she put it on one crucial occasion.

Sylvia had gone to the movies and Julian, telling himself that the time had come, pretended to be tired so he could stay home. In fact he was tired, but this did not prevent him from at once phoning Elaine to suggest, with a show of carelessness, that he was alone and she might if she liked come over for a drink; she had never before been in his apartment. He re-

211

gretted this step as soon as he hung up the phone, and twenty minutes later Elaine arrived.

She was dressed, with a kind of sacrificial simplicity, in black, without jewelry or any accent of ornament, and this costume, together with a kind of quiet tension in her demeanor, informed Julian plainly that she had come to him as his mistress. This was so, as even he had to admit, as a result of his own intentions, his own actions; he was delighted, of course, in a certain highly theoretical way, also frightened, but not merely in theory. At once he imagined Sylvia, bored with the movie, returning early. His own hypocrisy repelled him, but the idea of ignominious discovery (and possible violence — "I'd kill her," Sylvia had said so long ago, "and possibly you as well") inspired a kind of nervous terror.

While he fixed drinks in the kitchen, Elaine wandered around the living room, looked at the books, the furniture, the pictures (there was the picture of Sylvia, too, gazing around as if suspiciously) and said "What a lovely place." The dogs, Troilus and Cressida, frisked around her, and she admired the dogs ("What lovely dogs"). Julian brought in the drinks and suggested she might like to see the rest of the apartment. Elaine agreed, and they spent a few minutes in this way ("And this is the kitchen" . . . "Here is the bedroom") but as it was a small place there was not a great deal to be shown; also the furniture appeared to Julian to be staring at him in a peculiarly disagreeable and *knowing* fashion. Elaine conventionally admired everything; finally they returned to the living room, where she turned to him and said, with a grave sweetness:

"You asked for me, and here I am." And she put up her face to be kissed. Julian obediently took her in his arms. Out of the corner of his eye he saw Sylvia staring out of the portrait. The kiss was prolonged, and became quite impassioned;

212

it represented to Julian a new depth of self-disgust and, perhaps for this very reason, an intensification of pleasure; treachery, violation, hatred even, were the things which gave point to his love for Elaine.

"I love you, darling," he whispered, with an eye to the portrait.

"Do you want me?" she whispered back, and he replied "Of course I do." They embraced again. Through the charming, somewhat alcoholic and bitter fragrance of her perfume Julian unwillingly became aware of the sour smell of her body in heat; this is reality, he thought in desire and wild fear, and let her go.

"Not here, darling," he said. "Not this way."

"Oh, and why not?" She smiled at him her wicked, crooked, innocent smile. Julian glanced up at the portrait.

"She might come back," he said. "And anyhow — it wouldn't be fair."

"Who wants to be fair?" she lightly asked, turning her back on him.

"I love you, Elaine," he offered again, somewhat helplessly.

"Well, then . . . ?"

"We must be honest — that's the thing."

"And what does that mean?"

"Elaine, darling, if I told her — if we were perfectly honest about this — there's no shame to falling in love, is there? Would you marry me if I were free?"

The girl, her face still averted, was silent for a moment.

"No," she said then, in a tone of judicious reflection. "No, I very much doubt I would."

Julian stood aghast and frightened. She seemed to be leaving him alone in a house which they had robbed and ruined together.

"I don't love you, darling," she went on. "I don't want to talk about love. This is fun, or it was supposed to be. The last thing I'm interested in is breaking up one happy home" — she laughed angrily — "and starting another. That's not my dish at all."

"But I'm in love with you," Julian repeated.

"And here I am," said Elaine. "What do we do about it?" She turned back to face him, and there would have been perhaps another embrace, but Julian was becoming thoroughly miserable.

"Not here — not in this house," he said with somewhat absurd firmness, the picture of a man putting his foot down and finding quicksand under it.

"Your delicacy is marvelous," she said. "Sylvia would be delighted."

"Please don't say her name," Julian said between menace and appeal. Elaine looked at him with a remote, objective curiosity.

"Don't you believe I have some right in this?" she inquired. "I thought it was all so simple — you wanted me, you were attractive, I decided I wanted you — and now where are we?"

"Yes, darling, but not this way," he exclaimed. "Not with her looking on . . . and she might come back, there's that, isn't there?"

"Yes, there is that," Elaine admitted. "This is being damn badly managed, isn't it?" She seemed to consider for a moment, then asked, "Tell me, Jay, will you go away with me — will you meet me somewhere for the weekend?"

This proposition struck Julian as the perfect solution. *Away,* so long as it was anonymous and without particular character, and as it perfectly put off the embarrassment of the moment, appealed to him enormously.

214

"I'd have to make some excuse," he cautiously said even so, "tell Sylvia something, I don't know what. Where would we go?"

"I'm going to Hugo's place anyhow," said Elaine, "out at Lantern Point. If you want to come along — so. If you don't — so," she added carelessly. "I leave Friday. Tell Sylvia it's a business trip — I believe that's what people commonly do, isn't it?"

"But I never take trips in my business."

"Then this will be the first time, won't it?" she said sweetly. "She'll suspect, of course — won't she? But what's that? And we'll have a few days. We might even send her a postcard saying 'wish you were here.' "

"Don't, please don't be like that," he begged her.

"I only mean to say you must make up your mind." Elaine picked up her gloves from the coffee table before the sofa, looked up quizzically for an instant at the portrait of Sylvia, and said, "I'm leaving on Friday. You've got a couple of days to make up your mind and tell her some story or other. But it's got to be by then — or else never. If you came along," she added, "I might, I just barely might, decide to forgive your rudeness now. Don't imagine it's so pleasant for me, your conscience — such as it is."

"Darling, I'll think of something," Julian promised. "I'll call you Friday morning."

A kiss, somewhat grudgingly and coldly given, was his reward for this pledge, and then Elaine, to his great relief, left.

Almost as soon as the door closed behind her Julian began to wish things had been otherwise; now he felt not only guilty but humiliated as well, and this humiliation, he dimly recognized, increased his love for Elaine, and satisfied something in his nature which went deeper than his desire to be unfaithful to his wife. Thinking it over now, he found his original

215

motives almost impossible to recapture; what he had started out to do, possess (as he called it) another woman, could be viewed in several ways: as a simple desire for sexual experience (but it was certainly not simple, whatever it might be); as an assertion of freedom; as an expression of contempt for Sylvia (that one hurt, it hit close to home); as an enlargement of his own importance; as a wish for secrecy and even criminality; as curiosity about what evil was and where its place in the world; finally, as a wish to be punished, caught and punished — a wish to find, or if necessary create, an objective situation consonant with those feelings of guilt and insufficiency with which he had begun. The verdict of guilt had been delivered first, so long ago; what had to be discovered was the crime.

Like a murderer silently cleaning up the scene of his fatal action, Julian took both their glasses into the kitchen and washed them; he also scrubbed the lipstick off his face. Then he realized it would not look natural for him to have sat home all evening without a drink, so he made himself a highball which he did not want and took it into the living room.

"You're not going to offer me one?" asked Federigo, who was sitting on the couch looking at Sylvia's portrait. Julian gave a slight start, but only from the suddenness; it really frightened him that as a matter of fact he was not in the least surprised to see his curious acquaintance sitting there in the living room; also, while he was disturbed (naturally, who would not be disturbed?) he even, in a way, felt grateful to the presence of another person — especially one who was neither Sylvia nor Elaine.

"So it's you again," he said rather curtly, and made another drink for Federigo, who took it without saying thank you, and began to sip in an extraordinarily delicate way, as though he were not used to drink. Federigo was dressed casually in slacks and a shirt open at the throat; he also wore sandals instead of shoes, and looked very much at his ease; even impudently so, thought Julian — like a proletarian poet or some such individual.

"Now what is it you want?" Julian asked, determined upon boldness.

"I? I don't want anything, I'm perfectly content," said Federigo, looking indeed the image of a man satisfied with himself. "You're the one, my dear, who wants things." He laughed. "Though the Lord alone knows what it is you want, when all's said and done. As a lover, Julian, you'd make a wonderful real-estate agent — 'and this is the kitchen, this is the bedroom, here is the bathroom . . .'" Federigo imitated Julian's voice very accurately, with overtones of sarcasm at the same time. He laughed again. Julian was infuriated, out of sheer embarrassment.

"Damn you," he cried, "how do you know that?"

"Oh, I've been here right along," Federigo said, "only you overlooked me — as well you might, I suppose, under the circumstances. Julian, you remind me of a funny story. Do you want to hear a funny story?"

"No, I do not want to hear a funny story," Julian said between his teeth; but Federigo went right ahead anyhow, and Julian listened.

"There was this man, this drunk, at a bar — I'm sorry it begins in such a common way, but there it is, no help for that — and he made friends with a party of strangers. He fell more or less in love with them, the way drunks will, and when the bar closed he took them back to his house for one more drink. But when they got there he first insisted on showing them over his home. They were unwilling, but they went along for the drink, and he showed them everything in the most boring detail — here is the living room, here is the hall

217

and this is the closet, here is the kitchen . . . I won't take you through it all, I don't want to bore you, Julian. Finally he led them upstairs into the bedroom, where he turned on the light. 'And here is our bedroom,' he told them. 'That woman in the bed' (pointing at her) 'is my wife, and that man lying next to her — that's me.' " Federigo laughed at his joke, but Julian did not.

"I don't see anything so funny in that," he said with grumpy dignity, "and I don't see that I'm very like it, either."

"Oh, you don't?" asked Federigo. "Well, then, perhaps you're not — how should I know?" He looked curiously at Julian. "What are you like, then, do you think?" he inquired.

"If you know so much," Julian replied, "I suppose you know that, too."

"I've a fair idea," admitted Federigo, "but have you? There's the point. Have you ever used a camera with one of those split-image range-finders?" he asked. "The sort where you see two images of what you aim at, and you turn a knob until at the right focal length the two images coincide and become one? To me," he said, "you are a man looked at through such a camera, not at the right focal length."

"Looked at," Julian said doubtfully, "but by whom?"

"By yourself? By God?" Federigo spoke in a bored voice. "Who cares about that?"

"I care. Listen, Federigo," Julian said earnestly, "tell me this plainly. Are you the Devil?"

"My dear boy," drawled Federigo, relaxing on the couch, "that is your trouble, an all but incredible naïveté. Supposing I were the Devil, and you asked that, what sort of answer would you get — 'tell me plainly, be honest with poor me, dear Mister Devil' — how silly can you get? And even if it became quite clear to you that I was the Devil, what then? That's only a name, you would still have to ask what devil would so particularly belong to you. All this dramatic *me retro Satanas* kind of thing may be very well for the Saviour, but for you — no. You don't want him behind you, after all, behind you is the direction of danger and the unknown — a fact which, by the way, also makes toilet training such a profound influence on the Idea of the Good. And by the odd irony of history the great Descartes, inaugurator of the reign of reason, located the soul back there, behind the head in the pineal gland which is supposed nowadays to be the atrophied relic of a third eye which warned of danger from the rear. No, Julian, on the whole you had better have your devil out in front of you, in full view — like myself, for example."

"I knew that about the pineal gland," muttered Julian. "It was in Philosophy at college."

"Of course it was," Federigo easily agreed. "And now you are playing with the notion that I am some sort of subjective hallucination, because I know only what is known to you. Well, that is a nice notion, I suppose, and quite comforting even if it does suggest you are not quite right in the head, because it is better to be a little queer, isn't it, than to be diabolically possessed? Though some say, of course, that the two things are one. After all, the inner and the outer reality are very oddly married, aren't they? The outer reality has never been seen except by the inner one and according to its own rules — at least, so all reasonable people agree — in these *modern* times," he added sarcastically, "therefore you can see only the external world which is made a part of your internal world — so that knowledge becomes a kind of cannibalism, you digest the virtues of your enemy and they become you in the process — the courage of the warrior and the goodness of the missionary, all one in the stew. But of course even cannibals must be careful of whom they eat; you might bite on a coward, a lecher, a thief or murderer, and

219

become that — if the analogy is not getting a little too far-fetched to be followed."

"Then you are me?" Julian asked.

"I haven't said that either," said Federigo. "You're far too intellectual for your own good. Hasn't it ever occurred to you that this world is a real world, and that things are profoundly and beautifully, sometimes, just what they seem to be? Be more simple, Julian." Federigo stood up. "Come with me," he said, "for a walk in Central Park. There's something I want to put before you."

"But my wife," Julian objected, "she'll be coming back, she will worry . . ."

"You are admirably considerate," Federigo said. "Nevertheless . . ." And for reasons he could not compass, Julian felt impelled and even willing to follow, taking only one precaution before they left, which was suggested to him by the thought of Central Park at night: he left behind his wallet, thinking in confused shame that if his dead body should be found out there in the morning it would be difficult if not impossible to identify. Federigo noted this and seemed to approve it, though somewhat satirically, saying:

"I think you are wise to leave behind that little artificial heart (you notice men typically carry their wallets in pockets so placed as to suggest a right-handed heart balancing the one on the other side?) — not on account of the money, but the various civil identities it proclaims, the one hundred and one license plates which you usually wear on your public person. It is funny," he added, "you were robbed of your watch, now you leave behind your wallet. It suggests the not absolute impossibility of your ever learning from experience."

They walked together into the Park. Federigo insisted on linking his arm with Julian's in a disagreeable sort of intimacy, but on the other hand Julian felt quite safe with Federigo at his side. They skirted the dark bulk of the Museum of Art and climbed a small hill.

"This is Cleopatra's Needle," said Federigo, pointing to the little obelisk at the top, "but of course — I'd forgotten — you know rather a lot about Egyptian monuments by now, don't you?"

Julian did not reply.

"You will remember," said Federigo, with something of the lecturer's manner, "that this field over which we look was once water?"

"Yes, it was the Old Reservoir when I was a child," said Julian.

"Close your eyes," Federigo said. "Now look again."

Julian opened his eyes and looked. There before him was the Old Reservoir again, with its low retaining wall of rough stone. He stood on the path and marveled; it seemed to be daylight all around him.

"Over there, to the left, where the Old Fort is — that's where you used to play, most often," Federigo said. "Come, let's walk over that way."

They came to the place, which was full of nursemaids, children, baby carriages — exactly like real life, Julian thought, save that they seemed to see it from a great, empty distance. After a moment he realized this was so because of the silence; it was all exactly like real life except that nothing made any noise; there between the Reservoir and the playground, under the shadow of the Old Fort, he stood in mysterious and silent daylight, unseen by anyone, and watched the children at their play.

"That one in the brown corduroy shorts," Federigo observed, "that is you, Julian."

Julian looked at the little creature who at this moment was

sitting in some dirt beside the path. He remembered those brown corduroy shorts, which for some reason made him want to cry. Now a governess, whom he remembered quite well though he could not come up with her name, walked over and picked the little Julian bodily out of the dirt and slapped him. There was an expression of absolute rage on her somewhat shriveled face.

"That is Miss Collis," said Federigo. "She was with you for a long time, and loved you quite well, really, little horror that you were. She is still alive, did you know that? She slapped you in Central Park and she is still alive. She is in an asylum for the insane in upstate New York. It's odd, isn't it, what becomes of people?"

Julian heard all this as from far away. He began to cry, in part angrily because it seemed as though Miss Collis had really slapped him, hard, only an instant ago, and in part sadly because Miss Collis — he looked sorrowfully at her angry face in the playground — would one day be committed to an asylum for the insane. This feeling he had, of knowing the future, and knowing it also as the present, seeing all things, past, present and future, as one, was a feeling of strange power but also of reverence; he seemed to hear himself saying, "You see, one looks at these things, but one doesn't touch them." A moment later he realized this had been said, however, not by himself but by Federigo.

The little Julian had by now stopped bawling over the slap; he was playing in the midst of other children: Tommy Burns, Edward Cohn, Alexander something or other, a little girl named Genevieve, and two others whom Julian could not remember. Federigo supplied their missing names.

"Rita Larson," he said kindly, "whom you were going to marry when you grew up. No, don't worry, she is still among us, she married quite well — a banker in Trenton, New Jersey — she has several children, the eldest daughter looks rather as she did then — or does now, if you'd rather put it that way. The little boy you don't remember for a rather good reason; it was he who taught you about masturbation, you finally founded a sort of social club for the purpose and had an excellent time until the governess — not Miss Collis but another one — found you all in the bushes one afternoon. That little boy is Raymond Berenger, of course, and he now teaches at a prep school in New England somewhere, though unhappily he will soon be fired for homosexual practices with the students — you see, Julian, you had quite literally a hand in that as well.

"Alexander Hanson, now," he went on, "died in the war, at Bastogne. Edward Cohn never got that far, poor thing. Only a few days after what you are looking at now he came down with mastoiditis, was operated on and died in the hospital. You forgot about him, as children will, in a few days."

This seemed to Julian the most frightful and cruel outrage of all, though he did not see why. Tears of sorrow and long put-off mourning rolled down his cheeks.

"There, that's right," Federigo said, "you are weeping, aren't you, Julian? Tommy Burns is doing quite well, you'll be glad to know, as a certified accountant in this city. He never married, though. Elaine Leonard, by the way," he added, "has not yet been born."

Julian silently looked on at the scene below, watching the children playing in the shadow of the Old Fort which seemed to be also the shadow of futurity over them.

"I'm sorry," he said, still weeping. "Oh, I am awfully sorry."

He shut his eyes tightly for an instant of remorse and regret; when he opened them again the scene had faded. It was night, the playground stretched out where the Old Reservoir had been, but the Old Fort still stood on the rocks above. Julian turned to Federigo, but no one was there, and he had to find his way out of the Park alone.

As he went home, with eyes still wet, he began to lose the sense of what he had felt; secular considerations also obtruded themselves. Immense lengths of time seemed to have passed, Sylvia would have come home, she would be suspicious — unjustly, he cried in silence, unjustly — but there would be two glasses standing there because of that wretched drink he had made for Federigo. The silence of the house, and those two glasses, would surely betray him.

"He is a devil," said Julian of Federigo. "Only a devil could do such things as he did tonight."

And indeed it seemed as though Federigo must be a devil, or have some supernatural power, whether for good or ill, since when Julian arrived home he found that practically no time had elapsed whatever, since Elaine's departure. Sylvia had not returned from the movies, and two glasses, it was quite true, stood on the coffee table, but one of them bore distinct traces of lipstick.

The Devil, thought Julian, as he washed the glasses.

2

SYLVIA meanwhile, instead of going to the movies, was visiting with Marius in his room above the record shop, which was now, of course, quiet. It was an impromptu call, and not prearranged, she really had intended going to the movies, but when she arrived at the nearest theater she felt bored with the idea, in need of company, and rather resentful of Julian for being too tired to come with her; also, now that the wedding was over, her full, busy life seemed a little to have collapsed on her hands. Accordingly she decided that, as she had found no opportunity to tell Marius as yet the things she had thought during the party, now would be as good a time as any, so she phoned him and found him at home. It amused Sylvia, as with great poise she made herself comfortable facing Marius — she even sat boldly down on the bed — that the crucifix was not in sight on the opposite wall; she wondered whether he had removed it permanently or merely taken it away for the period of her call. In any case, she did not refer to it. What she had come for, she said, was to talk to Marius *sensibly.*

The substance of this sensible talk amounted to this, that Sylvia and Julian had been going through a critical time in their marriage — "the sort of thing that all married couples have to face sometime" — but that this time now was over. Anything Sylvia had said during that period, anything she had almost done, must be put down (of course) to her worry over the domestic situation (which conditioned, said Marius to himself, her foreign policy) — she had been almost mad with anxiety and doubt. But things had, as things will, righted themselves almost overnight; Sylvia wanted no uncertainty to remain in Marius's mind concerning her loyalty to her husband.

"Of course," she said lightly, "I should have been delighted to run away with you to some secret place for a mad weekend of delight — but you can see what my motive would have been, even then, I should only have been revenging myself on Julian."

"I see," Marius said, trying to look properly glum and rejected, while in reality he was almost hugging himself with glee, as people will whose exclusive possession of knowledge lets them play for a moment the role of destiny in the affairs of others. "What about the anonymous letters?" he casually inquired.

As for the anonymous letters, Sylvia said, that was something she did not understand, nor yet — she supposed — did Julian. Marius raised his eyebrows practically to his hairline. Doubtless some person had thought it a good joke, though the Lord alone knew who among their acquaintance owned so perverted a sense of humor; at any rate, there had been no more letters for some time, and Sylvia, in her new security, very much doubted there would be any more. "We've heard the last of Federigo," she said, and added that she hoped Marius would do her the favor of forgetting he had ever heard of such communications, implying that she in return would never mention to anyone any confidences Marius had imparted to her on the subject of religious faith (allowing her eyes to rest for a moment on the absence of the crucifix on the opposite wall). Of course, Sylvia concluded, she and Marius would remain good friends, and she would always be grateful for his having stood by her in the time of trouble.

"Sylvia," said Marius seriously, "supposing you should discover you are quite mistaken, and that the trouble is not over after all — imagine, for example, that Julian is actually deceiving you — what then?"

"Ah, no," she replied. "I worried over it — I thought that if he believed those ridiculous letters he might set out to show me that two could play at it — but I don't really believe he would. He does love me, and he is not a hypocrite — and besides, where would he find the time? I'd undoubtedly know about it at once."

"Undoubtedly. But still, supposing . . . ?"

"Why, then — " she laughed — "then, darling, I should

226

fly for refuge to your arms. I'd leave him at once," she added more seriously.

At this moment the phone rang, and Marius, answering, was shocked to hear Julian at the other end; it seemed impossible that neither he nor Sylvia could detect each other's presence in the situation, and Marius believed at first that Julian must have known his wife would be here. Instead, however, it turned out that Julian, speaking in a rather troubled voice, wanted Marius's help and advice "about a religious matter," and could Marius meet him for lunch next day?

"Yes, I suppose I could," Marius replied. "What do you mean, a religious matter?"

"I want to ask you something," Julian said seriously, "about the Devil — I thought you'd be the only person I know who would have a, well, a professional qualification . . ."

Marius, amazed, allowed Julian to set a time and place for their meeting, then hung up.

"Just a fellow I know," he said in response to Sylvia's slight, questioning glance.

"I didn't mean to pry into your life," she quickly replied. Nevertheless, she then went on to tell him, speaking as the Older Woman, that she thought it was time he married and settled down. She mentioned the name of Elaine Leonard tentatively — "for instance."

"I hardly know her," Marius said, adding with beautiful irony, "you know her much better than I do."

"I mean, of course," Sylvia continued, "you would have to give up your way of living, you would have to take a job — "

"But Elaine might not care to marry me," he objected, "she may have in mind to marry quite another person."

They talked for a few minutes about Elaine, agreed she was a charming girl; then Sylvia got up to leave.

"Julian thinks I'm at the movies," she confessed, "and I must get back at about this time."

Marius saw her downstairs and even to the corner, where he got her a taxi. Sylvia had, more strongly than ever, the feeling of being watched; but she did not think it right to involve Marius any further than she already had in the subjective problems of her psyche.

The matters of Dr. Thybold and Mr. Archer More, which had begun on the same day, the day of the first anonymous letter, as Julian recalled, settled themselves also on the same day, very abruptly. Julian had scarcely got settled in the office when there came a phone call; he heard a low, hoarse whisper at the other end.

"This is Doctor you-know-who," the whisper said. "Are you alone?"

"Doctor who?"

"Doctor — you know — lung cancer," the voice mysteriously went on.

"Oh, Thybold," Julian cried, "what can I do for you?"

"You can please not mention my name," said the doctor furiously. "Are you alone?"

"Yes."

"I'm phoning from a pay station. I daren't go home."

"You what?"

"I've received an anonymous letter," Dr. Thybold said in a quavering voice. "I'm afraid the cigarette industry is after me."

"An anonymous letter?" cried Julian in exasperation. "Oh, nonsense, doctor. You know perfectly well people don't do that sort of thing these days."

"Don't tell me, young man," the doctor said, "I have the letter right here, I'll read it to you."

228

In amazement Julian heard Dr. Thybold's voice, with an appropriate dramatic ominousness, read the following message:

It is not too late to mend. Retract your advertisement at once. Do not go to the police, you are being watched. If you go ahead with your plan consequences follow at once. You have been warned.

"Isn't it signed at all?" Julian asked.

"It is signed," said the doctor, " 'Nicotine the friend of man.' "

Julian controlled an impulse to laugh, not because it would be unseemly but because the laughter already felt hysterical in his throat.

"What do you want me to do?"

"Burn the letters," Dr. Thybold replied promptly. "I know when I'm beaten, I can't fight the cigarette kings."

"But some of the letters have already gone out," Julian objected. "Besides, as you said, you have to be prepared to suffer for your beliefs."

"Well, I gave up smoking, didn't I?" Dr. Thybold demanded. "But this is serious. Look, I can't talk any longer. A man is watching me. Please do something."

And on this the phone went dead. Julian sat for a few minutes feeling dazed, then gave instructions through Miss Duddon that no more of Dr. Thybold's circulars should be mailed until further notice.

"There are two men here to see you," said Miss Duddon, "a Mr. Archer More — he says you will remember — and friend."

"Send them in," said Julian.

Archer More was cold sober, and consequently looked frightful, with sagging cheeks and dilated eyes so bloodshot the pupils were nearly obscured. His relation to the gentleman with him was that of a prisoner to a policeman; the other man, holding him by the arm, pushed little Mr. More into the chair opposite Julian, but himself remained standing.

"How far has this ridiculous outrage gone?" he demanded.

"Just what outrage do you mean?" Julian countered.

"This — this advertising campaign," sneered the gentleman, "about love!"

"Nothing has been published yet," Julian replied, "I have the copy here waiting for Mr. More's approval."

"Mr. More will approve nothing," decisively announced the other man. "I am Mr. More's lawyer, my name is Henry Pratt, and I am delighted to be in time to prevent Mr. More from getting himself into serious trouble."

"The love of Christ Jesus," said Mr. More faintly, "serious trouble. Martyrdom. My head hurts."

"You may take it as a definite order," said Mr. Pratt, "that these advertisements are to be canceled — as of now. It is very fortunate that this got to my ears in time."

"I'm afraid I don't understand what this is all about," Julian said.

"The law, the law," said Mr. Pratt impatiently. "Surely you don't imagine Mr. More has any right to go around spending his money, much less throwing it away? Mr. More, sir, owes alimony to eleven women. These eleven women have eleven lawyers. If this nonsense about advertising became public these eleven lawyers would slap eleven injunctions against Mr. More before you could say — well, before you could say whatever you thought of saying. This gentleman," the lawyer continued, "exists, you might say, in order to go on paying alimony to these eleven women. If he died, that would be perfectly all right, quite legal, because the estate would be split up among the eleven former wives; if he married again,

230

that would be perfectly all right, so long as he could show, if necessary, that he could support another wife without reneging on the alimony payments. Mr. More," he concluded, "is neither more nor less than the living result of his actions, and he must take the consequences. That is all there is to it. Your firm, sir, may put in a bill for whatever expense this business has put you to; if it is reasonable, it will be paid. If it is not reasonable, you may go whistle for it. Good day."

The lawyer bodily pulled Mr. More to his feet; Mr. More groaned, wobbled slightly, steadied.

"Consider the lilies of the field," he cried as he was more or less dragged through the door.

These two crises, happening on the one morning, left Julian bemused by the idea that life was one grand theatrical performance. I live, he thought, in a world operated by Federigo; and he began to think that the actions of Dr. Thybold and Mr. More had run their courses together not as a result of coincidence but rather, though in an obscure sense, as demonstration: Dr. Thybold in his silly way a moralist, wanting to reform the world by works, and Mr. More in his silly way a mystic, wanting to redeem the world by advertising, which was after all a species of prayer.

"And I too," he reflected, "I wanted to change the nature of things, and I wrote anonymous letters. And now I don't know whether I'm coming or going."

This doubt whether he was coming or going formed the subject of his discussion with Marius Rathlin at lunch. Julian flattered himself that he conducted the inquiry at such a high theoretical level as to arouse no suspicion about his particular actions; he mentioned no names, neither of Federigo nor of Elaine.

The information which Marius already had, however, enabled him to see rather more than Julian imagined he saw. He knew, for example, about the letters, and he knew that Federigo exactly resembled Julian. The only thing that badly puzzled him was this, that Julian described his double (not mentioning the anonymous letters, of course) in such a way as made it seem this person could be no more than a hallucination, a *Doppelgänger* in fact; but Elaine had testified on the other hand — and if she were hallucinated, it would surely not be with this particular hallucination — to the real existence of a person with the odd name of Federigo, who, however, could not in her opinion be responsible for the letters, being away — and if that were true, neither could he be the person who haunted Julian.

"You know the thing that troubles me most?" Julian said. "It's that I am not even frightened when he appears, not even surprised, really. Sometimes I get angry with him — but I ought to be terrified, isn't that right?"

"If you want my honest opinion," Marius said, "it sounds more like incipient schizophrenia — you *know* the world is full of invisible enemies out for your blood, but at the same time you *know* that they can't hurt you, so as a result you're not even frightened."

"Oh." Julian took this information in reasonable calm, but was of course a little disconsolate. "You think I'm going insane, then?"

"Well, I don't exactly *think* so," Marius said. "You behave all right, though you look sort of pale and tired. It's not what I would think by myself, but it is certainly what is suggested by your story."

"But I chose you to tell it to," Julian explained, "because you're probably the only person I know at all well who really believes in the Devil — your religion does require you to believe in the Devil, doesn't it?"

"You mean you chose me to tell it to," said Marius, "because you believe I am a credulous and superstitious imbecile?"

"No, really," Julian assured him, "there's no need to be offended."

"But after all," Marius said, "what the hell would the Devil want with you?"

"Meaning I am damned already?"

"Meaning at least," Marius replied, "that it would not take any special concentration of effort on the part of His Sinfulness."

"You know," Julian said thoughtfully, "sometimes he seems to be a very nice fellow."

"Of course — I imagine his appearance wearing your face has predisposed you in his favor. I can only think, Julian," Marius added, "that you have done something so dreadful you refuse to face it, and finally it has caught up with you; the objective equivalent of your guilt is meeting you face to face."

"Oh — you think that?"

"I've no way of knowing what it is, of course," said Marius smugly. "Perhaps it's an analyst you need, not a priest. You might have an interview with Sylvia's man Mirabeau, who I believe is very hot on subjective impressions and fantasies and all that. You might become a classic in the literature of the subject," he concluded helpfully.

"I thought you might be able to tell me something," said Julian, "but never mind. I hope you won't mention this discussion to anyone?"

"The only advice I can give you," Marius said, "is, Be good and it will go away. As for your secret, it's safe with me — I shall be as the tomb, as the tombs of Egypt." He was unable to resist this final flourish, which he thought he had put in very aptly, and watched with a bland smile Julian's suspicious glance get nowhere and disappear.

Reflecting on this interview, Marius did not come explicitly to the conclusion that Julian had written those letters himself; nevertheless, he now decided upon his course of action, which struck him as villainous but irresistibly to the point: the letters had gone one way so far, now let them go the other way.

As he sat at his desk, occupied in the unfamiliar and tedious task of cutting snips of paper from the *Journal of the History of Ideas* and pasting them together, he smiled sourly, having thought of a charming parallel from history; when the young Louis XIV wished to impress Mlle. de la Vallière, he engaged M. le Marquis de Dangeau, a witty and eloquent man, to write his letters to her; the lady, duly impressed, thought herself insufficiently educated to write a proper reply, and in her turn engaged M. de Dangeau to write her letter to the King. Not a parallel, perhaps, perhaps a bit oblique, but at any rate (thought Marius) it must have been extremely amusing for M. le Marquis de Dangeau.

After what Marius had said, Julian was more confused than ever, and it seemed the mere operation of fate that Dr. Mirabeau should call him up at the office during the afternoon.

"Is your wife quite well?" asked the voice, after introducing itself.

"I suppose so," Julian said doubtfully. "Why shouldn't she be?"

"Well, she has skipped a number of appointments with me, just after one rather crucial session."

"Oh, I see."

"And I wondered if it would not be wise for you and me to have a little talk about the situation?"

Somewhat numbly, Julian heard himself agree to a time

late in the afternoon; it was with considerable nervousness, never having before been to a mind-doctor (as he put it) that he presented himself at Dr. Mirabeau's office.

Not being a patient (not being a patient as yet, Dr. Mirabeau's attitude proclaimed) Julian was not required to lie on the couch but sat facing the doctor across the desk; nevertheless the atmosphere was hypnotic and mystifying, all the room being darkened save for the single circle of light in which their four hands rested on the blotter, and Julian could see out of the corner of his eye *the couch* of which one heard so much and which gained, although an ordinary enough piece of furniture, something of the technical, scary mystery of medical equipment generally.

"To bring you up to date," said Dr. Mirabeau, "it all began over a question of anonymous letters — I take it you did actually get to see these letters?"

"Yes, I did," said Julian noncommittally.

"Ah. Now I must say that I at first made a mistake, a quite natural mistake. Mrs. Ghent did not actually bring the letter, the physical piece of paper, here to the office. From the way in which she spoke of it, I naturally concluded she had dreamed the whole improbable event, and she came in the course of the session to agree with me.

"But then," said the doctor impressively, "there came a second letter, and this one she brought to me. Of course I saw where I had gone wrong at once."

"You did?"

"Yes. For reasons which we need not go into, technical reasons having to do with the analysis, it became quite clear that Mrs. Ghent had written this letter at least, possibly the previous one if there was a previous one — "

"Oh, yes. There were two."

"Yes — had written them, as I say, herself. Now, Mr.

Ghent, it may be — none of us is perfect — that I made a further error here, a serious one, by treating your wife's relation with me as her primary motive in these communications. It occurs to me now that if that had been so she need never have brought you into it at all. But as you can testify yourself to the existence of these letters, it strikes me now that their major object was not merely an effect of the transference (which secondarily it was nevertheless designed to strengthen) but their major object was to involve you, to focus your interest and attention on whatever Sylvia — Mrs. Ghent — had done or was about to do.

"Now, Mr. Ghent, what I want you to tell me, in perfect confidence, as speaking to your own medical adviser, is this — is your wife faithful to you or not? That is, has she actually committed herself — in reality — to the fantasy proclaimed in the letters?"

"I don't know," replied Julian, "but I have reason to think not."

"Reason?"

"Detectives. I was, of course, bothered by those letters."

"Naturally, one would be bothered."

"Naturally."

"And you think there's nothing to it?"

"No."

"Ah," said Dr. Mirabeau, "I was afraid of that. It makes our problem more acute."

So this was psychoanalysis. Julian already had an impulse to confess everything, but he manfully resisted, though the sweat began to break out on his brow. He wondered, as though from a great distance, whether he would go with Elaine for the weekend at Lantern Point, and, if so, what excuse he would make to Sylvia.

"More acute," Dr. Mirabeau continued, "because, you see,

236

if she had in fact been unfaithful to you — these things do happen, do they not? — there would have been at least *some* connection with ordinary reality. As it is" — shaking his head sadly in the gloom back of the lamplight — "as it is, I must tell you that Mrs. Ghent is showing a detachment from the world, an apathy toward the daylight so to say, which I find professionally frightening. It suggests, even, incipient schizophrenia. And her refusal to return here after our last session seems, does it not, to support that judgment? She simply won't face up to the reality of her situation."

"No," said Julian simply in order to agree; he scarcely knew what he was assenting to, and only wanted to get out in the fresh air.

"Now I cannot force her to come back," said Dr. Mirabeau, spreading his hands in a gesture of easy helplessness, "but just there I think you might be able to help, if you are willing. Pick a time when she seems in a good, or at least not a bad mood; talk reasonably to her, do not appeal to her emotions or become emotional yourself — be rational. In such cases as these, we frequently find, the emotions are curiously uninvolved, stubbornly remote, while the reason itself is extremely susceptible of conviction, it follows and assents to even most ridiculous chains of evidence simply because they have the appearance of being rational rather than emotive. It is an odd condition in which, you might say, the loss of reason presents a symptomatic appearance which is more reasonable than reason itself, the patient will spend long hours analyzing causes, motives, and so forth. Do you see?"

Julian said he saw, and upon his promise of co-operation, over a manly handshake, was permitted to depart. In another moment, he thought, his head might have left his neck and gone spinning skyward, gently and slowly, like those children's balloons he had seen at the Zoo in Central Park.

Chapter 8

F<small>EDERIGO</small>'s third letter, which arrived in the morning mail Friday, outwardly resembled the other two save in one particular: it was addressed not to Julian but to Sylvia. Julian, who the previous evening had told his wife that he would have to spend the weekend in Philadelphia (why Philadelphia? He did not know) where the firm was planning to open an agency, and who accordingly would phone Elaine later in the morning to say he was going with her, did not even notice the arrival of this letter or Sylvia's reception of it, because he was engrossed in his own mail. This included a report from Mr. Bilsiter's office, that on the other night, when he had entertained Elaine and, later, Federigo, when that odd thing had happened in Central Park, Sylvia had been not at the movies but with Marius Rathlin at his apartment.

So! he was thinking, at just the moment that Sylvia opened her letter, so there is something in it after all. How fortunate that he had not called off those detectives. In order to keep the savor of his triumphant secrecy he looked at his wife, who all unaware was reading a letter. Julian felt, for her, pity and contempt — how secure she must imagine herself! — and, for himself, justification. Everything, complex as it was, had worked out; the idea of the anonymous letters finally justified itself in the only way possible, by being right, by referring to a real situation; his going away with Elaine Leonard likewise justified itself by means of what these letters brought to light.

Sylvia looked up from her letter, and said in a neutral

238

voice, "Why don't I walk the dogs this morning, darling, and you finish your coffee?"

"Of course, anything you say," Julian replied. Their eyes, however, did not meet. And when Sylvia had got dressed and put Troilus and Cressida on their leashes and left the apartment, the letter was prominently displayed on the table where Julian must presently see it.

Sylvia, with a grim expression on her face, immediately walked the dogs to the nearest drugstore, where she telephoned to Marius. It was difficult to do, as the door had to be left open and the dogs kept trying to drag her out of the phone booth.

She could see it all now, of course; and the worst thing in it, perhaps, was her own blindness and ridiculous sense of security, the feeling that the anonymous letters were past and gone, love re-established (when really it had been an armed truce) and life ready to go on in the normal way. She imagined Julian and Elaine laughing at her, and this idea horrified her so much that she could scarcely speak when Marius answered the phone.

He, having expected this result, had difficulty in sounding properly surprised, and then a more unexpected difficulty in sounding properly gratified, when it turned out that Sylvia would go away with him that very day, that she knew the place where they would go, that she realized (as she did not, in her extremity, fail to remind him) that he loved her whatever happened, and that she was coming at once to his room.

Do I love her? he asked himself while waiting, and had to allow that he did not.

"Still," he said, "it will be charming — if only it can be kept that way."

Sylvia in twenty minutes appeared, dragging the dogs upstairs.

239

"Queen and huntress chaste and fair," elegantly said Marius, for whom it was perhaps never too early in the morning.

"Listen to me," she said breathlessly, "and don't be silly. Listen — Marius, do you love me?"

"Of course, darling," he said lightly, and put his arms around her, "you know that."

Sylvia, however, having received this assurance, backed away and drew from her handbag a single key, which she presented to him. He stared at it doubtfully.

"It is the key to Hugo's place out at Lantern Point. We'll go there — it's lonely and beautiful. Marius — I want you to go out there first and wait for me. I'll come out later, but first I must go home to pack, and" — grimly — "have words with my wretched husband."

"This is all so sudden," said Marius. "What's happened between you two?"

"Oh, I'll tell you later, when I get out there. It was Elaine, all that time — do you know, he's actually going to Philadelphia with her, on *business*; he told me he was going to Philadelphia on business, and I believed it. Then, this morning, that letter came — I'll give him *business!*"

"Sylvia," Marius said, "are you going with me for love or revenge?"

This brought her to a stop for a moment.

"You don't know how it's made me feel," she said, "how horrible, how dirty it is."

"Ah, there," he said to comfort her, and put his arm round her shoulder.

"But it's not just revenge, Marius," she said. "It is you, truly it is."

"Of course," he said. The dogs had by now twisted the leashes quite around them both.

240

"Marius, it will be fun," she whispered. "But promise —
I don't know, I'm still ashamed — promise it will be dark,
and without saying anything."

"I promise," he gravely assured her. "In darkness, silently
— like strangers."

"Silently, like two strangers in the night."

Julian meanwhile had called Elaine.

"I was just about to leave," she said. "Are you coming?"

"Yes," he said into the cold phone. "Yes, darling."

"You'd better get over here in five minutes, then."

"Oh," he said. "I couldn't leave so soon. I'm not packed,
and really I'd better be at the office during the day — Sylvia's
got the idea I'm going to Philadelphia on business, you
see."

"Why, you clever lad," said Elaine, without admiration.
"Imagine thinking up a thing like that."

"Darling, don't — I love you, darling. Let me drive out,
I'll be there and meet you by early evening."

"You know, dear, I doubt you will," was the reply. "I
think you'll back out at the last moment. But it's your picnic.
I'll be there, and if you are not, that's the end. Understood?"

"I love you," said Julian into the phone which had gone
dead. Nervously he walked about for a few moments, went
to the dining room table and poured himself more coffee. So
it was all going to come true at last! At this moment his eye
fell on the letter, which so exactly resembled in appearance
the ones of his own composition. With shaking hands he
opened it and was shocked to read:

MADAME:
    Elaine the fair, Elaine the loveable,
    Elaine the lily maid . . . ?
                          FEDERIGO

For a moment Julian was capable of only one thought: I never wrote that. He sat down and looked incredulously at the letter, as though expecting it to dissolve in his hands and be no more. This was what it felt like to receive an anonymous letter; just so Sylvia must have felt.

Reality had spoken. At this moment Sylvia returned.

"So!" she said, upon seeing the letter in Julian's hands.

"So!" replied Julian, but less dramatically.

Because they were both highly moral, or moralistic, persons, an argument necessarily had to take place. This argument became passionate at times, at times bitter, at times, also, ridiculous (there was a passage of debate about who was to take the car, the dogs, et cetera); but this argument was on both sides corrupted by secrecy at the root, and by the uncertainties of desire, so that very little truth resulted from it. Julian, for his part, felt a sneaking gratitude at being caught out; the entire escapade with Elaine was by this means wrought up — a little hysterically — into honesty, he was no longer skulking behind Sylvia's back, everything was now brought out in the light of day (except, of course, the letters). And Sylvia in the same way felt a certain relief; it was now possible to have an affair without betraying anyone; she told Julian she was leaving him, what she did after that would naturally be her own business. Beneath their disagreeable tones, beneath the real but imperfectly apprehended consternation over parting, both were experiencing the same furtive jubilation, the random feeling of freedom and emptiness together; it is also likely that neither believed their separation would be permanent.

She loves me, after all, thought Julian. When she returns things will be as I wish. And he pictured himself as planning rationally with a much-chastened Sylvia the *modern marriage*,

242

marked by occasional light infidelities, which would exactly suit his requirement.

He can't live without me, after all, Sylvia thought. When he comes to heel, after a few days, I shall outline exactly what can be permitted and what cannot.

There were tears, a few, on her side; sullen gloom on his. At last they subsided into a kind of sad rationality (like civilized people, as Julian stuffily said) and Sylvia began to pack. Perhaps their closest appreciation of what was really happening came when they accidentally began to talk about their possessions.

"Since I'm the one who's leaving," Sylvia said, "I should have the car."

"I'm sorry," he replied. "I need the car, and besides it is registered in my name."

"I said I want the car."

"And if you take it, I shall report to the police that it has been stolen; instead, I give you all the furniture" — with a large gesture. "I'll put that in writing."

"What do I want with all the furniture — do I carry it away on my back?"

"The money in the bank belongs to you as much as to me. I can't stop you from buying another car — I regret to say."

"All right, but one thing I insist on — if I haven't the car, you must take the dogs."

"I don't want the dogs," said Julian. "I've never wanted the dogs. Hugo gave them to you, really."

"Hugo gave them to both of us, for a wedding present."

"And I know why," said Julian with a sour smile.

It was decided upon this that if Julian had the convenience of the car he should also undertake the inconvenience of the dogs, who at this moment were walking aimlessly around the apartment trailing their leashes which had not been removed.

"Where will you be, if I should have to get in touch with you?" Julian asked Sylvia. He had determined not to be the first to ask, but when Sylvia, with a suitcase, approached the front door in a decisive silence, he gave in.

"I don't see that is any of your business," she replied. "I won't be hiding, I assure you. You can find me if you want me badly enough."

"That's not what I meant at all," he said heatedly. "I meant, to arrange about the separation — lawyers, and so forth."

Neither Julian nor Sylvia had ever had any extensive dealings with the world of litigation and the courts; even the word "lawyer" frightened them both a good deal.

"We'll settle all that another time," Sylvia said. "But meanwhile, I think we ought to agree on one thing."

"And that is?"

"That neither of us will draw out all the money in the current account, or deliberately spend an extraordinary lot just to inconvenience the other."

"Well — I won't if you won't," Julian agreed. "But what is an extraordinary lot?"

"I merely mean," Sylvia said with excessive sweetness, "don't set up your precious little whore in the Plaza. Find her a cold-water flat, or let her live here so long as she doesn't use *my furniture*." Sylvia perhaps would have had a good deal more to say on this theme, once started; on the other hand, a better exit might be hard to find, and consequently the door slammed with dramatic finality on the word *furniture*.

As soon as his wife had gone Julian phoned Elaine, but found she had already left. He then phoned Mr. Bilsiter of the detective agency, whom he informed of what had happened.

244

"You suspect she is going to Mr. Rathlin, yes," said Mr. Bilsiter patiently, "and you want evidence, yes, of course. It shall be done, I'll see to it myself if possible. Now tell me Mr. Ghent, do you want us to phone you — quite plainly, do you want to be in at the death?"

"Certainly not," Julian cried.

"Well, some do and some don't," said Mr. Bilsiter carelessly.

"I merely meant," Julian added, "that I shall be away myself this weekend. You may simply send the results here to me by mail, as you did the reports."

"You shall have them, sir, if they are there to be had," Mr. Bilsiter promised. "Testimony and, to clinch it, photographs."

This last, which had not occurred to Julian, horrified him; he imagined himself staring, under Mr. Bilsiter's gaze, at a flashlight picture of his wife in bed with Marius Rathlin, and he shuddered. When one thought of it that way, the whole business took on a quite loathsome reality. But while he was shuddering, Mr. Bilsiter had said good-by and hung up.

Now there was no one left to phone. There was no one left. Julian had the apartment, save for the two dogs he did not like, to himself. Later in the day, to be sure, he would be with Elaine, and time would resume; but he stood now in an abscess in time where there existed only, it appeared, the fact of his being alone. He walked slowly but nervously around the room; the dogs walked around the room their leashes rattling on the legs of tables and chairs. Exasperated, Julian unsnapped the leashes, collared the dogs and locked them in the hall bathroom, turning on the light because they were afraid of the dark and whimpered if left that way. Now he felt more alone than ever, and confronted by the monstrosity of his nature. The accusations of the world were one thing, and occasioned mere secular anxieties; but the accusations from within, being inescapable, had a religious and exalted character, so that before he knew it he was pacing up and down like an orator on a platform.

The curtains were still drawn over the windows, for Sylvia had not pulled them back. Julian remembered reading that in a closed room one could have no way of knowing that the world still existed outside, and in a sudden access of anxiety he strode over and drew back the curtains; it was a gray, rather misty day, but the world, or at least this street of it, perceptibly existed.

An early fly crawled on the window pane and flew against it buzzing; for no other reason than that he felt miserable and full of guilt Julian devoted some time and attention to pinning this fly against the corner of the frame and squashing it. In disgust he rubbed its small black remains, with a little red blood (Sylvia's?) from his finger. Of course, the poor thing (he thought) had not suffered, there had not been time. But he could not, on consideration, admit this comfortable notion, for, how could he know what time might be to a fly? Perhaps that instant, in which his fat finger had descended on its life, had amounted, when gauged in fly-time, to some six weeks in agony in a hospital with, say, cancer, in human time. What was the world? In the bathroom, with the lights on, the dogs whimpered even so, and Julian walked the empty apartment.

The world went around, and he with it. His nearest evidence at this moment of the world's (and his) incessantly going around was the electric clock on the bedside table (he had wandered into the bedroom and stood abstractedly regarding the unmade beds). This clock read about a quarter to eleven and emitted a light, humming tone which he had always taken to be the domestic image and idol of the power behind the world going remorselessly about its interminable business. This clock was a machine more mighty, sacred and

246

dreadful than any rosary, for example, or prayer wheel of the Buddhist; under the appearance of an innocent, convenient recording device it exercised an absolute compulsion upon the waywardness of life; at this very moment, while he watched, it was going about its work of making him older, even while with the same three hands it brought some into the world and pushed others out, made this one punctual to tea and that one late for a plane in which he would have been destroyed. Everyone in society, it would be not too much to say, possessed a clock, or was possessed by one; portable models were also available, and their association with strap or chain was not accidental, for did they not everywhere demonstrate servitude? (Julian was reminded that he no longer had a watch; also that so far as marriage was concerned he had, more or less, his freedom; these observations failed somehow to impress him favorably.)

He sighed, he was alone. Sylvia's photograph on the dresser followed him with eyes of a terrible and accusing candor as he guiltily left that room.

The living room was of course no improvement, for there again was the portrait of Sylvia which he himself, Julian, had caused to be done, a long time ago, by a young artist who, for all the appealing expression he had caught, or put, in the face, had given the eyes a cold glitter and the mobility of swivel mountings. Was there not, he asked himself as he went on through to the kitchen, something morbid, something presumptively commemorative, in this making of images? Did it not — by its intention of preserving the past — give away the selfishness beneath its tender pretense? as in the anecdote which Marius had told him as coming from, of all people, Sigmund Freud, of a young man who sighingly remarked to his pretty wife, "Do you know, my dear, if either of us should die I think I would live in Paris?" But if some such wish lay

247

concealed in the black inward of the camera, in the mind which set the painter on about his business, the eyes took their revenge. "I know what you are thinking," was their word whatever one was thinking, and whatever one was thinking when suddenly made aware of the eyes, they were right, or at any rate convincing.

In the kitchen, where he went without any clear idea of what to do when he got there, he heard the subtle hum of the refrigerator, the domestic imitation of silence. Another emblem, this, of the power streaming ceaselessly through all things, the violent fluidity which itself enabled the world to look relatively solid and stable. He opened the door and stared objectlessly into the cold, lighted box, which contained a neat and sparing arrangement of foods, none of them at this moment very interesting to him: a package of bacon, a box of eggs, a bottle of milk which was paradoxically of all things in the world the coldest-looking and most forbidding; a thin, tall bottle of Niersteiner, and this he doubtfully reached for, held to the light, began to return to its place, and finally put down on the drainboard of the sink. This move brought him face to face with another electric clock: eight minutes to eleven. The sweep second hand moved with a dreadful smoothness.

There were sixty seconds in each minute, thirty-six hundred in each hour, thirty-six times twenty-four was already incalculable without pencil and paper, the result of that multiplied again by three hundred and sixty-five would be a staggering figure whatever it was, and, finally, *that* times an indeterminable (at present) number put by some authorities at seventy would be, leaving leap years out of consideration, the enormous number of seconds involved in measuring out a long human life, if anyone wanted to know. Julian observed with a sense of irritated anxiety that this problem had already cost

248

him some fifty seconds in the computing; moreover, about half his hypothetical number of seconds had already been used up. Of course, he might become a centenarian, or he might fall down dead in, say, twelve more minutes. The first possibility was statistically unlikely, the second did not seem probable under the circumstances unless he killed himself, which he now realized was what he had been thinking of doing.

He poured the wine into a squat, ordinary kitchen glass and returned with bottle and glass to the living room, where he sat down on the couch before the ornamental, empty fireplace. The eyes of his wife Sylvia looked down at a difficult angle, over her cheekbones, at the top of his head.

It was almost with gratitude that he saw, a few minutes later, Federigo standing rather shyly in the corner of the room, as though he had come through the door only a moment ago. Nevertheless, he put up a show of anger, and said:

"You had to send that letter, didn't you? I hope you're pleased."

"Ah, darling, I didn't send it," Federigo said, smiling.

"Don't call me darling, please," said Julian fiercely and with a surprising blush.

"I didn't send it," Federigo repeated, "and yet, you know, I thought you rather wanted some such thing to happen. It's been at the back of your mind for a few days, hasn't it, that the next thing on the program was to get caught off base, somehow-anyhow? Are you quite sure," he added, "that you didn't send this last letter as you did the others? You might have made it up and mailed it and then forgotten."

"No," said Julian, nearly in a shout. "That's ridiculous. You did it, you must have done it."

"I don't *do* things," said Federigo with a kind of disdainful dignity. "If I had, believe me, I should have chosen a differ-

249

ent quotation from Lord Tennyson — whose reputation, I believe, is going up these days:

> His honour rooted in dishonour stood,
> And faith unfaithful kept him falsely true.

Practically metaphysical, isn't it, with all that back and forth in the words; confusing."

"It's obvious you did it," cried Julian. "You knew it was Tennyson."

"They're very well-known lines," said Federigo evasively. "Still, that's not here nor there. The point is, what next?"

"I don't know," Julian sullenly replied. "And I don't much care."

"Go to Elaine? Kill yourself? Take a world cruise? Live elsewhere under a new name? Redeem yourself by missionary work in a malarial swamp?" Federigo presented these alternatives, if that is what they were, rapidly and in a neutral voice, adding in conclusion, "How far can you go by Ferris wheel?"

"I'm going to Elaine," Julian said. "After that — we'll see."

"Spoken like a little man," said Federigo. "As for myself, I'm delighted to see you do something straightforward. I'm sure it will work out for the best — so sure," he added, "that I've come to say good-by."

"You are leaving me? Now?"

"It's what you wanted, isn't it?" Federigo approached Julian casually, and before the latter was aware of his intention, heartily and disgustingly kissed him on the mouth, then quickly backed away toward the bedroom, with Julian angrily following.

"I'll just use your bathroom before I go," said Federigo,

250

pretending to be unaware of Julian's fierce expression; and he disappeared, leaving Julian to walk up and down the floor until his exasperation lapsed in moody inattention and sullenness.

He must have remained in this state for some minutes; he was never certain whether he had heard the toilet flush or not, but when he finally knocked on the bathroom door and then, hearing no answer, opened it, his strange companion was nowhere to be found.

"He must have slipped out while my back was turned," Julian decided as he packed an overnight case. His last action before leaving the house was to open half a dozen cans of horse meat, which he disposed at various points about the house, so that the dogs, liberated from the other bathroom, should not starve. But the image of them prowling the lonely rooms, and perhaps a certain vivid reminiscence of the smell of horse meat, remained with him all the day and night in resentment and reproach.

2

Far out on the northeastern end of Long Island Lantern Point jutted into the Atlantic; it was a desolate, haunted kind of country on the best of days, a land of shifting dunes and twisted, stunted pines, and today a thick fog from the sea rolled cold and gray over it all; out here, on a knoll which doubtless in good visibility overlooked the water — one could hear the waves through the fog — Hugo Alter's house stood alone.

Marius received directions at the station and decided, as he had plenty of time and not much money, to walk out; he invested a small sum, however, in provisions, reminding himself that even adultery marches on its stomach. The sand road off the highway was clearly marked, and the distance from there only about a mile; even despite the fog Marius became quite cheerful as he swung along carrying a bag in which were eggs and sausages and coffee and bread — there was a kind of biblical and ancient freedom about his having suddenly entered, only a couple of hours from the city, this loneliness.

This pleasant mood changed rapidly, however, on his entrance into the house. In the first place, the front door was not only not locked, it stood open; nothing could more have resembled a trap. Marius imagined that a party of tramps, escaped criminals, madmen, might have taken advantage of the loneliness of the place to hide out here. He reconnoitered, listened at the door, heard nothing, then at last took his courage and stepped inside.

Here it was very gloomy and cold, not only from the character of the day but because the windows were boarded up; the very air had that refrigerated stillness and staleness which suggested the tomb, the whitewashed walls were bare and dismal, one of them bore a calendar which had not been turned since February. It was the kitchen he had entered on, and here he stood for several minutes, while his hands and feet grew cold, looking at the black iron bulk of the wood stove and thinking that he ought to get busy at once cutting some kindling and lighting a fire; but he suddenly felt so depressed as to be unable to move. There was no doubt at all in his mind that Sylvia was a foolish woman; surely they could have arranged something more sensible than this? He himself would not have wanted a hotel room, for hotel rooms seemed to him, for such purposes as this, like re-usable coffins — but what in heaven's name would have been wrong with his own room, poor but centrally heated, and with the blessing of electricity?

252

Marius imagined how cold it would be in this house come night, and how utterly, utterly dark — how desolate. "I have my love to keep me warm," he murmured sullenly.

At this moment he heard a noise, a kind of scratching and dragging, from another room. He stood as if petrified. Human beings? Mice? He decided finally on mice, but the idea did not much comfort him. The noises began again — he imagined mice five or six feet high — then resolved into footsteps; a door swung toward him creakingly; Elaine Leonard came into the kitchen.

During a moment of astonishment, neither spoke, for each determined not to be the first to show surprise (*nil admirari,* Marius told himself proudly; one so seldom met situations surprising enough to let this motto be serviceable), and at the end of this moment each was ready with a *clever remark.*

"Dr. Livingstone, I presume?" said Elaine.

"A small world, is it not?" said Marius.

"You are aware, I guess, that this is private property?"

"I just happened to be passing by, and thought I'd drop in."

Another silence followed, then Elaine said:

"While you're here, you'll find some kindling in the shed round the corner to the right as you go out; also an ax and some logs. If you will first bring the kindling and then go off rail-splitting, I'll try to see that we don't freeze to death."

Marius did as he was told, with some difficulty; he even brought the ax, luckily wedged in a chunk of wood, down on his toe, but without serious harm since he had already got too tired to hit very hard. He also, at Elaine's instruction, pumped water up from the well. In half an hour or so they had the kitchen warming up to a reasonable temperature and had even made coffee. During this time they scarcely spoke; each was wondering what was to be done with this odd situation. They drank coffee and smoked cigarettes; the kitchen was quite

253

cozy, and (thought Marius) as full of suspicious tension as it would have been had they been married and living there for months.

"I could have the police come over and get you out of here," Elaine observed in a highly theoretical tone, not moving from her chair.

"Isn't that sort of elaborate?" he asked, as though also prepared to theorize. "There's no phone, you'd have to walk down to the village — I mean, you could hardly send me, could you? If you're very determined, probably you could persuade me to leave — but I wonder if there isn't a better way?"

"I wonder," said Elaine, and a moment later proposed they take a walk on the shore. "I am afraid," she said, "we are going to have to explain ourselves, or each other, somehow."

Down on the shore, below the dunes, the fog was close and cold about them. The waves washed with a sound of sandpaper at their left as they walked along; it was possible to see barely twenty feet out on the black calm of the water and the breaking white of the small waves; not even a bird cried in the calm.

"Like the beginning of the world," she said.

"Or the end of it," said Marius, feeling however that this was not so much a difference as an agreement between them. He boldly took her hand, which she did not remove, and they dawdled slowly down the shore, idly swinging their linked hands.

"Do you love him?" Marius presently asked; Elaine looked up at him and grinned.

"You seem to know a great deal," she said. "But, as I told you the other day — no, I don't. This was designed, sort of hopelessly, for pleasure. And you — you followed me out here, I guess?"

254

"Well, as a matter of fact — no," Marius said. "You see," he began to explain, "we seem to have got hooked up on the same circuit. Sylvia's coming down, too."

"Oh, my God," Elaine said. "And he told her he was going to Philadelphia on business." After considering this for a moment, she began to laugh.

"I think you couldn't have heard the latest," said Marius. "The Philadelphia version has been seen through — your friend Federigo," he added with conscious malice, "has struck again." And he explained what he had heard from Sylvia that morning, reporting the text of the letter as if she had told it him but not by any means admitting his fateful rôle in the business. "Elaine the fair, Elaine the loveable," he said, partly to see her blush and partly for the pleasure simply of saying this to her, "Elaine the lily maid — and there, with a question mark, it ends."

"It does, does it?"

"Yes, and I very much fear that in the sequel the Ghents have broken up. At least," Marius added, "Sylvia gave me that impression this morning."

"So that Julian, when he gets here, if I know Julian, will be desperate with *love*. Oh, dear," Elaine sighed. "With large, moony eyes and a serious expression and talk about honesty and wanting to marry *me* to make everything all right again. Oh, dear."

"I think," said Marius, "that Sylvia has some such notion about me. I got the idea this morning that love alone would save everything — it also seemed, and this was not so nice, as if she was retreating on prepared positions, and I was to be the prepared positions."

"You mean she arranged this with you before she broke up with him?"

"I am afraid there was this element of calculation in it,"

255

Marius said. "But it didn't seem right for me to back out just then."

"Oh, dear," Elaine said once again. "Do you suppose it is marriage makes people like that — or are they that way to begin with?"

"Maybe they get married because they are like that," said Marius.

"Of course, you led her on," she said. "That was wicked, wasn't it?"

"Let not the pot and the kettle begin slanging one another," Marius reminded her. "You are here, too, you know."

They became aware just then of a strong, disagreeable smell. Just before them on the sand lay a big, dead fish with a huge head of which the lower jaw protruded in a kind of grin studded with sharp, uneven teeth. Flies flew about intensely buzzing, violent with black life in the midst of the calm of the fog. On seeing this sight they both turned in silent agreement to walk back the way they had come, and as they turned Marius took Elaine by the shoulders and kissed her, with consent. Then, hand in hand once more, they walked away.

"What's to be done?" he asked.

"We might simply run away," said Elaine. "After all, if this is funny for us, think how it will be for them to find each other here."

"Yes," Marius agreed. "Quite literally, the bonds of matrimony."

"Are we, do you think, wicked people, you and I?" Elaine asked. "Or are we only younger and a little more gay?"

"I simply don't know," Marius replied. "I suspect we're wicked enough to live. Probably it would be best to run away — that is, you're not dead set on meeting him, are you?"

"No," said Elaine, "I think I could live without."

"I feel the same way about her."

256

They walked in silence for some minutes. When they had almost reached the break in the dunes which led to the house, Marius said:

"There is another way, you know. It's difficult, and it's devious, but it has a certain decisive charm — as we are, you and I, difficult and devious persons. As I imagine it now, things would go roughly like this . . ."

3

Human actions, of course, are natural and realistic — or are they? The things which take place in our lives take place from, we presume, the more or less accidental complicity of purpose and accident; we may believe the result to be predestinated by powers watching over us, or we may believe the result to be consequent on our own rational cleverness, or we may believe things happen mostly by chance. In any case, we seldom and only under special conditions — ranging in kind from jokes to tragedies — believe our actions, which so resemble products of freedom and the free operation of our wills, are in fact compelled, ourselves all ignorant, by other human wills; and if we believe it seldom, we never believe it willingly. Such things have to be forced upon our notice: a man moving across an open field, under the open sky, naturally refuses to believe he is moving through a dark, narrow tunnel from which there is no escape; yet frequently, so far as his will is concerned, the latter is the more accurate version.

What Sylvia saw, what Julian saw, what they saw who watched behind the scenes, or knowingly and with a charmed sense of power acted a part upon the scene — as a matter of fact, no one *saw* a great deal, for the greater part of the action was acted after dark, Marius and Elaine had hidden all but

257

one lantern in order to simplify the plot, and this darkness, it ought to be remembered, was the darkness that was before electricity, the divine and awful darkness which people who live in cities experience only in the midst of a war, and which they otherwise tend to forget about, telling themselves (if they think of it at all) that it could not be, really, so terribly dark — but, of course, it is.

Already when Julian came on the scene, in the late afternoon, he had the headlights on, mostly because of the fog — but the fog seemed to bring the night down earlier. As he stepped from the car he saw Elaine emerge from, oddly enough, not the house but a clump of trees. She greeted him with a kiss, and he began to feel better, a little, than he had at any time since early morning. It was still with a reckless and glum sense of desperation, however, that he returned her kiss, thinking dismally that he felt, absolutely and physically felt, that he was being watched, probably by Sylvia, absurd as it was to think so. He wondered where she was.

While Elaine led Julian into the house — he proudly showed her the bottle of whisky which he had been sensible enough to bring — Marius dutifully trudged back to the village of Lantern, where he met Sylvia, who arrived on the only train it had been possible for her to get, the last one of the afternoon.

"Oh, dear God," she thought miserably as she stepped down on the platform and saw her lover, "dear God, this is really happening. My marriage is over, seven years are gone, now I am doing *this*." She embraced Marius with considerable fervor in order to conceal this feeling, and at this sight Mr. Bilsiter, standing in the vestibule and preparing to dismount with two cameras and a black valise, turned to smile wisely at his assistant, and wink.

258

Marius had decided, he told Sylvia, that it would be best to dine in the village, which they accordingly did. Marius was tender, charming, even rather sentimental than witty; also, he paid the check. Sylvia began to feel somewhat more secure, though this probably was as much as anything a result of having dinner. She felt also, and accordingly, as though she had arrived at the end of a road; this, whatever it turned out to be, was the place of decision; and she was free for the first time in days of that annoying sensation of being followed. From time to time, however, she wondered bitterly about Julian and his Elaine in Philadelphia — how could he, knowing that she knew, go on with such a thing?

Elaine, carefully watching the time, cooked Julian a thin sort of supper, with which, however — or more likely with the mere spectacle of her domesticity — he was charmed. She then insisted on making him go for a walk along the shore, in the course of which she said to him:

"Julian, please promise me, when you come to me tonight, it will be dark, and you won't speak?"

Julian expressed surprise.

"Please, darling, let it be that way. I am not so used to these things," Elaine added, "as you are."

This unlooked-for hint of innocence — and indeed, Elaine seemed, out here in the lonely wilderness beside the sea, less sophisticated than he had thought — quite charmed Julian, who tenderly promised they should be silent.

"There is a dead fish somewhere about," he said, sniffing. "Let us turn back." He kissed Elaine as they turned, and had the weather been much warmer a complication might at this point have developed in the scheme; as it was, however, they slowly walked back toward the house, where Marius and Sylvia, a few minutes before, had arrived by means of the single taxi operating from the village of Lantern. (Mr. Bilsiter and his assistant at this moment awaited the return of this same taxi; they stood shuddering with cold in the shadows of the station platform, while they munched sandwiches they had thoughtfully purchased before leaving New York City.)

"I lit a lamp in the kitchen," Marius said, "thinking it would be dark by the time we got back." He also pointed out the open bottle of whisky on the table as evidence of his solicitude.

"There is a smell of cooking," Sylvia said doubtfully, looking around into the deep shadows cast by the lantern.

"I made myself lunch when I got here, darling," Marius told her, "and brought stuff for breakfast as well." With the lantern he showed Sylvia into the bedroom down the hall, away from the kitchen. "There is only the one light," he said, "but that is as you would have it, isn't it?" And he respectfully withdrew, saying he would come to her in fifteen minutes. "Silently," he added, giving the girl a light kiss and hug.

Marius replaced the lantern on the kitchen table, and left the house.

("It is Mr. Alter's place," Mr. Bilsiter was saying to his assistant. "Give them another hour, I'd say." And he arranged accordingly with the driver of the now-returned taxi.)

"There's the house," Elaine said, seeing the light in the kitchen. "We almost lost it, I thought for a moment."

"Darling," Julian whispered as they entered the kitchen. "Darling, I love you. Do you love me?"

"Of course I do," she whispered back. "Remember — silence," she added, still whispering, and pointed down the hall. "Come to me in ten minutes," and, taking the lamp with her, she vanished toward the bedroom. Sylvia, lying tensely alone in the bed, heard footsteps; she shivered, perhaps as much from cold as apprehension, but the footsteps went on. Sylvia sighed; the time was not yet.

Elaine passed the bedroom as softly as possible, stepped out the side door at the end of the hall, and blew out the lantern.

"How goes it?" whispered Marius from the pines.

"It goes," she whispered back.

"Should we take their car?"

"It would make too much noise."

"It's a long, long walk to the station." And they vanished silently down the path.

Julian stood alone in the kitchen. He had taken off his clothes, and it became very noticeable that the kitchen stove was going out. Surely ten minutes are up now? he thought, but between eagerness and doubt he gave it a moment or so more. It was cold, and dreadfully dark except for the slight glow from the rim of the stove-plate; he wished Elaine had left him the lamp.

At last he tiptoed down the hall to the bedroom, opened the door, tiptoed across the floor, and drew in his breath sharply as he hit his bare toe on the bed post. Very creditably, he refrained from saying anything, and got into the bed all naked as he was, and lay beside the cold, naked body he found there. They both lay quite still for a few moments.

Scruple, doubt, unwillingness, guilt, anxiety, are all very human; but what presently followed went according to nature, which is perhaps not so human as all that. The thoughts of the two persons in the bed — two persons whom it would be very difficult, at this moment, to name accurately — were, allowing for differences in the pronouns, as though thought by the same mind; a mind with two backs.

The night was deep, dark; the waves washed ceaselessly up and down, back and forth, on the sandy, stony shore; the dead fish on the beach, as the tide moved in, was nudged uneasily, stirred back and forth — the flies departed — turned over in a lifelike motion, and taken back into the sea which had tossed it up.

She found herself thinking fiercely, with an effort of concentration, of Julian; just as Hugo had told her he likewise had thought of Alma; it was a slap in the face and a revenge.

He thought of Sylvia, rather miserably it is true; at the same time he knew she could not compare with the beautiful young girl who now lay in his arms. They both found each other highly satisfactory, and, being prohibited from the release of talk, all their concentration went physically into this act of darkness which they committed, even while mentally it turned back so that each fed fiercely on the matter of his own mind.

"Darling," he whispered at last, and she too broke the silence to whisper, "Darling." The two characterless and disembodied ghosts of voices met in the stillness and hung there. She thought of Julian, and he of Sylvia.

So this is what it is, thought the single mind between them. This is the great secret that everyone knows, this is the Whore of Babylon, the pleasure of Judas, the object of all the movies, the space between the lines of newspapers and the silences of mother and father; what is wicked is the wish to be wicked, and this, this, is wickedness.

The silence was broken by the sound of footsteps, creaking of doors, muffled voices. The bedroom door flew open, a flashlight directed itself imperatively at the couple in the bed, a voice was heard to exclaim "This is them" and, almost immediately, there followed — as Julian and Sylvia sat bolt upright in the bed — two blinding flashes of light, as if the heavens had opened and judgment day peremptorily been declared. Then darkness descended, there came the noise of feet running, a terrible thud as someone bumped into a door,

262

a dirty word loudly shouted, footsteps vanishing, silence again.

Even then, in panic and consternation (looking for a match), they each suspected any and every incredible thing except their own continued — and, it seemed, compulsory — innocence of any infidelity save that of the mind; which some strict authorities have declared to be equal and tantamount, as sin, to that of the flesh.

Among other things, they discovered that Marius and Elaine had vanished — not, perhaps, as though they had never been; but sufficiently vanished. They stared at one another, Julian at Sylvia and Sylvia at Julian — across the small, new flame of the match.

This is a very old story, and when it used to be told in what may have been in some respects a simpler age, it would have ended, perhaps, like this: ". . . and the married couple, when they perceived how astoundingly and justly they had been diddled" — or "saved," depending on the sort of person narrating the tale — "resolved ever after to be true to one another."

We no longer dare to say so much; that "ever after" phrase does not come easily to us. Yet it remains to sum up the short-term results, so to say, of this witnessed action, which took place not so very long ago:

Julian and Sylvia Ghent are still together, without being altogether certain why; though it is true that there was born to them a child, whose creation could have been dated to that night. This child was a boy, whom they named Peter. Mr. Bilsiter, by the way, sent Julian prints and negatives of the photographs taken in the night; there was no comment, but the bill, while it could not under the circumstances be called blackmail, was extremely high. It seemed to bear out the truth of

Hugo's aphorism about free love; that love was never free, and seldom even inexpensive.

Marius and Elaine were so charmed with the cleverness and success of their plot that they were unable to resist getting married themselves, and are now experiencing some of the delights and difficulties of that state. On this account, and because of the child, the Ghents were able a little to revenge themselves on the new couple, to whom for a wedding present they gave the dogs Troilus and Cressida. This might have offended Hugo, but Julian and Sylvia decided not to care, and at all events Louisa had made Hugo settle down in Italy, where it is regrettably true that she betrayed him with one gentleman after another, and some not so gentle.

Mr. Archer More, it appeared in the papers, took his twelfth wife amid great celebrations, and divorced her one year after. Of Dr. Thybold, nothing so happy can be reported: Julian's attention was caught by a small piece in the paper about a man answering his description who had been found shot to death in what was called a "hide-out" in Canarsie; the victim had evidently been chain-smoking for several days before his demise, which was ascribed to gangland warfare — but Julian looked up the account in several papers, which reported the poor man's name variously as Dybold, Dybbuk, and Dr. Hy Ball, and was sadly satisfied that it had been indeed his late client, caught up with at last by the cigarette kings.

Of Federigo, nothing more was heard after Sylvia had asked once, "But who was Federigo?" and Julian had replied, "Oh, he died during the war, in the Coral Sea" — actually filling his mind, at that moment, with the peace of that translucent coral image.

Yet Julian saw him once again. It was at a party, in a brilliantly lighted room with crowds of people. They came face to face.

264

"Federigo Schwartz," Julian said boldly; but the other, looking him straight in the eyes, said: "I beg your pardon, you must be mistaking me for someone else." To which Julian replied, quite gaily: "Oh, very well, if you want it that way. Incognito again, I see. But," as he turned away, "I understand now what you meant." And this phrase might have covered a multitude of sins.